I0545169

You
Take
Yourself
With
You

Clare Josa

© Clare Josa, 2017
www.ClareJosa.com

Published by Beyond Alchemy Publishing, UK, 2017
For bulk orders, contact hello@beyond-alchemy.com

A CIP catalogue record for this title is available from the British
Library.

Paperback ISBN 978-1908854-88-9
Kindle ISBN 978-1908854-89-6
ePub ISBN 978-1-908854-90-2

Cover design by Andrew J Becker

This is a work of fiction. Any similarity between the characters
and situations within its pages and places or persons, living or
dead, is unintentional and co-incidental.

Printed and bound in Great Britain by
Clays Ltd, St Ives plc

Join the Readers' Club:

Members get full access to:

Exclusive deleted scenes
Casting sheets for your favourite characters
A Spotify playlist for the big scenes
Recipes from Nonna's kitchen
Interviews with the author
The first two chapters of book two of the Denucci
Deception series: The Tainted Diamond

Join free now:

Dedication:

To Gita Faux and Hazel Shrimplin

who proved that a
great teacher can change the world

Also by Clare Josa:

Fiction:

The Tainted Diamond - Book 2 of The Denucci Deception

Non-Fiction:

Dare To Dream Bigger
52 Mindful Moments
A Year Full Of Gratitude
The Little Book Of Daily Sunshine
28 Day Meditation Challenge

November

Autumn's siren call
Marches us into winter
The final leaves fall

1. Taking A Big Risk

I was taking the biggest risk of my career. It would either get me promoted or arrested - for running a male brothel. All in the name of market research.

"We're nearly ready," I said to my boss, as Lucy's nearly-on-maternity-leave bump walked through the door several seconds before the rest of her. "Are they all here?"

I was asking about the ten women for tonight's focus group. It was the first one I had run without Lucy in the background, because she was going home before it started. I knew I could do it, but that didn't stop me feeling nervous about going solo. I ignored the squirming in my stomach and tried to drown out the thoughts about everything that could go wrong.

"It's all fine, Sophie," Lucy replied. "You've done a great job. I have complete faith in you. I'll just pop into the back room for a moment to check everything's ready in there and then I'll head off home. I'm done in. I can't wait for my maternity leave to start. Only two more weeks!"

I smiled politely. I'm not looking forward to Lucy leaving. She is my best friend, as well as my boss, and the thought of a whole year without having her to bounce ideas off makes me want to take a sabbatical. I don't want to think about how being a mum will change her – will change us. But I had to concentrate on the focus group first. It was my Big Chance to Shine. I hadn't told Lucy, but this was my last-ditch attempt to impress Harry, the owner of our agency, to make him change his mind and let me cover for Lucy while she's on maternity leave.

Over the past few years I've run focus groups on everything from cars to condoms, but this one was different. I had something extra special planned. I was pushing the boundaries of what I would normally do with research, to get the client the answers they were looking for, so we would know which direction to take the advertising campaign in. And I was praying it was going to work, or I might be out of a job.

The wine was chilled. The bowls were full of nibbles. The notepads and pens were on the table. The sound and video recording was all set up. I was glad the client wasn't sitting on the other side of the two-way mirror, for once. The last thing I wanted was to have 'helpful suggestions' or 'spontaneous questions' being passed into the room every ten minutes by a blushing intern, destroying the flow and rapport. And I wanted to trial tonight's approach without an invisible audience. I have always hated that feeling of being watched – analysed – second-guessed – even criticised by the faces I can't see behind the mirror.

Lucy has been encouraging me to take on more responsibility, to get me ready for her maternity leave. Some guy called Stuart is going to cover for her, but Lucy wants to get me ready to step up to lead the team, to be a Planner – like she is – in an advertising agency. A Planner's job is to do the initial research before a firm pitches for an advertising contract, to find out more about the market and uncover potential opportunities for the product. Then the Planner does the full research and testing once the agency has got the contract and has developed more concrete advertising concepts.

Ever thought that those ad-memes get into your brain by

accident? Think again! It's a deeply scientific process, which then gets gloriously muddied by the artistic temperaments of the *creatives* who do the actual ad design. Then it's watered down by the I-need-my-bonus fears of the marketing director of whichever client is investing millions in raising their brand awareness or flogging the latest hot idea to people who don't really know what they want, and almost certainly don't need whatever they're being persuaded to buy.

So tonight, I was doing something new. It was either going to be a raging success and make our agency's name in the industry, or get someone calling the police. I smoothed out the non-existent wrinkles in my skirt with slightly clammy hands and checked my reflection in the two-way mirror for the twentieth time. The face smiling back at me looked confident and calm, proving that mirrors can and do lie.

I checked my watch. Time to get this show on the road. I dimmed the lighting and plumped up the cushions and then invited the 'delegates' in.

In came our ten lovely ladies, nervously choosing seats on the sofas, in an impromptu game of silent musical chairs. I asked them to help themselves to wine, soft drinks and nibbles. Hardly anyone ever chooses the soft drinks and that first glass of wine always goes quickly. Being in Central London meant no one would be driving.

We used to run our sessions in people's houses, so that everyone would feel at home. But these days it's hard to find a home with a big enough lounge or kitchen to comfortably seat eleven, plus the video and audio recording kit, and without bouncing kids or barking dogs. Lucy and I finally gave up on the idea when a host's children were discovered to have been eavesdropping on the stairs during a particularly sensitive focus group on 'feminine toys'. We only found out after they had uploaded the whole thing to YouTube. I still have no idea how Harry managed to hush that one up.

When Harry told us we were moving offices, we insisted on having our own focus group space. It's kitted out to look just like someone's home. No office furniture or strip lighting in sight.

It was time for the warm-ups, explaining how the evening would work, making sure they knew that anything they said would be confidential and that what they would be shown was confidential, too. I even remembered to check that they had all signed their non-disclosure agreement forms. The 'recruiter' – the person who finds the right people to come to the focus group – did the initial checks on background, lifestyle, attitudes and stuff and, from the initial vibe of the group, she had done well.

They were a mixed group of early-thirties women who looked dissimilar – ranging from jeans and Goth-black hair to a designer suit with perfectly styled highlights that must have cost a week's rent – but who should all have common educational backgrounds and attitudes to life. Tonight's group was full of working professional women who were in a long-term relationship with a man, with no children. They were opinionated enough to give their man 'constructive feedback' on his appearance, with an unspoken veto on his wardrobe choices. It was going to be interesting.

I did the usual introductions, breaking the ice, some fun stuff, getting everyone used to talking in front of the group. I let them know that there was no such thing as a stupid question or comment; I wanted to hear all their thoughts on the stuff we were discussing, even if they disagreed with what everyone else had been saying. They nodded obligingly - the first glass of wine was working its magic already.

Tonight's research was for a men's deodorant spray, I told them. This was the first time they had heard this and they looked surprised. The token Brave Soul asked why the group was full of women. I love it when someone ask questions. It gives everyone else permission to speak.

We were talking to women because our client has a theory that girlfriends and wives have more influence over the purchase decision for male deodorants than men do: they care more about how their men smell than their men do. And, no, I explained, they would never be told which brand this is for, but they might guess in about three months' time, once the ads have come out.

We did the required 'brand awareness' stuff, with magazine and TV ads. We talked about how their partners smelled: what was good, what wasn't. It could have got a bit awkward here, but the wine helped keep the conversation flowing. I needed the detail: the words they used; the facial expressions; the body language.

We did the classic 'sniff-sheets' test for different fragrances – the kind of thing you find in glossy magazines that never quite represents the real smell. Everyone was polite. And tipsy. We were making great progress through the evening's script.

And now it was the Big Moment. I wished I could rush to the loo, I felt so nervous, but once I was in the room and leading the research, I couldn't leave my post for the full two hours. One of the joys of this job: bladder of steel.

Oh God! I've been talking to myself in my head and the room's gone silent. They're looking at me as though I'm supposed to be saying something. I am. Okay, deep breath. Here goes. I'm either going to make my career or …

"Okay, ladies, now I have a treat for you. If you'd like to look over towards the door at the back of the room, I hope you're going to enjoy what's coming your way!"

As I walked to the door and opened it with what I hoped was a sense of occasion, I was trusting (an unusual experience for me) that Lucy had got everything sorted before she went home. I felt ten pairs of curious eyes on me, as though I were unveiling an invisible plaque.

"In you come, boys!"

Four drop-dead-gorgeous male models entered the room, shirtless, looking like the stars of those iconic 1980s jeans adverts. Two blonds with blue eyes. Two with a decidedly Mediterranean appeal. All with rippling abs betraying years of dedication in the gym and biceps to make you dream of them sweeping you off your feet. All four of them shuffled uncomfortably under the scrutiny of these women-turned-teenagers. This clearly wasn't the behaviour they were used to from photo shoots.

The women gasped. Then giggled. And grinned.

"What do you want us to do with *them*?" asked the Brave Soul.

"Smell them!" I announced. More giggles. Thank goodness they had been drinking.

"Here's the thing," I explained, having to talk more loudly because the ladies had started to whisper to each other. The models were looking self-conscious. I wished I had thought of putting on some background music, but that might have made it feel like a Chippendales performance. "Fragrances smell different on real people compared with pieces of card. And our client *really* wants to know what you think: which you love; which turn you off. So these four gorgeous gentlemen are each wearing one of the fragrances the brand is considering releasing. We need your unbiased opinions. So I'd like you to take it in turns to *experience* the fragrances on our models."

Waves of embarrassed snickering filled the room. I felt my stomach clenching. Was this going to work? Mike in the office had volunteered to help with this, but his man-bun and beer gut might have biased the results. It was hard to break that one to him, but he had taken it like a pro.

"As you know, this is market research and we want to make sure we get your true response, not one biased by the visual appeal of these lovely gentlemen." The models shifted awkwardly. I needed to speed this up. "So to make sure no one accidentally chooses based on the model they find most attractive, you're going to be blindfolded."

I had to let them have their moment to snigger and talk, as they got their heads round this.

"In the bags in front of you on the table, you will each find a blindfold and a medal on a ribbon. In a moment, we'll move to the empty area at the back of the room and I'll ask you to put on your blindfold. I'll guide you to where the models will be standing and I want you to experience the fragrance on each of them in turn. It's up to you how you do that. But please – no touching!"

Eyebrows were nearly meeting hairlines as these thirty-something, professional women turned back into starstruck girls at a pop concert. I was half-waiting for one of them to scream with excitement. How did these models compared with their men back at home, I mused.

"When you have *experienced* all four fragrances, I'd like you to hang your medal around the neck of the model whose fragrance most appeals to you. Then we'll come back to the sofas to discuss which smell you preferred and why. Is everybody clear about what we're doing?"

Yes. Nods. Good. Okay!

I guided them through the process and, being the only sober and non-blindfolded woman in the room, I had to admit it was hilarious. The models were getting into the mood. The women kept bumping into each other, with hands stretched out in front of them. There was a certain amount of tipsy flirting going on as the ladies each hung the medal around the neck of their favourite fragrance.

"Please, no hugging the models or touching them!" I had to remind them, as things threatened to get out of hand.

There was a minor moment of panic, as multiple women each tried to hang a medal on the same person at once and a fight risked breaking out, but I managed to calm them down. I could see this was working, but I sensed that we needed to finish this and move back to the talking, before I lost control of the group and it turned into a hen night. I needed to keep this professional.

Lucy and I had been to so much effort to make this work. All the women had been told not to wear perfume or strong scents for the evening. Ditto for the models. We had even given the models unfragranced shower gel and shampoo to use before the event. One had also insisted on a very expensive moisturiser; he said he couldn't go 'on stage' without it. We supplied them each with a pair of identical new jeans, too, so there wouldn't be any laundry detergent or fabric conditioner to contaminate the results. Lucy had to spray each model in a separate room and then keep them in separate corners of the waiting room until we were ready, so the fragrances wouldn't mix and confuse the results. My favourite part of our preparations had been looking through the online profiles at the modelling agency to choose the four most gorgeous men I could find for tonight. Talk about feeling like a kid Christmas shopping in Hamley's toy department with a blank cheque!

I felt sorry for my favourite model. I've always had a soft spot for the Italian types. By the end of the voting, he didn't have a single medal. The blindfolds had worked. I took a moment to reassure him, though the dejected puppy dog look in his eyes made me want to take him home.

I was in the process of removing one of the women's arms from around the neck of her favourite model as she pretended she was checking if her medal was there, when the main door opened, without warning. Everyone jumped.

"What the hell is going on here?" boomed a confused and angry voice.

Silence.

Then giggles.

Then silence again.

Harry. My Big Boss. He wasn't supposed to be here! My insides lurched into my shoes as I realised that 'promoted' was now off the table and 'fired' was looking the more likely winner.

"I thought I'd pop behind the mirror to check everything was running smoothly before I went home, given that it's your first time without Lucy. I did *not* expect to find you running an orgy! Outside please, Sophie. Now!"

Somehow I drowned out the blind panic that threatened to make me vomit in front of the group and managed to claw back enough dignity to suggest they sit down and chat amongst themselves, asking the models to get dressed and go home, but first to write down how many medals they had each got.

"I'll be back in a minute," I told the group. I knew I might be lying.

2. The Truth In The Mirror

T he last time I looked in this mirror Dad was alive and I was free.

I found it in a box of stuff I had brought back from the farm last weekend. I had been putting off going through it. I knew how much it would hurt.

I was back in my flat in Milan, shaving with Dad's old mirror; the one he had when he taught me to shave, just four short years after Mum left. I checked my reflection to make sure I hadn't missed any patches, then I found another grey hair. I winced as I pulled it out with a pair of tweezers that had been lurking in the back of the bathroom cabinet. I knew I shouldn't care. It was vain. But I was only in my mid-thirties, and it really showed against my dark brown hair.

Crow's feet had started to garnish my mother's chestnut-brown eyes like dill leaves on a salad. I didn't look like this a year ago. That was *before*.

Tired eyes. A worry line forming between my eyebrows. My face too thin. My skin pale, despite the Italian sun. When did I last cook a proper meal?

The kitchen in my flat in Milan is sterile and functional – barely used. It's too easy to grab food on the run in a city like this and I can go weeks at a time not being here, travelling with work. White and black and stainless steel dominate, with tiles that are strangers to the splash of passata; worktops that have never made fresh pasta; an oven that prefers to reheat than to cook. Such a contrast to the warm chaos of my grandmother's kitchen back at home on our cherry farm. There I am welcomed by the smell of delicious food, whatever time of day I arrive, echoing to the sound of Nonna's loving scolding. *Christof! You are looking too thin!* The shelves happily carry the weight of generations of pottery jugs, heavy-based pans, boxes of hidden luxuries. Wall and floor tiles in every shade of terracotta are stained with stories, dripping with the laughter, worries, and gossip of nearly 300 years.

The room is dominated by a heavy, old, oak table, which my grandparents bought when they got married. It's strange to think that my Dad ate his first ever food at that table. You can still see the scratches he made with his first penknife, shortly before Nonna showed him how much her biggest wooden spoon could hurt, allegedly leaving him unable to sit down for at least two days. It's strange to imagine that I ate my first meal there too, sitting on Mum's lap and stealing cherries from a bowl, causing blind panic when everyone thought I had swallowed a cherry stone and would choke to death, only for them to find I had already spat it out onto my white baby vest. And my parents ate their last meal together there. Before Mum left. But that was too long ago. I was ten. I don't want to go there again. She was never mentioned by Dad or Nonna, or anyone else at the farm, after that evening, as though she had never existed. But I was living proof that she had.

I finished drying my face with a comfortingly soft towel and walked towards my kitchen. It wasn't far. Flats in central Milan aren't huge, though I was fortunate when I bought this place: mine is larger than most, with a high ceiling and windows that actually let in a breeze when the sun is stifling, which is most of the summer. And I'm spared the incessant traffic noise by living up a quieter side street, more useful for parking than for driving. So the air is fresher here, too.

I made myself an espresso using Dad's battered old stove-top pot. It makes me chuckle when I see people spending hundreds of euros on barista-quality home coffee-making machines. I prefer the results from this dented metal contraption, with all its history, that would cost less than ten euros to replace, yet it's irreplaceable. As the water hissed its way through the pot, the room gently filled with that slow aroma of the perfect espresso. No rush. No queue. No paying extra for sitting down. I thought about the nuances of how to make it, with just the right amount of coffee, compacted to just the right degree, with the right surface area, the right speed of the water and the steam, all controlled by the temperature of the hob. Rush it and it would be a weak disappointment. Too slow and it would be bitter and stewed. But I knew I was just distracting myself from other thoughts.

I poured my drink into a small, bright blue, china espresso cup, ignoring the saucer – Nonna wouldn't have approved – and took it to my sofa, to sit and enjoy. I leaned back with my feet on my coffee table. Its battered cherry wood was warm and friendly. It looked out of place against the modern lines of the rest of my apartment. I had rescued it from an old barn at the farm, when I first bought this place. I wanted to bring a piece of home with me. I'd describe my flat more as 'functional' than 'cosy' – the exact opposite of the farm. But with the amount of work and travel I do, I don't have time for fluffing cushions or arranging vases. I like how it feels calm and clean, with nothing I don't need. It's easier that way.

I took the first delicious sip of the espresso. Perfect. Not bitter. Not too strong. No sugar needed. The taste hit my nose before my tongue. But it didn't change anything. I had hoped it might.

It was Saturday - a day off – the first one in I couldn't remember how long. I didn't know what to do with it. I felt like I was bobbing at sea with no oars and no anchor, craving a breeze to give me direction. I wasn't used to freedom like this: being able to choose; no concrete mission.

For years I had worked late nights and I would even bring work home at weekends, on the rare weekends when I was in the city instead of at the farm. But Nonna had kicked me out, telling me I needed to 'go back to my old life'. It was my first weekend in Milan since the accident. I didn't want to be here. But I didn't want to be at the farm either.

I shouldn't be here. I don't mean the flat. When Dad's ancient Fiat left the road and flew down the hillside, I thought that was it. I felt the roof smash as we landed on it. My seatbelt pinned me back, crushing my ribs as it fought to protect me. We rolled. Just like we did as kids when we would lie on our sides and roll down hillside meadows, out of control and crying with laughter and excitement, loving the thrill of it, drowning in the scent of the wild flowers we crushed. Before Mum left.

But cars aren't meant to roll like that. Roof. Side. Wheels. Side. Roof.

I knew Dad was dead even before I looked over at him. He wore his seatbelt loosely, as a token gesture to road safety. Gravity and momentum killed him.

I didn't remember anything else until I was in the hospital, waking up in a white room with white sheets and white lights, and white nurse uniforms and white-coated doctors. I laughed to myself at how it felt like a cliché of comedy hospital heaven. Then I remembered. And I stopped laughing.

No one will ever know what caused Dad to lose control on

the bend he must have driven a thousand times before. The weather was fine. The sun was hazy. The police found no trace of mud or oil that might have caused a skid. From what was left of the wheels, the tyres looked fine. I had been reviewing some financial figures, preparing for the meeting with the bank manager we were driving to, to talk about getting a loan to rebuild the packing barn at the farm. Then suddenly we were flying. And then he was gone.

Luca, my boss, gave me two months off to get over my injuries and sort out the mess that a person leaves behind when they didn't know they were going to die.

I had a few cracked ribs, a dislocated shoulder, whiplash, a few cuts and plenty of bruises, and a decent dose of concussion. That last one was my fault. No one tells you that when your car lands upside down and you take off your seatbelt you'll land on your head. And it will hurt.

The physical wounds healed soon enough. But the rest of it?

It took weeks before I stopped waking up screaming, reliving the accident in slow motion, suffocating under the fear, racking my brain for anything I could have done to prevent it, wishing for a time machine. And it took a month before I could get back behind the wheel of my car. Luca suggested counselling, but what good would that do? There were too many boxes from my past that I'd carefully locked away and I wasn't convinced that 'talking therapy' was going to keep them that way. I'm not ready to deal with them yet. I don't want to talk about it. Any of it.

I sipped more of my espresso and remembered how things used to be, back when I knew how to laugh.

I used to have friends who, like me, loved to drive to the lakes and the mountains at weekends. We worked hard and played hard. We would go off-road mountain-biking, risking our necks on treacherous descents that forced us to pay 100 per cent attention to the slightest movement and change in the track, becoming one with our bikes, and regularly being grateful for the safety gear we had all given in to wearing.

We would hike for hours up hidden tracks that the tourists never found and swim naked in secluded glacial lakes. We would climb rock faces and picnic on the cliff-tops, before abseiling back down. One summer we all got addicted to base-jumping, throwing ourselves off death-defying sheer drops with nothing but some nylon string and an over-ambitious sheet strapped to our backs. The feeling of sheer terror as we jumped was instantly replaced by a profound sense of total peace and calm, a oneness with the air around us, as we floated and glided and, if we were lucky, caught a thermal to add a few precious moments to the exhilaration. The jumping was the easy bit. The only tricky part was landing, which we usually got away with.

Life was full of love, laughter, fun. Summer romances would consume our every waking moment, only to peter out before the first hot chocolate of autumn, but no one cared. We were so free. We felt so alive.

Had I known those days were numbered, would I have appreciated them more? I'm not sure. We all started turning thirty, and with each wedding I attended, another one left the group, never intending it to be permanent, until the christenings started. And after a few years, I was the only one of us left, and I started to fill my weekends with work, instead.

I'm not sure how that happened. It wasn't for want of trying. It would be unoriginal for me to say I had never found the right woman, but I hadn't. I had thought I had with Isabella, but that was perhaps one of the worst calls I ever made.

My friends all came to visit after Dad's funeral, which I had missed while I was unconscious in hospital. I hadn't seen most of them in over a year. They all offered to help. But what could they do?

I feel the pressure of the farm each and every moment of the day. Pietro has run the estate for years – decades – but he's a manager, not a decision-maker. He made that clear to me, once the funeral was over. He runs a team of up to twenty people, who come and go through the seasons, doing everything the farm asks of them. And now paying their salaries, keeping a roof over their heads and shoes on their children's feet and food in their bellies, is my job. Sometimes I wake up in the middle of the night, drenched in icy cold sweat, wondering what would happen to them if I messed up. The fact that I survived, not Dad, puts them at risk. It wasn't their fault that life chose me instead of him. I don't want them to have to pay if I make mistakes.

And Nonna – Dad's mum – pretends she's as strong as an ox, but I know she's not. Not anymore. No woman should have to bury her husband and her son, or raise her grandson without his mother. But she's right. I need to get back to my life – what's left of it.

So I am back at work in Milan, pretending that everything is okay. I'm good at pretending. It's one of the reasons why Luca relies on me. Pretending is a core part of our job, except that the company's official term for it is 'building rapport' – to gain confidences, hear secrets, solve riddles and make the decisions that no one else wants to make.

We're part of an international business consultancy and clients call us in when they know they're just heartbeats away from having to close their business down. Maybe they need to restructure. Maybe someone has been fiddling the books. Maybe their product market is dying and they need new innovations to survive. Finding the answers is our job – those secret solutions that you can only see if you're an outsider. I used to love it.

Maybe one day I will again.

Luca said last week that he's got a new project for me, but this one will be slightly different. Not a company but a 'business', in the southern Italian sense. The file had the name *Denucci* on the cover when I saw it on Luca's desk, just before his holiday. It's going to be a stretch for us all and more dangerous than usual. I need it to wake me up, drag me out of this *stuckness*. I want to feel excitement again, even if that means feeling fear too; to remind myself that there's more to the world than my worries.

So I downed the rest of my espresso and headed to the door, grabbing my keys. I was going to drive into the mountains a few hours outside of the city, and walk until I was too tired to do anything else. I always keep an overnight bag in the boot of my car, because I never know where I'm going to sleep if I'm in the middle of a case, so all I needed to do was to pick up my hiking boots from my lock-up in the musty cellar of my block of flats and I would be on the road.

The sky was blue and cloudless once I escaped the city. The roads were busy. The cars were crammed with families and bike racks. The good weather meant everyone else in Milan had had the same idea. But they would all be heading for Lake Como and the hills around it: to weekend homes and crowded restaurants, and overpriced boat cruises and sunburnt tourists.

I was going an hour or two further up the valley, skirting Como via Lecco and heading past Sondrio and into the mountains. I knew the perfect spot where I could park the car and then walk for hours uninterrupted, falling in love with those views all over again. Alone with just my thoughts for company. As usual.

3. Repercussions

I had been up all night. My stomach was so knotted I hadn't been able to eat and I'd lost count of how many times I had been to the loo. I was convinced I was going to be fired by Harry when I went in to work. He had really lost his rag with me during the focus group. We all know he's a 'creative type' and he tells us that this is why his volatile emotions are never far from the surface, but I had never seen him explode like that before.

"Thank *God* the clients weren't there!" he had roared at me, his face going a shade of red that had made me wonder if I should phone an ambulance. I gave silent thanks for the sound-proofing of the focus group room. "They'd have fired our agency, and do you know how much that would have cost us? Not to mention the damage it would do to our reputation to lose such a Big Name client! We'd have been a laughing stock. It could have been the end of my business! What the hell got into you?"

Every cell in my body had been shaking with fear, trying desperately hard not to show it. Somehow I had managed to explain enough about the plan to persuade him to let me finish the focus group. After all, we had paid the recruiter and the attendees for the event and needed to get some return on our investment, even if I had created a disaster.

I don't know how, but I managed to do a good job for the last fifteen minutes. Luckily the women had thought the whole thing had been hilarious. We had got the descriptive language we needed from them to help with the ad campaign, and I had reminded them that they were sworn to secrecy about the evening's research, at which most of them looked disappointed. Thank goodness their bags and phones had been left in lockers before they went into the focus group room.

At the end of the evening, several of the women had approached me with a smile and a wink, and asked me to let them know if I ever needed help with focus groups again. I'm not sure how I could ever top last night's performance, but at least they enjoyed it.

Harry had gone home after his outburst after telling me he couldn't face watching any more of 'that French farce'.

I had left the clearing up for the cleaners, packed my bag and got the Tube home. It was too late to call Lucy. She would have been asleep. And anyway, I didn't want to stress her. There was nothing she could do before the morning and nothing she could say would have made me feel better.

I had a bottle of white chilling in the fridge when I got back, but I didn't dare open it. I was scared I'd finish the lot, the state I was in. So, instead, I went to bed with what was usually a good book, but the words swam in front of my eyes. I couldn't stop replaying the events of the evening in my mind. And with each retelling they got more exaggerated, blending together with every memory of the many times I had screwed up in my life, until I finally fell into a nightmarish sleep filled with scenes from my mind's special version of its *Day from Hell* movie.

I woke up at 3 a.m., icy cold, pillow and sheets drenched, heart racing, thirsty. I reached out for my glass of water and knocked it all over the bed. *Shit!* I decided to get up and make a cup of tea. Fixes everything, according to us Brits. Well, that's a lie.

I can't lose this job. I can only just afford my rent and there is no way I'll get work elsewhere if word of last night's disaster gets out. And I don't want to go freelance: you need to have been a Planner to get decent work at that. I would need to have been doing Lucy's job for a bit.

As I sat on the sofa, wrapped in the fluffy old blanket that compensates for the rubbish central heating in my flat, my mind ran through every mistake I had ever made at work, as though wanting to make sure I was suffering sufficiently for my crimes last night. It wanted to convince me that the more I tortured myself over my incompetence, the less likely Harry was to fire me. Crazy 3 a.m. logic.

I've been with the agency for four years now and the only person he has ever fired was Simon and that was because he had told a client to f– off. And the client did ... along with their six-figure contract. Was what I had done that bad?

If last night's client hears about it, it could be much, much worse. They could take our other clients with them. It's a small world, the advertising industry, and the business magazines make a big fuss about who works with which brands and agencies. Firms get to do the public 'walk of shame' if a client 'no longer wishes to retain their services'. It wouldn't take long for word to go round and we could lose all of our clients. Or, at least, they might not renew their contracts with us. And bang would go Harry's hopes of selling the agency when he hits fifty, and retiring to his very own, private desert island with Tequila on tap.

And it would all be my fault.

Inspiration struck.

I could phone in sick. Yes. That's what I'd do. Switch off my mobile. Pretend I'd got some terrible, contagious disease. Silent shafts of grey light through a chink in the curtains told me it was now a normal person's time to get up. I checked the clock opposite my sofa: 7 a.m. I'd text Lucy now and tell her I was ill. Dodgy takeaway after the focus group. Maybe that would give Harry time to calm down.

I picked up my phone and turned off the flight mode I use overnight, so it doesn't nuke my brain in my sleep. *Ding ding.*

A text from Lucy. I didn't want to read it.

I peered at it through squinted eyes, the way I used to watch Dr Who on TV when I was a kid, as though that would somehow make the message easier to digest.

Harry called me. What a night you had. Don't you dare phone in sick. I know you. Meet me at the coffee shop at 9. We can fix this. Lucy.

I did as I was told. I showed up at nine and Lucy was already there, her bump meaning she had to stretch to the table for her chamomile tea. My favourite Americano with almond milk was already waiting for me.

"You look crap, Sophie."

One of the things I love about Lucy is that you always know where you stand with her.

"Harry phoned me at some God-awful time this morning and told me what happened. First, I'd like to thank both of you for not calling me about it last night."

"Has he fired me?" I blurted out, interrupting.

"Give me a second!" Lucy took a sip. She was enjoying this. Cow! "No, he hasn't."

"Am-I-on-probation?" It came out as a single word.

"No."

"So where do I stand?"

"Look, it wasn't great. Harry was pretty pissed off. Actually, that's putting it mildly. Very. You know what he's like. He had been telling himself stories all night about how you could have closed his agency down. It's his baby, you know. He's built it up over two decades and it's worth millions. That matters more to him than market researchers expressing their inner creativity. Anyway, he was already at the office when he called me."

"Crazy sod! Does he ever sleep?"

"He's a genius workaholic insomniac, with caffeine flowing through his veins instead of blood. We all know that. Stop changing the subject, Sophie."

I grunted. I was going to be sick. I could feel waves of panic rising again. Breathe! What was it that book said I should do when I felt my heart start to race? Why couldn't I remember?

"Stop holding your breath, Sophie. I told you, we're going to fix this. I have complete faith in you. Anyway, I have persuaded Harry that he took the evening out of context. He has agreed to watch the two-hour video of last night's focus group in full, before he decides what to do."

"So he might still fire me?"

"I don't think so. I can't make any promises, but you and I have a meeting with him at ten. He won't want to stress me in my current *condition*, so at least he'll be civilised."

I looked at my watch. It was 9:45 a.m. I had approximately 15 minutes of employment left.

At 9:50 a.m., Lucy and I crossed the street to the agency. I tried to sneak past Smiling-Susie-in-Reception, who gave me a knowing look. So the word was out, then. Lucy took the stairs to the second floor slowly these days, which I loved, because it meant I wasn't breaking out in a sweat or out of puff by the time I got to the top, like I would have been if I had had to race up them with one of the guys.

I focused on my feet: one foot up on the next step; other foot up on the next step. Gripping the handrail, more to give myself something to hold on to than for balance, I felt the world starting to spin around me.

Fired at thirty-three for gross incompetence and possible criminal activities. That wouldn't look great on my CV.

Lucy walked me up to Janet's desk, Harry's assistant. She always sits in front of his closed office door, keeping guard more effectively than a hungry Rottweiler that's several hours past dinnertime. Her poker face gave away nothing.

"Is he ready for us?" asked Lucy.

Janet nodded. "In you go."

Lucy opened the door. I tried to hide behind her. I didn't want to see Harry's face. He had his back to us. He was watching the last few minutes of the focus group video.

"Bloody brilliant!" he said.

I couldn't work out if he was being sarcastic.

He spun his chair round to face us. He was grinning.

People didn't normally grin when they're about to fire someone… unless they're psycho. Maybe he was a psycho! Maybe he liked firing people.

"Look, I owe you a bit of an apology, Sophie. I was tired last night. I'd had a nightmare conference call with our least-favourite client all afternoon and I walked into the viewing room to see you throwing my business down the pan with some crazy porn movie trailer."

I wasn't off the hook yet. I could feel my nails digging into the palms of my hands.

"I've watched the whole tape. It was a brilliant idea, and you pulled it off. I'm really impressed, Sophie."

"So you're not going to fire me?"

"No! I'm not."

I sank into one of the chairs next to his desk, my legs giving up on me in relief.

"But I do have a serious request for you. In fact, it's going to be a new Agency Rule."

"Yeees?"

"Next time you have a fantastically creative idea to spice up your focus groups, would you please fucking tell me first?"

"Of course!" I said to my shoes, grinning.

He's not firing me!

"Okay. I think we're done here. I reckon you've probably got a report to write up?"

"Sure! I'm off!"

Lucy and I turned to leave his office.

"By the way," Harry added, as we turned round one last time, "those guys were gorgeous! Wish I had been there for the whole thing. Not that I'm gay or anything."

"No, of course not," I mumbled, though we have all suspected it for years. "Thank you. Bye," I half-stuttered in my need to leave the room and gulp fresh air.

I still had a job. And he liked my idea!

"Sophie lives to face another day in the agency world. I told you we'd fix it!" said Lucy. "Now get on with that write-up. I want it on my desk after lunch."

4. The Client's Verdict

L ess than forty-eight hours and two more focus groups after I had rescued my career, the client wanted to know the initial results of the research. They were hungry for answers like children at a chocolate fountain, ready to drink in the data, gorging their appetite for answers, secretly hoping that the results would back up their gut assumptions.

Lucy and I are always strict about that. We don't want to hear about hunches or intuition or best guesses, when the clients brief us. The mainly qualitative nature of our work means that, unlike scientists, it's almost impossible for us to avoid influencing our analysis, if we know the person paying for it has an agenda, though we do try hard. And, from what I have read in magazines lately, it seems that quantum physics could really mess things up for us. But that wasn't something I was going to worry about today.

As part of her strategy to raise my profile with Harry, Lucy wanted me to give the presentation to the clients. I had done it before, but never with him watching and only with the smaller clients. I was wearing my 'posh' skirt and I was aware it was probably a few months past the point where I should have admitted it longed for me to go back to the gym. I had my killer heels on, too, so I was going to need to be extra careful about balancing, but they gave me an extra three inches, which made all the difference when I was standing at the front of the room. Why was it I felt I had to be as skinny Kylie Minogue to get away with being short?

My palms were clammy and I hoped the client didn't notice me wiping my right hand on my skirt, before I shook hands with their team when they arrived. If they did, they were polite enough not to mention it. We all found our seats.

The boardroom's glass oval table was overflowing with presentation folders and chilled water, coffees and sweets, in case someone might pass out in the thirty minutes until lunchtime, if they couldn't get a sugar fix. Every chair was taken and a few spares had arrived, to accommodate the client's marketing and research team, as well as our *creatives* – the people who needed this research to give them inspiration for the adverts they would design. But they weren't allowed to dive in and dream up their crazy ideas until the client had decided which direction to follow. They would make that decision based on our research advice – my advice. That's why I was nervous. The campaign budget was over a million, and if I had got it wrong this past week, they might as well flush crisp £5 notes into the nearest sewer.

No pressure then.

Lucy had given me a brilliant pep talk before they all arrived, reminding me how often I have done this, reassuring me that she agreed with all my conclusions, begging me to speak more slowly than usual and to actually ask them their opinions, instead of forcing them to endure Death by PowerPoint.

Harry was cold with me. He might have let me keep my job, but his expression as we walked into the room together made it clear that I was still on unofficial probation as far as he was concerned, and it was obvious he would rather Lucy had been presenting.

All too soon, Harry announced that it was time to start and

he introduced me to the team I had already met at least ten times. It was as though giving my presentation a sense of formality would prevent the disaster he feared. I stood up from my metal chair, grabbed from the canteen at the last minute, and it scraped across the slate-tiled floor, screeching like chalk down a childhood blackboard. People visibly flinched and gritted their teeth. Great start.

I picked up a can of deodorant from the table and lifted off the lid. It was the winning fragrance and my presentation was to explain why, as well as to give them pointers on marketing messaging that would motivate women to hassle their men to buy it. We were suggesting a totally new approach, but Lucy and I hoped they would love it.

I walked to the front of the room to switch on my laptop, praying that the connection to the projector wouldn't play up again. My plan was to start by passing the deodorant can round for everyone to sniff. There was no need to spray it. There was enough fragrance left in the nozzle to get an impression. Instead, I tripped over the laptop cable and hurled the can at the far wall, where it bounced off the nozzle and filled the room with more of the spray than a typical nightclub.

The air was so thick that it was hard to breathe.

Silence. Apart from muffled coughs, and a sneeze.

Ground. Swallow. Me. Up.

More silence.

Everyone was pretending it hadn't happened, while sneaking glances from their respective bosses for an indication of how to respond. I held my breath.

Then the client manager laughed. He walked over to the window. "I think we'll open this, don't you?" Everyone else joined in with the laughter. *Thank God.* "I hope that wasn't the strategy you used in the focus groups!"

Harry breathed again and the tension eased. I had got away with it.

The rest of my presentation went without a hitch.

They loved it.

They were happy with the results and excited by my recommendations. Even the unorthodox research method got their approval.

After much hand-shaking and back-slapping, it was time for lunch. Officially it was our treat to the client, though we all knew it would end up on their expense account at the end of the project.

Now it was over to the creatives to come up with advertising concepts. My job was done for the moment, until I would get pulled back in to test the ideas out. And that wouldn't be until after Lucy had gone on maternity leave.

But I refused to worry about that right now. There was a glass of Rioja with my name on it and a plate of fresh pasta calling for some *parmigiano* to top it off.

Lucy gave me an affectionate hug.

"You did grand, girl!" she reassured me. I could tell she meant it. And for once I could feel myself starting to believe in my abilities almost as much as she always tells me I should.

5. Worth The Risk?

Our office is on the tenth floor of a glass-walled building that would save a fortune on air-conditioning had someone chosen to put in real walls instead. There are about 200 of us in the Milan team, doing corporate business consultancy work; the usual bread-and-butter stuff. It's cubicle heaven. The only difference in the past ten years is that now the cubicles are arranged in 'group pods' and the walls are half-height, so no one can scratch their bum or pick their nose without someone seeing. And the only way to make a private phone call is to book a meeting room. Even then it would be on speakerphone.

If you know where to look, you'll find us, our team of five – all men for some reason – tucked away at the far side, in front of a north-facing window with a view of the concrete facade of a neighbouring building, across the road. Our boss, Luca, reports direct to the MD. We get the Special Projects, the ones where the stakes are higher and there's a strong chance of someone going to prison. We specialise in run-of-the-mill fraud investigations and embezzlement paper trails, but sometimes we get projects that are out of the ordinary. And today was one of those days.

Luca is short for Gianluca, but he scowls at you if you use his full name – he says it makes him feel too grown-up. He has been my boss for about five years now and he knows that one day I want his job. But I'm in no rush, especially not at the moment.

So he promised that the next time we got a juicy case – one where I could show what I'm made of to the promotions board – he'd make sure it came my way. He's fair like that. I value his level-headed approach and he's a genius at seeing the missing part of the solution if one of us is drowning in the detail. He's also an expert strategist.

We once had a client who was sure there was internal fraud running in their business, but it was too well hidden for their accountants to find. It was the classic reason for calling us in. The fraud has to be big enough to warrant our fee and, when it is, it's always worth them finding it. Luca and I worked on the numbers, asked some awkward questions and found the leaking tap within the first forty-eight hours of taking on the case. I was so excited I was about to call our contact when Luca stopped me. I was confused. Why not tell them? Surely they'd think we were amazing for finding in just two days what they have failed to spot for over a year?

No. That wasn't how it worked. He insisted that we make them wait for at least four weeks, giving them weekly updates, to keep them interested and help them to trust us. And, sure enough, at the four-week point they were blown away by how quickly we had solved the problem and how much evidence we had found for them. They could then hand the entire case over to the police to finish off.

Why did we make them wait? As Luca pointed out, they would never have believed us had we gone back to them after just two days. They needed to believe the fraud had been hard to spot. Otherwise it might have seemed too obvious, like a lucky guess, and they wouldn't have believed us. And we'd have hit the ego of their Financial Director hard, because his team should have found it if it were that 'easy' to spot, and they would never have given us any work again.

We have to be master problem-solvers and genius game-players in this team. A decent poker face helps too, so you never give your emotions away. In addition, the ability to ask the 'obvious' questions that others have overlooked or assumed the wrong answers to will often be what unlocks the final piece of the puzzle.

I walked into Luca's 'office', which is demarcated only by the walls of filing cabinets – our entire floor is noisily open-plan, which means that confidential conversations normally have to happen in meeting rooms. Luca was sitting behind his desk, waiting for me. His desk was empty apart from his three-tier filing tray, a framed photo of Daniela and their two children, and the obligatory brown-stained cup for coffee. He picked up a heavy cardboard file, grey-blue, overflowing, and dropped it on the table in front of me with a decisive *thunk*, leaning back in his swivel chair and gesturing me to sit down.

"The Denucci case. It's all yours. Good luck."

I felt a tingle of excitement. It was a relief after the numbness of the past few months. A thrill shot up my spine. I could still *feel*. A chink appeared in the frozen desert of my emotions. The project would be something to distract me. I was hungry to know more.

"That's not much of a briefing. I'm guessing you might have more to tell me?" I could tell he was teasing me.

"Oh, go on, you've twisted my arm!" he joked. Discretion – secrecy – is vital to the success of the work we do. Those we are hunting cannot ever know we are on their tail. The risks are too great, both to the Special Project and to us. Knowing when to talk and when to shut up and listen, hard, is possibly the most important skill I learned when I cut my teeth on my first few cases in the team. Luca is a great boss. He lets us have a long lead, but we know he's there to support us if we need him. We can feel how much he trusts us, but he won't let us drown.

"Denucci – from the South – has somehow stolen many, many millions from our client, who wishes to remain anonymous, so we would have a code name for him to use in any conversations that could be overheard. It usually only happened when the political or publicity risks of the truth coming out would be too damaging for them.

"The police weren't interested, for the usual reasons," Luca rubbed his thumb and fingers together, letting me know that substantial bribes had been involved, "so they tried to take matters into their own hands. They found the person Denucci had been using to funnel out the cash – one of the company's employees. The thing is that guy is no longer with us, metaphorically or physically. He disappeared shortly after he was discovered. His wife claims to have buried him."

Again, a mystery that may never be solved and wasn't important. However, knowing how things run down there, there is a strong chance that the guy was murdered for incompetence, for letting Denucci down, for being discovered.

"Then, last week, the managing director was found drowned in his swimming pool. It looked like an accident. It looked *too* much like an accident, if you know what I mean."

I nodded. I did. We didn't have to get involved with this kind of thing very often, but it wasn't pretty when we did.

"The local police closed the file, saying he was drunk and fell into the water. But the toxicology report from the post mortem makes that look unlikely. We're pretty sure the police were *persuaded*," more finger and thumb rubbing, "to ignore the death. And the company's owner, who was the MD's best friend, has called us in to help. He doesn't believe his own life is in danger, because it was the MD who had been running the internal investigation. There's nothing to say that he, personally, knew anything. But he has hired bodyguards and added security at his home, just in case."

Luca gave me a moment to mull this over. He knew as well as I did that there would be risks involved in us taking on this Special Project.

"What do they want from us?"

"Enough evidence to put Denucci behind bars. The police have been incompetent or, more likely, intentionally blind. That's where we come in. They want someone invisible, who won't be suspected, to uncover the hidden trails."

I knew what he meant. "Why me?" I asked.

"Because you're ready for this. You're the best on the team. You've got the experience, the confidence and the calm head to handle this, even if it gets messy. And it's a chance for you to prove yourself to the promotions board. Not that I'd want to lose you."

It's not unusual for us to have to 'hide' our investigations from those in the company we're working with. In fact, if someone is suspected of criminal offences, but the client doesn't know who that person is, then it's essential that we don't inadvertently tip the person off. Otherwise they'll cover their tracks and the problem will become unsolvable. But there are ways to do it, questions to ask, patterns to look for. The stakes were higher this time though, as there had almost definitely been a murder, if not two. And that meant we would have to work even harder, not to be seen.

According to Luca's briefing, Denucci is believed to be one of the most secretive leaders of the Camorra: the Naples version of the Mafia. He's so good at keeping himself hidden that even rival clans won't admit to knowing who he is or where to find him. His nickname is 'il fantasma' – the ghost. And that's why we need as much evidence as we can get, to find a way to trace him.

This wasn't the only theft he's wanted for, but he has a habit of making trails run cold. His clan has been growing over the past three years and he's wanted for a string of 'disappearances' and implicated in at least twenty serious fraud investigations. It's said he has a way of *persuading* insiders in firms to help him.

Going after him was going to be a big risk, but it carried big rewards too.

"You know I'm up for this, Luca. But I need to ask … what kind of risk am I going to be taking? How can I make sure I don't end up taking an unscheduled swim next?"

He looked at the photo of his family and sighed, then looked back at me, straight in the eyes. "I won't lie to you, Christof. I can't make any promises, but we'll be invoking enhanced procedures to make sure you're safe. And you're going to have to be careful. Extra careful. It's vital that you keep me in the loop, especially if you spot anything suspicious. Denucci has made it really clear that he is prepared to take whatever action is necessary to cover his tracks on this. And once we're on his tail, I'm assuming we're going to find a rabbit warren of activities he'd rather the authorities didn't know about."

I nodded and picked up the file. It was as heavy as it looked.

"What's next?" I asked.

"Have a good read through that lot and we'll get back together at nine tomorrow. You can take me through your action plan. We need to move fast. Hot trails go cold when people die. This one is already down to lukewarm. Denucci has a head start on us. We're going to need to sprint, to catch him up."

December

Branches dance naked
In the savage winter winds
Time to hibernate

6. The Focus Group From Hell

I took the red-eye Eurostar to Paris this morning at some ungodly hour, to supervise a series of five focus groups we have organised on behalf of a UK client. It was the first time I've been *allowed* abroad for this kind of thing. Normally it would have been Lucy's job, but she was way too pregnant to risk the journey now and she said she'd rather stay in the UK, making the most of her nesting instinct, than lug heavy bags of samples and potential advertising materials halfway across a continent.

It was a stretch for me, but Lucy and I had agreed I was ready for it and it would help to raise my profile with Harry. Lucy has been hinting that she might not want to come back full-time after the baby and she has been grooming me for a job-share with her, though she has sworn me to secrecy, in case Harry finds out and tries to cut the generous maternity leave package she negotiated.

So I was getting to play with eco laundry detergent. Useful stuff, but far from glamorous. The research we had already done in the UK had identified a potential gap in the market and the client wanted to own it.

They are rebranding their current product because apparently its old name meant something rude somewhere else in Europe, and we have got the job of testing out the new name and positioning in the UK, as well as getting them feedback from their three key European territories: France, Germany and Belgium. We are starting with focus groups in Paris before Christmas and Cologne in the spring, moving on to Brussels afterwards, if they still needed more feedback – and have the budget. I speak fairly decent French, having studied it to A level, and I've managed to keep it going over the years, but there is no way I could lead a focus group in the language. I could, however, be the client-behind-the-mirror, supervising them to make sure the focus group leader was sticking to the agreed script and letting him or her know if any burning questions came up. It's something I enjoy. It's like running the group but without the pressure.

We had commissioned a third-party research agency to set up the sessions. The agency is owned by an Eastern-European businesswoman called Katja, who always looks like she has just stepped out of the pages of *Vogue*, with not a hair out of place and perfect nails that have never seen a dishcloth. Her wardrobe manages to make even Parisian women look frumpy. Every time I see her, I subconsciously tot up how much her clothes must have cost and compare it to the monthly mortgage on a small house. The answer always makes me wonder if we're paying her too much. Maybe there's a sugar daddy somewhere behind the scenes. I always feel self-conscious when I'm around her, so I was relieved when she told me that tonight's focus group wouldn't be run by her – she had some formal event she couldn't get out of – but by one of her team, François, who she described as 'a bit of a lady's man'. I smiled to myself. I could do with a bit of harmless flirting with a sexy French accent.

They had hired a room at a focus group facility near my hotel and I was met at the bland (they'd call it 'neutral') Reception by a scruffy looking man in his late forties whose jeans were so dirty I considered offering him one of the bottles of laundry detergent to take home with him. I could see the grease tracks where he has wiped his fingers on them. I didn't want to know how many days ago that had been. His shirt was untucked on one side and was a living memorial to the egg he had eaten at some point in the day – or perhaps week. His straw-coloured hair had the look of a mad professor who pulls his fingers frustratedly through his mop at least every sixty seconds, trying to figure out problems that would have made Einstein cry. And the stench of Gauloises hit me, as he moved towards me, flashing his so-yellow-they-were-nearly-green teeth at me in a smile guaranteed to give young children nightmares. His chins were sprinkled with a week's worth of mottled grey stubble and I tried not to recoil as he held out a stubby hand for me to shake in welcome. I didn't want to know where it had been and I felt an overpowering need to wash mine as soon as I could afterwards.

I assumed he was an assistant and instantly dreaded being locked up behind the two-way mirror with him for the evening. I wondered if there would be wine to help me get through it.

"Bonsoir, Mademoiselle Sophie," he growled, with a guttural accent that sounded like iron railings being dragged over cobbles. He was careful to take a good look at my cleavage, despite it being hidden by the woollen scarf I had wrapped around myself against the December frost, before reluctantly returning his focus to my eyes, lingering on my curves like a sugar addict imagining the flavours of a particularly delicious dessert on his favourite restaurant's menu. I cringed.

"Je suis François."

Shit! Really? This can't be him? Come back Katja with your £2,000 skirt and tights that cost more than my last holiday. All is forgiven.

This couldn't be the man we had hired to lead tonight's research! If he made me feel nauseous, how were our female focus group delegates going to react?

He misinterpreted my shock as having not understood him.

"*Desolé*. I was told you speak French. I am François."

"I do speak French," I stuttered. "I just hadn't expected …" I couldn't stop myself from looking at his filthy clothes.

"Oh, we're not all as formal as Katja. For the evening research groups, we find a more relaxed approach gets better results."

I wasn't sure when the last time was that this level of lack of personal hygiene had been justified as being 'more relaxed', but the research participants were due in fifteen minutes and I knew there was nothing I could do except to hope for the best … and keep my distance. His smiles and gazes made it clear he thought he was irresistible and he was doing his best to flirt with me.

I felt relieved as François closed the door to the client room behind him, but I also felt a quiet dread at what might happen over the course of the next two hours. Maybe the women he was going to be talking to were used to men who looked like him, and wouldn't mind. I felt guilty at inflicting him on them. We weren't paying them enough for this. Respondents would only be getting a token payment that was intended to cover the costs of travel and childcare and a small contribution for their time, but they can't make a living by attending focus groups. And they were certainly going to earn their money this evening.

I had agreed the format for the evening with Katja when I was back in England, drawing up a list of questions and prompts to ensure consistency. All of this series of focus groups will follow the same script. The researcher is allowed to ask probing questions, to get more details if something interesting comes up, but they must always come back to the outline we have agreed.

The women walked into the room, trying to create space between each other in the circle of chairs, staring silently at the walls, the pictures, their handbags, just as women would in England. I had a clear view of them but the mirror on the wall meant they couldn't see me, though legally François had to tell them I was there. I waved. Then felt stupid.

A teenager in understated black slid into the room with a tray of wine glasses and offered them round, before leaving as silently as she had arrived. François started with the introductions, explaining the 'rules' of the evening: that everything was top secret and that whatever they told him would be strictly confidential. They fidgeted nervously in their seats as he gave them a knowing smile and raised an eyebrow.

He moved to the table at the side of the room where a white linen cloth covered a range of boxes and unidentifiable lumps. With a swish that would have made a showman proud he pulled off the cover and revealed tonight's fun: bottles of laundry detergent the women had never heard of and mock-ups of a supermarket shelf display, placing the detergent in context with its competitors. He looked disappointed as his revelation failed to get the gasps of surprise and excitement he had hoped for. The women were still looking blank.

"This, ladies," he said dramatically, picking up a bottle of lavender-scented gloop, "is the reason we are here tonight."

Fortunately he returned to his chair – he had chosen the most comfortable armchair, which he placed right in front of my viewing window, which meant I didn't have to stare at his face – and he went back to the script. It was working well. The women were soon on their second glass of wine and the invisible teenager in black had refilled the nibbles. It was good news for our clients back at home: the market seemed ready for their product, there wasn't much competition in their sector and the women looked intrigued. We were getting great insights to help with the advertising slogans and messaging and I was feeling hopeful.

But then François, obviously yawning, went so far off-script that the train derailed.

It started when he stood up and moved behind his armchair, one hand either side of its back, leaning forwards over it, and started asking the women about washing their underwear. Katja and I had explicitly agreed not to go there. We knew it would make the women clam up and we didn't need to know about it. So when I heard what – to my schoolgirl French – sounded like François asking the women how they knew when it was time to wash their trousers ... their shirts ... their underwear... I choked on my wine, dropped my notebook and was glued to the mirror, terrified about what he might do next.

I didn't enjoy the view. His bottom was hanging out of his trousers as he leaned over, beautifully framed by the fraying waistband of his grey-white boxer shorts, and I was being treated to a view I hoped no one had seen since his mother last changed his nappy. I couldn't imagine anyone ever wanting to get intimate with this guy. It was a very big bottom and his even bigger belly had now escaped from the belt that had been the only thing maintaining any decency in his attire. His stomach was resting, naked, on the back of the chair and he was gently swaying his backside to and fro. Everything was wobbling. He was clenching his buttocks like he was fighting to hold back diarrhoea and I though I was going to vomit. Thank goodness the women couldn't see the view I had.

He leaned over to hand a fragrance sample to the woman nearest to him. She didn't want to take it. Was he staring down her top? I couldn't believe this guy. I really hoped it was just the angle I was looking from. But she must have felt it too because she pulled her dress up, to cover more of her chest.

In the meantime, the women were doing their best to

handle the situation, struggling to give him answers to questions they must have known he shouldn't be asking.

"I change my underwear every day!" volunteered the token Brave Soul who has appeared in every focus group I have ever run.

"What? Even your bra?"

"I don't wash bras in the washing machine. I wash them by hand."

"And does your current laundry detergent get your underwear clean? How can you tell when it's clean?" He was grinning, loving this.

The women were visibly recoiling. One even went so far as to pick up her handbag, as though considering leaving.

That was enough. I had to intervene. He had gone too far off-script and there was no way we could ever use this material for the ad campaign. Our client was clear that they are a family-friendly brand. I left my viewing cocoon and, for the first time in my career, went to the door of the focus group room, knocking once to warn the women I was coming, and walked in. Silence filled the space as everyone turned round to look at me.

"Oh, this is our Client, everyone. Please welcome her! I'm afraid I have already forgotten her name, so I can't introduce you." Everyone mumbled *bonsoir*. The spell had been broken. They had forgotten they were being watched.

"François, I need a quick word with you, please."

He pulled a funny face at the women to signal that he didn't normally take orders from younger women, but that he was making an exception to humour me.

The moment the door closed behind him the fear and frustration I had been feeling exploded.

"You have gone too far off-script. Get back to the questions we agreed or I'm pulling the plug on tonight and I'll make sure that Katja takes the costs out of your wages."

He looked at me blankly. "But it was interesting, *n'est-ce pas*, what they do with their underwear?"

Rage gave me courage. This man was four times my size and had a severe lack of understanding of appropriate behaviour. I took a deep breath. He needed to know I meant this.

"No," I hiss, "Script, or you're fired."

I tried to look dignified as I turned my back on him and went back to the client's viewing room.

He cracked a joke I didn't understand as he scratched his bum and went back into the room. He reluctantly went back to the script and the rest of the evening limped on.

At the end of the night, once the women had left, I joined him again in the focus group room.

"I need to show tonight's research group recording to Katja in the morning, so we can agree what needs to change before we run any more of these sessions. Please give me the tape."

I say *tape*, but we haven't used tapes for many years. These days it's all digital.

François laughed. His gut wobbled with his chins. "Oh, yes, that. I forgot to turn on the cameras." And he walked out of the room, without saying goodbye, leaving me, the paying Client, to clear up.

I made it back to my hotel room at midnight, exhausted, stressed and half-wondering if I was about to get a visit from the police. I wasn't sure whether François' behaviour this evening had been legal.

It had been so bad I would have laughed, had my career not been hanging on getting a successful outcome from these groups.

I lay in my hotel bed, reliving the evening in glorious technicolour. Yes, it had been every bit as bad as I had thought it was. In fact, my internal replay was pointing out bits I hadn't noticed when we were live. It had been a disaster.

There were another two nights and another four focus groups still to do. We couldn't use François again. And I wasn't sure tonight's research was of much use, especially after the underwear incident. I was going to have to talk to Katja first thing in the morning. I was dreading it. I hate confrontation. But if I let the rest of this trip run the way tonight had, I'd be unemployed and homeless by Christmas.

7. The Chateau's Memories

I was heading back to Paris for the first time in years, running a course for Head Office in a beautiful chateau in the countryside, north of the city. We have been developing a new international database with programs that can check for common patterns in companies' financial data, to make it easier to detect fraud, embezzlement and theft, and I needed to train my colleagues in how to use it.

I'm not usually one for standing up at the front and presenting all day, so I had designed the training to be more of a workshop, where we would all get to share the latest developments and best practices from our individual branches. I planned to slot the software part in early on, before lunch, or no one would be paying attention any more.

The chateau is beautiful, requisitioned from its aristocratic owners when the State relieved them of their heads during the French Revolution. It has since made its way back into private ownership and its thirty bedrooms are all decorated with exquisite attention to historical detail. It's not uncommon to have a four-poster bed and an antique chaise longue to relax on, with a dressing table whose mirror has been reflecting faces and emotions for centuries. When a company hires the whole property, you get a free bar, with local wines, beers and liqueurs. So lunch was likely to have a strong liquid element. It was going to be great for networking and we were all staying overnight, with a presentation from the Managing Director of our European Operations on the second morning, before we left. Luckily he was going to be with us this evening, so would get to follow his lead on pacing ourselves at the bar.

It was also going to be the first time I had seen Isabella, since we split up eighteen months ago. Actually, it's nearly two years now. She went back to the Paris office afterwards, leaving me in Milan, and I haven't heard from her since. I was hoping she was going to behave herself. After all, it was she who left me. That's another box best left well and truly locked.

I was in Lyon with a client yesterday, so I stayed there overnight and caught the 7 a.m. train, reaching Paris Gare de Lyon just after nine. A twenty-minute taxi would get me to Gare du Nord, for my train to the chateau, but I asked the driver to drop me at a nearby *boulangerie* instead. I had missed breakfast at my hotel and the food on the train was predictably bad, but I would have just enough time to grab some croissants and a filled baguette before my train left, if I was quick.

The taxi wound its way past the familiar sights. The slow traffic of the morning rush hour meant he gave me a great view of the Place de la Bastille and then he took me way off course, past Notre Dame, which was a treat in the early morning winter sunshine. I found myself remembering the last time I had come to Paris. It was also the time I had got together with Isabella.

The chateau is stunning, but it has the classically unreliable plumbing you might expect from a property that was already ancient when the Republic of the New France was born in the late 1700s. That plumbing got me into a lot of trouble the last time I stayed here.

Ten of us had been dragged up to Paris for a conference. I already knew Isabella from her visits to the Milan office and, as the only other Italian at the meeting, it was no surprise when she sat next to me at dinner. She was so stunning that most men melted in her path. Fortunately I knew I wasn't in with a chance – I wasn't her type; I didn't own a yacht – so she held less power over me.

After dinner we headed to the free bar and made our way through yet more glasses of really good local red wine. The owners bought it by the barrel, so it was served in lightly chilled stoneware carafes, adding to the testosterone as the men competed with each other to identify the grapes and the region, to impress Isabella. It didn't work.

We walked back up to the floor our rooms were on and said goodnight. No spark. No tension. I was tired, and a long way the wrong side of light-headed. But I couldn't help but feel the inevitable male instincts sparking up as I watched Isabella's eternally long legs and impossibly high black heels walking confidently away from me, back to her room. I couldn't deny a twinge of disappointment.

I smiled to myself as I closed my bedroom door behind me, feeling secretly proud of the jealous looks the others had given me this evening, when it appeared – to them – that I had monopolised Isabella's attention. And, of course, the fact that we had chatted in Italian meant that none of them could understand a word we were saying. No doubt I'd come in for a ribbing at breakfast as they jumped to conclusions.

I tried to clear my head with a large bottle of water from my room's ice bucket and a re-read of the figures I would be presenting the next day. It didn't work and I had just decided to give up and go to bed when I heard a knock at my door.

The chateau didn't do room service and I wondered who it might be, as I could still hear the guys laughing in the bar downstairs. I opened the door and standing there, in a luxurious, fluffy, white hotel dressing gown and those dangerously high heels was Isabella.

"My shower doesn't work. I don't want to wake up the caretaker. There's no guarantee he'd be able to fix it tonight, anyway. Could I use yours?" My head took a few moments to get itself round what she had said. The thought of sitting just the other side of a plasterboard wall from a naked Isabella getting hot and steamy sent me into a spin.

"Please, Christof. Does your shower work?" I managed to nod, unable to speak. She walked into the room, closed the door behind her and untied the belt of her dressing gown, letting it fall to the floor. She was wearing nothing but a black silk camisole, black lace-topped stockings and those shoes. I stood in stunned silence. Her confidence made it clear that it wasn't the first time she'd had this effect on a man. And she loved it. "I have no intention of showering alone, Christof."

It was an incredible night, one I will never forget, and the start of an unexpected love affair. As soon as I let down my defences I fell head over heels in love with her. What else was there to do? She got a secondment back to the Milan office and it was the most intense summer of my life.

Her socialite contacts meant we lived through a whirlwind of moonlit balls, crammed with power-hungry politicians and breathtakingly beautiful celebrities. We spent long, lazy afternoons on yachts, surrounded by Adonis-type men and nearly naked women who wouldn't know an ounce of fat if it smacked them in the face, drinking Champagne that had been bottled before I was born. We attended film premieres in Cannes, staying in luxury hotels, wearing full black tie, despite the heat. And I had Isabella on my arm. It was most men's idea of heaven.

Although I was swept away by it all, daring to dream that Isabella might be the woman I would spend the rest of my life with, deep down I knew it felt fake, though I would never have admitted that at the time. It's funny how hindsight changes the past. I knew Isabella loved me, in her own way. But the life we were living was as unreal as the love: ungrounded; superficial. It couldn't last. And it didn't.

8. The Boulangerie

I was so stressed about last night's focus group I couldn't have had more than a few hours' sleep. Part of me couldn't believe that Katja would employ François. Part of me was scared that Harry would say this had all been my fault, even though it wasn't. I didn't want to phone Lucy to ask her advice. It wasn't fair to stress her, at least not until I had tried to sort it out for myself.

So I texted Katja this morning to ask if I could meet her in her office at ten, to talk about some important changes for today's focus groups. She agreed. I felt nervous, but it was going to be easier to do this face to face. I had to keep reminding myself that *we* were *her* paying client and that last night's fiasco could not be repeated. It should be *her* feeling nervous. But her perfect sophistication always intimidates me, even when I'm wearing my smartest clothes and manage to get my hair to behave. I had slapped on enough make-up to force my face to pretend it had got enough sleep, but I knew that none of this would be enough.

Her office is near Gare du Nord and I was over half an hour early, so I decided to grab a quick coffee and a croissant and maybe find a bench to sit on, to watch the world go by for a while. I was glad I had brought my winter coat. It was freezing. It was December, so why was I surprised it was so cold? I saw a *boulangerie* over the road and managed to cross to it without getting run over – a feat I always felt proud of in Paris.

I hadn't seen Isabella her since the moment she walked out of my life, leaving my heart, my hopes and my dreams shattered like an opera soprano's crystal glass. What she did was unforgivable. It's locked in a box, like so much else in my life, and I didn't want to think about it just now.

My stomach was rumbling with nerves and I kept rehearsing things to say in my head. I was glad we would get a networking session before my presentation, so I would have a chance to say hello to her before I had to stand up and speak in front of her. I was dreading seeing her. I had no idea what it might dredge up for me. But there was nothing I could do to avoid it. I was going to have to go straight through the middle of this one.

I knew I had been secretly holding on to the pain of our ending. It has been nearly two years since I last took a woman out for dinner, let alone opened up enough to start a relationship. Part of me was hoping that seeing Isabella again today would prove to me – and to her – that there was nothing there anymore. But, after what she did, I still had no idea how long it might take me to trust someone again.

I was grateful to my taxi driver for leaving me to my silence and I gave him a generous tip as he dropped me at the *boulangerie*. I grabbed my case and looked at my watch as I got out of his car. Just enough time, if I was quick and there wasn't too much of a queue.

I was lost in my thoughts as I reached out to open the door of shop and bumped into a stranger who was hurrying with a suitcase.

"Ouch!" He pretty much crashed into me.

"Oh, I'm sorry. I wasn't concentrating. Are you okay?" he asked me in perfect English, but with the slightest hint of an accent. I couldn't place it.

"How did you know I'm English? It's not that obvious, is it?"

"No. It was the 'ouch'. English word."

My embarrassment crept up over my face like a shiny, red mist.

"Actually," he continued, "I know it's not very English, but I'm in a real hurry. I've got a train to catch. And I'm starving hungry. Would it be okay if I jump the queue, please?"

Chestnut-brown eyes. Dark brown hair. Mid-thirties? A sad look about him. Tall enough to be elegant, but not so tall that you'd need a stepladder to kiss him. Broad shoulders. Nice strong chin. Just my type. And then he smiled at me. My knees wobbled. How could I refuse him?

"Of course," I mumbled, cranking up the blushing at the thoughts this stranger was inspiring in me.

"Thank you." He moved up to the counter and ordered a croissant and a Brie and tomato baguette. I had my eye on a solitary slice of one of my favourite desserts – black cherry *clafoutis*. It was sitting on a little cardboard tray behind the glass counter, ready to be taken to the park. It had my name on it.

I had been putting off having to think about what I was going to say to Katja, so I stood behind the stranger, allowing myself to daydream about running my fingers through his hair, wondering what it might be like to kiss him. God, it had been too long! I found myself admiring his backside, which looked fantastic in his navy trousers. And a white linen shirt. Suddenly I had a flashback to last night and François: his backside; his half-mast jeans; his filthy white shirt; his wobbling belly and chins. I shuddered with an audible 'urghh' sound. It wasn't in the dictionary. Mr Tall-Dark-And-Handsome heard it and he turned round, looking confused. I turned as red as the tomatoes in his baguette.

"Thank you again." He smiled, this time with his eyes as well as his mouth. I watched him turn his attention back to the shop assistant and suddenly I realised he was pointing to my slice of *clafoutis*.

"No!" escaped my mouth in panic, before I could stop it. Both the stranger and the shop assistant were now staring at me.

"Is there a problem?" the stranger asked. But I was back to that familiar feeling of wanting the ground to swallow me up. I struggled to speak, but everyone was waiting for me to say something.

"It's just that I really love cherries. I haven't had *clafoutis* for years. I was about to buy that slice!" The stranger nodded, as though I had been sharing a universally important nugget of wisdom, before turning back to the woman who had been serving him.

"Do you have any more?" he asked her. She shook her head. He turned back to me and smiled, telling me it was mine. He would take the *tarte au citron* instead. I beamed and watched him leave. My heart was fluttering. He had disappeared. He hadn't been lying about being in a hurry.

After grabbing my breakfast I had to jog to Gare du Nord, fumbling in my coat pocket for my train ticket as I ran, dragging my suitcase behind me. I made it with a minute to spare and got on at the first carriage, squeezing my suitcase through the narrow aisles as the train started to move, trying not to run over strangers' feet, until I finally made it to my carriage.

I performed the ritual of trying to get my suitcase into the overhead racks – surprisingly difficult, despite it being small enough to fit in the overhead locker of a plane. Then I somehow managed to take off my bulky winter coat without injuring anyone and without dropping my breakfast on the floor. It made me glad I wasn't carrying a coffee, though I needed one. My neighbours muttered with displeasure at me upsetting the peace of their morning commute. I also annoyed the woman sitting next to me in the aisle seat by asking her to move, so I could reach my seat. She made it clear that she was very comfortable and I should have shown up sooner if I wanted to sit next to the window. I hoped this wasn't a sign for how the rest of my day was going to go.

It was my turn at the counter. I bought myself thinking time by pretending to inspect the options behind the glass, forgetting the queue behind me. I wondered how the *Mr Clafoutis'* (my new name for him) English was so good, and what he was doing. Where he was from. I had forgotten to check for a wedding ring:

occupational hazard of dating once in your thirties. Even if there was no ring, he would probably have a girlfriend or a messy divorce behind him. Or he would be freaked out at the fear that my biological clock might be ticking so loudly it could serve as an alarm for a whole city and I only wanted him as a sperm donor. Anyway, it wasn't like I was ever going to see him again. He would be on his train any minute.

"Madame?" abruptly interrupted my thoughts.

Jolted back to the *boulangerie* I saw a middle-aged woman in a white apron looking at me with a bored expression. "I'd like two croissants, the *clafoutis* and a black coffee to take away, please," I said in my best French.

She shook her head. I was confused. Didn't she understand? Was my French that bad? She pointed to the tables at the side of the shop and told me they didn't do takeaway coffee, as though the idea disgusted her. If I wanted coffee, I could drink it there or go to Starbucks.

I needed coffee, I had got so little sleep last night. I wanted real croissants and I wasn't missing out on that *clafoutis*, so I shrugged and nodded. A table in a café was as good as a park bench when it came to wasting time, and the extra I would be paying would go on my expenses, anyway.

Luca had said Isabella might be coming back to the Milan office for a while. I had no idea why. She would be working with Luca via the Paris office in the meantime, joining us in Italy in the spring. I wasn't sure how I was going handle working with her again.

My train arrived promptly and I took a taxi to the chateau. It hadn't changed since I was last here. The taxi driver was impressed, as he pulled up the long driveway through the avenue of old trees. I couldn't tell what they were without their leaves.

I could feel its history: the joy, the love, the war, the hatred. It was all there, piled into the bricks and stones and plaster and woodwork. My history, too. I was stupidly tense about meeting Isabella again. I had no idea how I was going to feel about it – or how she would behave.

I paid the taxi and carried my suitcase up the steps to the front door. In the olden days, someone would have met me there, to carry my bag and even unpack for me. It was funny to think how much change this place had seen. Part of me wished it could talk. But knowing how the French Revolution ran, most of me was pleased it couldn't.

I stepped up to the heavy oak door and listened to its hinges creaking as I pushed it open. I walked inside and my heart stopped. Someone was there waiting for me.

"Hello, Christof," she said, looking as beautiful as I remembered. Even more so, if that were possible. "I thought it would be good for us to clear the air before the training starts. How are you?"

She accepted the two-sided kiss of a friendly business colleague. I managed a 'hello', but that was it. A knife twisted inside me. Was she as beautiful as I had thought? I was sure I could see traces of coldness in her face. She was outwardly stunning, yes, but maybe I knew her too well to be able to find it on the inside.

"I thought we should put the past behind us and make sure it doesn't get in the way of our work. What do you think?"

She was acting as though nothing had happened. I hadn't

seen her since she dumped me. Even that she didn't do face-to-face. Surely I was entitled to explanations? I wanted to talk about this. I wanted to know why she had done what she did – what I had done wrong. Or did I? Wouldn't I rather just move on? It was all crammed into that tiny box in my heart. Surely talking about it would open up the old painful wounds again? Isabella was standing opposite me, smiling professionally, waiting for an answer.

"Of course. That's fine." I would have to make sure it was.

9. Afternoon Tea At Claridge's

I t was the final week before Lucy was due to leave and we were putting the finishing touches to her farewell do. It was a far cry from the last party we planned for her – her hen night, two years ago.

Anything even hinting at being racy had been strictly forbidden, in case it pushed her blood pressure over the limit or kicked off labour. She wasn't due until January, but she had some annual leave to use up, so she was leaving before Christmas. She didn't feel there was much point in coming back in January for just a week or two. And she was feeling tired most of the time now, so whatever we chose had to be easy and low effort for her.

She finally agreed to let us do something she knew she wouldn't be able to do for a while, once the baby had arrived: afternoon tea at Claridge's. She figured that the baby would smash the delicate china tea cups and smear the chairs with clotted cream, so it was now or never. And with 'eating for two' she wasn't fussed about the calories any more.

Harry had agreed to us all finishing early, so that the ten of us could go on a weekday afternoon, when it would be quieter. The tearoom was filling up fast with Christmas shoppers at weekends.

We arrived on time, but having already been to the pub, we were perhaps a little louder than their usual guests. We started with a tour of the Christmas tree, which had been designed by Dolce and Gabbana. It was simply incredible. At 8 metres in height it dominated the foyer, rising up past the staircase. There were life-sized moving deer below it in a forest scene that even had a small fire burning underneath the tree – health and safety compliant, of course. The baubles were made of clear glass with hand-painted flags on them and the lights made them twinkle and shine. The tree was topped by lights that looked like they could be the Snow Queen's winter crown. It was beautiful.

The tea room was full of retired *Ladies Who Lunch* and tourists, trying to look like they fitted in. Harry had arranged it all. We weren't even allowed to look at the menus (he said the prices would have made us cry) and he was picking up the bill as his gift to Lucy. She has worked for him for five years.

Someone had let slip that Lucy was expecting a girl, though she had tried to keep it a secret, and Harry had told the restaurant when he made the booking. So there were pink smoked-salmon sandwiches, with green peppercorns, and pink raspberry choux pastries called 'choir boys'. The Cornish clotted cream was generously domed over the top of its beautiful mint-green and cream striped cups: none of the 'level teaspoon per scone' nonsense that normally passed for a cream tea. We had over twenty flavours of tea to choose from, though most of us didn't know where to start. And the sandwiches went beyond the traditional 'crusts removed' and were cut into exquisite 'finger sandwich' rectangles, lined up on the plates like a child's toy train. Even the traditional 'egg mayonnaise' had been made with duck eggs, chopped by hand, with home-made mayonnaise. It was all so very civilised.

I tried a freshly baked scone, still warm from the oven, with Christmas jam (they called it something eyebrow-raisingly fancy – *Marriage Frères Noël gelée* with orange zest and vanilla pods –

Madagascan, of course) and more clotted cream than my arteries would thank me for. My first bite was enough to confirm that these chefs knew their stuff. As I raised it to my mouth, even before I tasted it, the smell was heavenly. It made me forget the stress of work and presentations and research, and the absence of a life partner (don't get me started on my pre-thirty-five life plan failures). The first bite melted in my mouth. I would be doing it an injustice to describe it as 'delicious'. The cream was so fresh. The jam – sorry, *gelée* – perfectly sweetened with just enough fruit to remind you it was real. The scone was delicate, but not too crumbly. The tea was loose-leaf, in a proper teapot, with a silver strainer and fresh milk in a jug. The pastries were sublime. And the service was attentive.

We finished with a mini Christmas pudding, made to the same recipe Claridge's has been using for one hundred years, served with cognac custard. I had never tasted anything like it! It was a million miles from the heavy stodge that normally left me unable to move after a family Christmas lunch at home.

Lucy was beaming and it was clear to see that this was a wonderful choice for her leaving celebration. Of course, we are all hoping it's not really a 'leaving' celebration. We want her to come back in twelve months' time at the end of her maternity leave, but employment law means that's a topic Harry is not allowed to discuss with her. He has hinted that he'd like me to find out more, once the baby has arrived, and to let him know. We'll see!

Everything was very polite and civilised until Harry announced, "Sod this for a leaving party. Let's get some Champers!" Pink, of course, though Claridge's preferred the term 'rosé'.

Two hours later and we wondered how often people were asked to leave Claridge's, after having chalked up that particular achievement, assisted by a refined but firm restaurant manager. We got taxis back to the office, where we had left our laptops and a fluffy bear so enormous it was bound to psychologically scar the baby for life.

Lucy had asked us not to buy her baby clothes or kit, because she was going to be borrowing most of it from her older sister. So, instead, we clubbed together and bought her a year's nappy laundry service. Glamorous, not! But she was over the moon.

"Now I won't have to wash a single nappy for a whole year!" she chimed, with delight in her voice.

"Yes, but you'll still have to change them!" Gary threw back at her. He has vowed he will never have children, despite the adoption and surrogacy options now available to gay couples. "They're far too much hard work and I'm way too selfish to bother. And Harry doesn't pay me enough to hire a nanny!" he would retort, whenever anyone asked him why.

The next morning, I was sitting in Lucy's office for the last time in a while. It was hard to imagine the place without her. Tomorrow was going to be her last day. That was when she would introduce me to Stuart, the guy who is taking over from her as her maternity cover. I had heard rumours that I hoped weren't true, but Harry said he's an old friend from his uni days, so I was keeping my fingers crossed.

I took a slurp from my coffee and watched Lucy sipping her pregnancy-friendly herbal tea. I wondered how her life would change in the coming weeks. Could she still drink hot tea with a wriggling baby in her arms? When might she next get peace and quiet? Time to herself? How would it change her? Would she still have time to be friends? Would she want to come back to work?

"Spill!" she instructed, interrupting my musings.

"What?" I replied, for once not knowing what she was talking about.

"You're lost in thought and this might be the last time in who knows how long that you get my undivided attention. How can I help?"

I plucked up the courage to ask the question I had wanted to ask her since the day she told Harry she was pregnant.

"Why couldn't I cover for your maternity leave?"

Lucy paused and smiled at me. She knew how hard it had been for me to find out that someone was going to cover for her.

"You're already so busy," she replied.

"But we could have hired a freelancer to cover my old work."

"Yes, but that would have cost more."

"What's the real reason, Lucy?" I replied, sensing that she wasn't telling me the whole story. "I even gave up my Italian night class so I could work longer evenings and do more focus groups! It was all that was left of my social life."

"Okay. You asked for it. It's Harry. He doesn't know you as well as I do and it doesn't matter how often I tell him you're great, he hasn't had a chance to see that yet. He thinks it's down to me, even though it's not."

I pretended to be fascinated by my mug, by the swirling patterns the steam from the coffee was making.

"But it's a good thing, Sophie."

I gave her a look that told her what I thought of this comment.

"Really! While I'm off, you can shine. He'll see it's really you, not me. You'll be helping Stuart to find his way around, so you'll be stepping up to the next level. Harry was pretty impressed by the way you handled the disaster with that horrible man in Paris. He'll think more of you once I'm not there as a go-between."

She waited to see if this cheered me up. It didn't. She tried again.

"And remember, we've got our master plan – our job-share – once I'm back from having the baby. I'll be there to help you while I'm off, to make sure you're lined up for Harry to say yes in a year's time."

"I suppose so," I grunted, conceding that she might have a point. But I was still feeling hollow inside. Seeing Lucy going off to have her baby, just two years older than me, reminded me how far behind I was on where I thought I'd be by this stage in my life.

"What else is up?" she asked gently, really wanting to know.

I didn't want to admit it, even to myself. And saying it out loud to someone else risked making it too real to ignore. But Lucy gave me a look that told me silence wasn't one of the available options, so I took a deep breath and started.

"I'm fed up with being single." There. Said it. No more pretending. "I'm not sure I want babies, like you obviously do, but I don't want to be on my own either. I'm really busy, but I feel lonely. I'd love to have someone to go home to. And Jamie phoned me last week."

Lucy sat up as straight as her bump would allow and gave me her best headmistress look.

"Do. Not. Go. Back. There." She punctuated each word with a wag of her finger.

"Is that an order?" I replied, cheekily.

"You bet it is. Don't you remember how he behaved?"

How could I ever forget? Nearly six months ago, after treating me like shit for two full years, he had run off with some disgustingly rich heiress or other who had shimmied her double-Ds at him, along with her daddy's country pile. I never even got a goodbye. The night he dumped me, I had thought he was about to propose. He stood me up at the poshest restaurant I have ever been to, without even the decency to send me a text. I cried my way through the most expensive bottle of wine I had ever bought, as I waited for him to arrive. It was the longest evening of my life. It sounds flippant when I talk about it now, but at the time it tore me apart in ways I didn't know love could.

"Anyway, what did he want?"

"Dinner."

Lucy's eyebrows looked like they were trying to hide in her hairline. The look said it all.

"What happened to his heiress?"

"I don't know. He said he doesn't want to dwell on the past. He wants to see if we could have a future together."

Lucy gave me what Paddington would have called a 'hard stare'.

"How convenient," she answered, with a concrete mixer full of sarcasm. "And what do *you* want?"

"To not be lonely anymore."

"I hear you, sister." There is obvious compassion in her voice. "But is Jamie the price you want to pay for that?"

I didn't know, but surely anyone was better than no one? Wasn't it like job-hunting, where it is always easier to get a new job if you already have one, and people can smell desperation even before you put your interview suit on? Didn't long-term single girls have neon signs above their heads that warned potential suitors about ticking biological clocks and a dangerous need for near-instant commitment?

"I just thought I'd be settled by now. I can't even be bothered with dating any more. And in this line of work, nearly every attractive man I meet is either gay or married."

Lucy nodded in silent agreement. There hadn't been anyone since Jamie. When he left me, at the start of the summer, I lost contact overnight with our network of friends. They were his friends, really. In fact, looking back, I'm not entirely sure they were ever my friends. And after two years of being part of the 'in' crowd, I had lost touch with most of my old friends. It took me a while to rebuild any form of social life. And that was just me and the girls once in a blue moon, because we were all too busy working. Pizza, wine and a DVD. Unless we wanted to pick up the delivery guy, the chances of romance were slim.

"Make me a promise, Sophie?"

"Maybe."

"Be very, very careful. And don't trust a single word that piece of shit tells you."

She had a point. But surely going out for dinner couldn't hurt?

Lucy read my mind. "And remember to take your wallet with you if you go out for dinner with him. When was the last time he ever paid the bill?"

10. Trampolining

Luca lives about an hour outside of Milan, in a suburb where people can still afford to buy a place with a garden. He lives with his wife, Daniela, and their two young boys. This weekend he was dragging me over to show off his latest acquisition: a trampoline.

"When was the last time you jumped up and down like a lunatic, Christof, just for the fun of it?" he asked on Friday morning, as he told me about the invitation. He had a point. The answer was probably twenty-plus years ago and that wasn't on a trampoline.

"Anyway, Daniela is expecting you. She's going to be making gnocchi and, frankly, you look like you could do with feeding up. You're going to need to put another notch in your belt soon, if you keep losing weight like this. I know you've been through hell, but don't you deserve some fun?"

I had nothing else planned, so I drove out to Luca's place late on Saturday afternoon. He and Daniela had invited me to spend the night, so we would have plenty of time to relax. But Luca had forbidden me from talking about work. The Denucci case was pretty busy and he knew we both needed some time off.

I arrived to the sounds of children screaming in the back garden, their noise reaching as far as the front door. I couldn't tell if they were having fun or trying to kill each other. It turned out to be both, as I found them running around the garden with water pistols, drenching anyone or anything that got in their way, covered from head to toe in waterproofs and wellies, to protect them from the December cold. I did a double-take at them playing what I had always thought of as a summer game just before Christmas.

Luca handed me a lightly chilled beer and Daniela gave me a welcoming hug and the Italian double-kiss.

"Dinner will look after itself now," she said, "and I want to see if you look as stupid as Luca on the trampoline." She grinned as she issued the challenge. I couldn't refuse. I was grateful for my winter jumper as I headed out into the back garden.

There was nothing else for it, I was going to make a complete fool of myself. But I knew they wouldn't hold it against me. We didn't have a trampoline when I was a kid. Such a thing would have seemed frivolous when the farm was always trying to find ways to fund its costs and pay its staff. And there was only me. No other children. When Mum left I had to become a mini-adult overnight. She had been the only one who remembered I was a child. Everything got so serious. I've seen trampoline parks in various places on my travels, but there has always been a good excuse not to use them, so I was a trampolining virgin, halfway through my fourth decade.

It was time! I handed Luca my beer bottle and climbed up the steps. It was about a metre off the ground and at least 3 metres across, with a 2-metre high netting enclosure to stop the kids from breaking their necks. They came running over, excitedly shouting hellos. One of them pointed his water pistol at me. "Go on, Uncle Christof! Otherwise we'll have to shoot you."

I made my way awkwardly to the centre of the trampoline, my sense of balance maxing out as my feet got confused by why the ground beneath them wasn't behaving the way it should. I stood there, confused, realising I didn't know what to do. It suddenly felt so frivolous to be bouncing without a care in the world, when the fate of at least ten families rested on my decisions. I felt like they were all sitting on my shoulders, weighing me down as I tried to jump, egged on by the cheers of Luca's family in the softness of the early evening sun. The farm-workers' faces are always there when I fall asleep. They haunt me in my dreams. I don't make a single decision in life any more without thinking about how it might affect them.

It has only been a few months since the accident. I suddenly realised I was about to cry. The tears were stinging my eyes and a torrent of emotions was threatening to take over. I hadn't cried since the *accident*. I called it that in my head; it was easier than saying 'since Dad died'. I felt a wave of panic rising inside me. I couldn't cry in front of the kids. If I started, I was scared I would never stop.

Daniela, like the angel that she is, guessed what was happening and stepped in to rescue me.

"Uncle Christof is clearly hopeless at this. Perhaps one of you could get onto the trampoline with him and show him how it works?"

Alessandro, their elder son, obliged by leaping up the steps and crawling through the gap in the enclosure netting, bouncing towards me with a grin the size of a large banana on his face. He grabbed my hands and told me to copy him. It was clear he was a seasoned professional. His bouncing forced me to bounce and soon we were lifting each other higher and higher into the air, as one's landing launched the other. It was fun. I was laughing. I felt like a bird: that moment of airborne stillness at the top of the jump where your stomach does a somersault.

I know this feeling, this weightlessness – like being in a car that is flying over the edge of a steep drop, preparing to bounce and roll. I have to stop. I freeze, but the trampoline beneath me doesn't. I have to get out of the car. I don't want to die. I'm trapped. I'm not in a car. I'm on a trampoline. It has to stop. I don't want to scare the boys. I don't know how to make it stop! Their screams of laughter echo the smashing and crashing of the windscreen and bodywork and wheels and branches. Please make it stop! I have to get off. Now.

I tried to smile at Alessandro and pretended I was feeling seasick because he was so good at bouncing. He bought my lie. The fear was taking over. I wasn't sure how I was going to get away from this. I clambered through the tiny gap in the netting and fell down the steps, twisting my ankle. I yelled out in pain. I managed to tell Luca and Daniela I needed the loo. They knew I didn't. I ran into the house, ignoring the screaming pain in my ankle, and made it to their lounge where I collapsed on their sofa.

The sobs took over. They wouldn't wait any longer. I muffled the sounds with a cushion.

They tore at my throat. I couldn't breathe between them. I was suffocating. Drowning in the grief I had pretended wasn't there. The anxiety was rising. My whole body was part of this wave upon wave of letting go.

The guilt of surviving. Of not being good enough. Of being the one who should have died.

After a few minutes Luca came in, quietly shutting the door behind him, and put his arm round my shoulder. I was exhausted. The sobs were less physical now, but they still wouldn't stop. He sat with me, hugging me gently for as long as it took until I was done.

"Thank you," I said, with a final sigh, feeling a gentle sense of release and relief that I didn't have to keep holding the emotions in, pretending they weren't there, pretending to be strong when I felt weak and useless. Luca had been such a good friend to me. Understanding, still interested, when all of my old friends were too caught up in their family lives – when I wouldn't let them in, when I wouldn't tell them I needed them. But Luca has a vested interest. He needs me to function at work. He can't risk me breaking down on the job. He wanted to support me this evening. And I let him.

"I've known that was coming for a while, Christof," he said kindly and without judgement. "It wasn't my intention to provoke it, but I'm glad I was here to help."

"Thank you." I said again, really meaning it.

"Now, you look like shit. I suggest you go and freshen up and then join us outside. I'll have another beer waiting for you."

11. A Fairy Godmother?

J em is my bonkers godmother who has been my rock whenever I have needed sound advice or a kick up the backside. She went to school with Mum and they have stayed firm friends ever since. She never had kids and she travels the world, living life to the full, being godmother to other people's children instead. She claims it's much more fun that way. She and her friends even formed a Godmother Club that she once, accidentally, told me about. It's supposed to be top secret.

She has been in Bali for most of the autumn, so I haven't seen her for ages. And today she took me out for a 'welcome back, Jem' lunch. She always picks up the bill and I'm eternally grateful to her for the many ways she shows her generosity

She showed up at the restaurant wearing brightly coloured cotton clothes that were well-suited to the Bali climate, but had been beefed up against a British winter with thick leggings and a thermal top that, she confided, with a giggle, had come from Damart – her token concession to now being nearly sixty, she chuckled. The combination of floaty tropical fabrics and black lace-up Doc Marten boots made her look nearer twenty. She doesn't seem to have aged much and she swears she has never been under the surgeon's knife.

"I've brought you a present," she announced, as we browsed the menus the waiter handed to us. "Cute bum," Jem commented, slightly too loudly, as he walked away. "Pity he's gay," she whispered to me, handing me a small, beautifully-wrapped box. I opened it eagerly – she didn't force me to wait for Christmas – another one of the great things about having her for a godmother. I unfolded the pastel blue tissue paper and gasped as I felt the softness of the black silk chemise, folded lovingly inside it. I risked holding it up, to admire it, despite the looks it brought me from neighbouring diners.

"It's for whenever you next get lucky, my dear!" *That could be a long way off.*

"That's the thing, Jem," I replied, "All the attractive men in London these days are either gay or spoken for or lunatics."

"Going through a bit of a dry spell, then?" With Jem is there's no pretending; no politely British tiptoeing round the edges of a problem. She aims straight for the bullseye and it saves a lot of stress.

"Yup. No one since Jamie, and it's nearly Christmas. I don't want another Christmas and New Year on my own."

"Not even a nice bit of internet dating? You know, a few romantic dinners? The odd movie?"

"I just can't face it, Jem. It took me a while to pull myself back together after Jamie, as you know. And the whole 'online shopping' internet dating thing just doesn't do it for me. Plus, work has been so busy and my social life so thin that the likelihood of meeting the perfect guy by chance feels sub-zero."

"We need a plan, my girl." Jem gave me that look that said she was reading my mind. "Tell me …" It's an instruction, not a request.

"Jamie called last week. He's asked me to go out to dinner with him, to see if we have a future."

"And I'm assuming you told him exactly where to go!" retorted Jem, almost before I had finished my sentence.

"Well …"

"There's no *well* about it, young lady! That guy was a shit and he broke your heart. Even before that bit, he treated you so badly I'm amazed you were still functioning. Don't you remember?"

Of course I remembered.

Jamie had swept me off my feet in a torrent of It-Party invitations, last-minute reservations at the best restaurants and back-stage passes at concerts that had sold out months before. Life with him had been exciting … and dangerous. I knew, deep down, I couldn't trust him. He struggled with simple things like telling the truth. I remember how much of a fuss he had made at one particular party about going to school at Harrow, trying to impress the Rich Set, even though I knew he had only been there for one term before he had been expelled. He never told me why.

He always seemed to be living beyond his means, but somehow found the money for the expensive weekends and parties. Until he didn't. And that's when I started having to pay for everything. It began with just a dinner here and there. "Oh, I forgot my credit card. I'm so sorry Soph, could you sub it to me?" Then it moved on to the occasional long-distance, late-night taxi and when it ramped up to 5-star hotels it quickly emptied my savings account.

But we were having fun, weren't we?

Looking back, I could see that the relationship had always been on his terms. It was always Jamie who decided where we would go and when and with whom. The people I thought of as friends never phoned me, only him, which is why they melted away like ice cubes in the Indian sun the moment we split up.

It wasn't as though he treated me like a princess, either. If we went back to his flat, he was always on his mobile, doing deals and sorting out his social life. I rarely got a moment of genuine attention. And he took *mansplaining* to new heights, especially in public where he excelled at using me to show everyone how clever he was. I felt stupid, but at least I wasn't on the shelf. Looking back, the whole episode had trashed my self-esteem and I wasn't sure I'd got it back yet.

It was easy to see it, now it was in the past, but why did I stay with him? Because the world he was living in was intoxicating. Exciting. Full of parties where the press showed up to take photos for the society columns, with people I had actually heard of, and he was gorgeous. I felt amazing walking into a stately home for the weekend with his arm around my shoulder and a man in a spotless uniform would carry our bags to our room. I convinced myself he really cared about me. And the sex was great. I could get lost in those memories for quite a while.

Jem gave me a few minutes to muse before reminding me we needed to choose what to order. I obliged, choosing a starter and main course that would make sure I still had enough room for the home-baked cherry pie I had spotted on the specials board. Order placed, menus collected, Jem launched back in.

"Sophie, what on earth would possess you to get back together with that guy? Really? You can do so much better than him."

"Can I?"

"Yes! There's more to life than exotic parties and *who you know*."

"Says the woman whose life revolves around both of those things!"

"Yes, but that's different. I know who I am. And I am making my own choices. That's not how it was with Jamie, was it?"

I shook my head. I knew she was right.

"I've just had enough of being single. Surely it wouldn't

hurt to go out for dinner with him?" But even as I said it, I could hear how stupid that sounded.

"Sophie, you haven't heard from him for, what … over a year?" I nodded. "He didn't even talk to you to tell you he was splitting up with you. You heard it through gossip on Facebook." I nodded, again. "Did he apologise when he phoned you?"

"No. He said he didn't want to dwell on the past."

"How very convenient. For him!" She echoed Lucy's sentiments. "So why do you think he wants to see you?"

I couldn't think of a single genuine reason. Yes, of course I was deluding myself that he had suddenly realised he loved me and wanted to be with me for the rest of his life. That was less likely than me winning the lottery, two weeks in a row, with tickets someone had dropped in the street.

"Just remember, Sophie, with that guy there will always be more in it for him than for you. I have seen his type too often to kid myself. He's not worth the effort."

I sighed. It was heartfelt. I knew she was right. I was only going to go out with him because I'd had enough of sitting in front of the TV with a microwaved dinner after long days at work. I was fed up with having to fill my weekends with stuff to distract me from the empty feeling inside – that sense of longing to be part of a relationship that was bigger than me, to have someone to snuggle up with to watch a film on TV, to have someone to make it worth cooking for, to have someone I looked forward to going home and seeing.

The idea of getting back into the social set for Christmas and New Year really appealed. But they all knew how Jamie had treated me. And they hadn't done anything. They weren't my friends. They were no more real than the fairy on top of the Christmas tree.

"You're right. I'll leave it."

Jem looked relieved.

"Fantastic. For a moment there you had me worried. I thought I was going to have to cancel my winter in Sydney to stay here and make sure you don't dial the wrong phone number!"

"Australia! Wow! What are you going to be doing there?"

We spent the rest of the evening discussing her plans and enjoying the delicious food.

"I'm back in a couple of months," she said, as we hugged goodbye. "Before Easter. Do you think you can look after yourself until then?"

I promised her I would.

But, back in my beautiful flat, with its oversized windows that always make me feel like I'm living in an artist's studio, it's so light and airy, I sank onto my comfy old sofa and wondered what the future held. I could feel thirty-five steam-training its way towards me and I had thought my life would be sorted by then. Husband. Kids if we wanted them. Career well on its way. I felt scared I might end up a spinster for the rest of my life. But, unlike Jem, I knew it wasn't what I wanted.

Maybe that's why I have been considering letting a third-rate arsehole like Jamie back into my life. Because I'm desperate and I don't feel like I have any other options.

Despite my recent successes at work, I was feeling really nervous about meeting my new boss, Stuart. He would only be covering for the year of Lucy's maternity leave, but it felt like starting a new job. Harry has known him for well over twenty years. They went to university together. He told us that Stuart was doing him – and us – a massive favour by agreeing to stop being freelance for a year to run our research team.

Lucy had had to give me yet another pep talk, complete with

coffee at our favourite coffee shop. I felt really sad that we wouldn't get to do this for a while now. It wouldn't be the same with a baby in tow. Lucy is so large that she struggled to find a safe path between the tightly packed tables and she had to apologise to each person she bumped into as she made her way to our favourite seats. She gave a loud sigh of relief as she sat down on one of the tiny chairs.

"I wish I could put my feet up!" she exclaimed. "Swollen ankles are a killer. I feel like a beached whale."

"How long to go now?"

"They say that first ones are always late, but I should be down to the last few weeks, which means any time now, really. Or five weeks' time. I'm hoping for sooner rather than later, to make the most of my maternity leave. The clock starts ticking on that at 5 p.m. today."

"Wow! A whole year off! I can't imagine it!" But I could. Lounging around, drinking tea with other women, while the babies sleep or play. The occasional bit of housework, and cooking. Pure bliss.

"It's not a holiday, Sophie. It's hard work. Apparently. One of the mums in my NCT antenatal class said it took about three months until she found time in the day to shower and brush her teeth. She's having number two now and she said that going back to work was the holiday, not maternity leave." I found that hard to imagine, but I was sure Lucy would keep me posted.

"Then there's the sleep deprivation. Apparently they wake up every few hours for feeding, until they're about six months old. If you're lucky, they'll go back to sleep after about fifteen minutes. But if you're not, it can take an hour to settle them again. There are some who sleep through from six weeks, but they're a rarity from what I've heard. In fact, there are rumours that they don't actually exist and it's just alpha mums showing off. It turns you into a zombie. You know they use sleep deprivation as a form of torture?"

It didn't sound like much fun to me. I found myself wondering why women did it. I wasn't sure I wanted to. But, as Lucy always says, when I tell her that, maybe I just haven't met the right man yet?

I wasn't convinced that meeting Mr Right would be enough to make me want to go through all of that. But it was all a bit hypothetical at the moment.

"So are you ready to meet Stuart yet, Sophie?"

We were due to meet him at ten, in Harry's office. He was going to be spending the day with Lucy to be briefed on the current projects and to meet our team. Then it would be just him. Lucy would be gone. Harry's HR Guru told him we're not allowed to phone her about work stuff while she's away. At all. Though I know I will. She won't tell anyone.

We headed back to the office. "Am I allowed to tell you you're waddling, Lucy?" I asked, rudely pointing out the truth.

"You don't need to tell me, you cheeky mare!" she replied, giving me a friendly punch on the arm. "The midwife said it's something to do with the head engaging. It means the baby is nearly ready."

Lucy puffed her way up the stairs to our offices. I wondered if I should plant my palms on her bum and push, but I wasn't convinced I'd get away with it. Sure enough, Harry and Stuart were waiting for us, proving that they had spotted we weren't in the office yet.

"Ah! Here they are!" Harry announced to Stuart, as though we had been declared missing in action and the search teams had already been scrambled. We were still ten minutes early, though I did feel guilty, carrying my second coffee in its takeaway beaker. It made it obvious that we had been playing truant.

I looked over at them and saw Stuart for the first time. Not what I had expected, given how flash Harry is.

My heart sank. Stuart was a slightly less unhygienic version of François. But it was a close-run thing, if I ignored the laundry. This didn't bode well.

Short and 'portly' with watery blue eyes set too close together, a weak chin and nasal hair that was competing with the tufty mop on his head for both length and quantity, he had already shaken hands with Lucy, who maintained the appropriate professional dignity. Now he was moving towards me, extending a podgy-fingered hand, not unlike François'.

"And you must be Sophie!" he declared, stating the absolute obvious. He flashed me a grin that turned my stomach. The state of those teeth: he must have had an extreme fear of dentists since childhood. I shook his hand, trying not to display my reluctance. I wanted to instantly wipe it on my skirt or empty an entire bottle of hand sanitiser over it. I resisted.

A whole year of this? How? I want to hide under my desk for the next twelve months.

"I'm so pleased that Stuart has been able to join us," announced Harry. "Not many people with his experience would be free to cover such a high-profile role on an interim basis. It's wonderful to have you on the team, old boy!" He slapped Stuart on the back. Stuart looked very pleased with himself. I looked at my shoes.

"Come on, Sophie, there's no need to be shy! I don't bite!" Stuart was mistaking my horror for nerves. Or was he? Was he just trying to prove who was on top in this power game? "It's going to be great having you work for me." The emphasis on the 'you' and the 'me' made it clear where I stood. For the next year I was going to be his dogsbody. And he knew that I knew it.

Christmas

Candles in the tree
Excited children wait for
Babbo Natale

12. The Office Christmas Party

My phone beeped at 7:30 this morning, just as I was getting out of the shower. It is the final week of work before Christmas and tonight sees our annual office Christmas party. There won't be enough time to go from work to home and back to the venue, so my bag was crammed with the obligatory Little Black Dress, a pair of shoes that give me vertigo and enough make-up to fool people into thinking I'm awake.

The text was from Jamie.

Want to meet me at the Ivy for dinner at 8 p.m. tonight? Managed to get a cancellation.

In other words, he had been stood up.

No, I wouldn't like to meet him. Especially since I knew there was no way I could afford to pick up the bill at the Ivy if he *forgot* his credit card again. I was going to follow Lucy's advice, and Jem's. It didn't matter that I was genuinely busy already. I didn't want to let him back into my life.

"Sorry, I'm washing my hair," I typed, left-handed, arguing with my phone's autocorrect, as I brushed my teeth. Send.

I was feeling proud of myself.

It has been a week since Lucy left and working with Stuart has been bearable as long as I do what he tells me to, give him all the credit for my best ideas and allow him to pretend to the outside world that I don't exist. He never lets me finish a sentence, if there's someone listening he could impress. And he carries his 1990s Filofax everywhere. The papers in it are always falling out and he freaks out when this happens, as though he has mislaid his firstborn.

The day after Lucy left I had a meeting scheduled with him for first thing. I made extra sure I was on time. It was a jolt to see him sitting in Lucy's chair, at Lucy's desk, touching her stationery, reading her files. I wondered if she would get them disinfected, when she comes back.

I sat down in the chair opposite him, determined to make the best of the situation, which had been Lucy's advice. He didn't give me much chance. I had popped into the coffee shop, extra early, to get my Americano with almond milk. They had stopped asking what I wanted to order years ago. I had got my notepad and pen ready, tucked under my left arm, and I was holding my coffee in my right hand. I put it on his desk, taking my pad out to make any notes that would be needed. I smiled at him. He didn't return it.

"Let's get one thing straight, before we start, Sophie," he said, applying the full frost treatment to his words and leaving me in no doubt as to who is the boss. "You do not bring coffee into my office. And you certainly don't leave your coffee rings on my desk. Coffee is for break times, not working time, and I hate the smell."

I was blown away. And put in my place. I mumbled an apology and gestured towards my cup, silently asking him what I should do with it.

"I'll wait for you to put it on your desk, Sophie." He tapped his pen irritably on his desk as though already counting the seconds until I returned, like a human stopwatch.

"But it will go cold!" I protested. I really didn't understand what the problem was. It had a lid on it. He couldn't smell it.

"You should have thought of that before you bought it."

It went downhill from there. He has taken all the interesting projects off me and left me with the work that I only used to put up with because I had the fun stuff too. He is going to be taking the lead on everything, even the eco laundry detergent project, where I had finished the hard part and I had written up most of the presentation, ready to debrief the client as soon as we were back from Christmas. He's going to do the presentation 'on behalf of the business'. He convinced Harry that was the best option. He'll be taking the credit for my hard work, including sorting out François, despite it all having happened before Stuart joined us.

I had been hoping Stuart wouldn't come to the Christmas party tonight, but that was wishful thinking. "I wouldn't miss it for the world!" he responded gleefully, when I dropped it into conversation this morning, telling him I assumed he was busy, since it was such short notice after him starting. Free food and booze and lots of women in short dresses were an offer he couldn't refuse. My insides tightened as I wished I had brought a kaftan with me, instead of my Little Black Dress. Hopefully I would be able to avoid him as much as possible.

There are only eleven of us on the team, so we usually go to one of those 'multi-company' Christmas parties. It's more fun than a restaurant. Although we sit on one table for the meal, there's always a disco afterwards and you can escape from anyone you'd rather avoid. Lucy wasn't going to be coming this year. She didn't think it was right, given that she's now on maternity leave. And she said she could barely walk now, even though she's not due until January. She told me the midwives were already threatening her with something called an induction if she dares to go eleven days past her due date. But Lucy's not having any of it. She said that most first babies are late, so the due date is wrong, and that in France a pregnancy is forty-one weeks, not the forty we count in the UK. Twenty-six miles of sea couldn't possibly make that much difference to human gestation, in her view. And she read that getting induced increases the risk of a caesarean, which she really wants to avoid.

So tonight it was going to be just me, Harry, Stuart, Susie-from-Reception, and six guys from our creative and reprographic teams, most of whom are gay – the ones who aren't are married, of course. Janet, Stuart's PA, never comes to these things. She's in her sixties and takes being stern to Olympian heights. Letting her hair down to hang out with us wasn't something she would ever agree to. And I was glad that, for once, the party fell on a Friday, so if it did turn out to be a good night, I would get a lie in the morning after. A whole weekend to recover, in fact.

Six p.m. and Harry instructed us all to disappear and get ready. The taxis were booked for 6:30, so we could be at the venue by seven. There was going to be a free bar until the meal at eight. I hadn't had time for lunch today, so I was going to need to make sure I ate plenty of nibbles with the first drink, or I could end up tipsy enough to break my neck as I wobbled in my heels.

Susie and I were the lucky ones. We got to share the ladies' toilets between the two of us, as we changed our clothes, did hair and used the dim lighting to apply make-up that hopefully wouldn't make us look like clowns. We were squeezed together in front of the only sink, sharing a mirror so small it must have been a bloke who chose it. But we were managing. It was fun.

It took me back to the time when I managed to wangle tickets to the Last Night of the Proms at the Royal Albert Hall with my friend Claire. It's almost impossible to get them, but between a group of us at my old work we booked enough tickets throughout the season to be entitled to two precious Last Night tickets, up in the gods, soaking up the incredible atmosphere of the evening. We all pretty much ignored the first half of the concert. Nobody really wants to hear it. We all want the Last Night classics: 'Fantasia on British Sea-Songs', Elgar's *Pomp and Circumstance March*, *Rule Britannia*, *Jerusalem* and *Auld Lang Syne*. It's the one night of the year in the UK when being patriotic is permitted. I looked down at myself this evening and realised I had been wearing exactly this Little Black Dress, though the heels on my shoes were slightly less scary that evening, due to the long walk from South Kensington Tube station to the Royal Albert Hall. Claire and I dutifully sat with 5,000 others though the first half of the concert, with the Promenaders down at ground level whooping and letting off screaming balloons and waving their flags, raising money for their charity as they passed round big white buckets, making the most of the vibrant mood.

Then, in the interval, we had sprinted for the loos, our bags clutched to our chests. The queue was horrendous, as always. Maybe, in Victorian times when the building was constructed, ladies didn't need to go to the toilet as much. There were half as many toilets as would reasonably be needed, and the intervening 100 years didn't seem to have changed things much.

We jumped the queue, which is unforgivable in the UK, telling angry women we needed the mirrors and reassuring them we weren't stealing their cubicle slot. We got to a sink and emptied not make-up but packs of children's face paints onto the shelf in front of us. It was time. When we were done, we both looked ravishing in our Little Black Dresses, high heels and sheer black stockings, but our faces were adorned with Union Jack flags. And I mean full face, not just a little flag on a cheekbone.

The brilliant thing about wearing enough face paint to make people stop in their tracks with surprise is that they can't see who you are. It's like wearing a mask. It gives me the most incredible confidence.

We wore our faces with pride and sang our hearts out for the whole of the rest of the concert, trying not to cry with emotion as the music reached its climaxes and the atmosphere in the auditorium went wild, the usual British reserve thrown away for the night. We even wore our flags all the way home, though we could easily have washed them off. I don't think I have ever been stared at by as many people. It wasn't the 'done thing' to be dressed like that without wearing football kit. It was so much fun. An evening I will never forget.

I doubted, somehow, that tonight would top it. And today I was going for 'subtle', rather than 'national flag' for my make-up.

We piled into the taxis. I managed to avoid Stuart, and we were soon propping up the bar at the hotel that was risking taking 200 Christmas office party revellers into its bosom for the evening. Those living outside of town were getting an overnight stay, courtesy of Harry. I didn't fall into that category. Tight-arsed git. But I didn't mind too much. Stuart was staying and the thought of sharing a roof with him while I was asleep freaked me out, even with a lock on the bedroom door.

Dinner passed without too much excitement. The food was good, but there's only so much a kitchen can achieve when it has 200 people to serve at once and the staff are doing it for the twentieth time that month. Then the music started. Susie and I had an unspoken pact that we would stick together, accompanied by a couple of the gay guys on the team as we cased the joint for eligible males before we split up. Safety in numbers.

It didn't take long for Susie to spot a group of likely males, just her type, and she was the first to split off to dance with them. Gary and Oliver, my two gay escorts, soon tracked down the gay crowd, congregating on the far side of the dance floor, harassing the DJ until he played them their favourite songs. I had no doubt that *I Will Survive* would be up before long. I said a silent and sincere thank you to the party organisers for the absence of karaoke.

And that left me, on my own, missing Lucy like crazy. It was the first time I had done the Christmas party without her and I hadn't realised how we kept each other company as the others drifted off. Harry was off power-networking, yelling above the music at the owners of firms who might become clients next year. I decided to go and play wallflower at the bar. It was too early to leave without offending Harry and I wasn't the type to want to dance on my own. Sitting at the office table would have encouraged Stuart or some other saddo from another firm to assume I needed company.

There was no free bar after dinner, so I was going to have to pay for my next drink. In an effort to avoid ruining the last weekend before Christmas (aka present shopping hell), I opted for a mineral water, saying yes to the offered ice and lemon. As a single girl in London, I quickly learned the signals to give off to make men leave me alone: closed body language, looking intently at something in front of me, tapping my fingers on the bar, as though I were waiting for someone who had the lack of courtesy to be late. It's not a long-term strategy, but it normally buys me enough uninterrupted time to finish a quick drink. I was using all of them tonight. I hadn't seen anyone here who I might want to approach me, other than a couple of gorgeous guys who already had women dripping off their arms like diamond bracelets.

I decided to use the label on my mineral water bottle as my *object of study* and I was making a good job of the 'leave me alone or regret it' vibe when someone stood next to me, slightly too close. I worked hard to ignore them. My peripheral vision was telling me it wasn't Adonis, so I didn't look up.

"Sophie," slurred a familiar voice. "What are you doing here all on your own when you could be sitting with me?"

It was Stuart. He was drunk. He was hitting on me. Trying to flirt. Yuck!

I ignored him, hoping he would go away.

"Oh, I know that you're shy. I remember that from the first time we met. Did you feel the electricity, too?"

I looked at him. Horrified. Was he being serious? I looked in his eyes. Yes, he was.

The stench of his aftershave was starting to overwhelm me and my nut roast with mushroom gravy was threatening to revisit. Suddenly I felt his arm around my shoulder.

I recoil. My heart starts to pound as though it senses the danger. I have to get out of here.

I pull away. He tightens his grip, drawing me closer to him. He leans over. He's whispering in my ear as he blatantly stares down my top. "I've got a room upstairs, you know. Big double bed. Bouncy. Let's go!"

He's not asking me. He's ordering me. I'm frozen to the spot. My body won't move. My voice isn't working. His fingers are hurting my arm.

He lunges at me and he's kissing me with the bravado that only alcohol can bring. My body screams the 'no' that my mouth is too stunned to speak. It's disgusting. I struggle. The arm over my shoulder is pulling me in more tightly and his hand is reaching for my breast, his fingertips brushing over my skin. I feel his tongue touching my lips, pushing between them, and that's finally enough to shock me out of my frozen terror.

"No!" I scream so loudly that the barman drops a bottle of orange juice he has just pulled out of the fridge, the glass shattering on the floor.

"Don't touch me!"

Stuart looks stunned. And then angry.

I've already backed far enough away that he can't reach me.

I'm wiping at my mouth with the back of my hand, trying to get rid of the taste of him. A small crowd is gathering around us, silently watching the drama unfold. No one steps in to help me. He moves towards me.

"Get away from me!"

I'm screeching. Panic. Nausea. I want to wash my mouth out but it will never be enough to remove the memory of the last sixty seconds.

With a dark look in his eyes Stuart stands facing me, his hands on his hips, his too-tight trousers bulging, showing the world how much he was enjoying himself.

"You will regret this, Sophie. You shouldn't have done that."

And he walks away, without a care in the world.

No one stopped to help me as I sprinted my way through the dancers to the toilets. I didn't care about the queue, or the women complaining at me pushing past them. This wouldn't wait. I rushed to the sink and turned the tap on full, rinsing my mouth and spitting. Even after a full five minutes it didn't feel like it had made any difference. No one asked me what I was doing. Or why. Or whether they could help.

I remembered a bottle of out-of-date mouthwash at home; something a dentist once recommended. I imagined the sting of its chemicals the one and only time I used it. That was what I needed.

I ran all the way to the Tube, pulling my shoes off the moment I realised I couldn't run in the heels without breaking an ankle, holding them in one hand while I clutched my Tube ticket in the other, as precious as Charlie Bucket's Golden Ticket for Willy Wonka's Chocolate Factory. I was willing the minutes away once I finally stood in the train, gasping for breath, the stitch in my side distracting me from what had just happened. I ran all the way from the station back to my flat, my feet feeling like Hans Christian Anderson's mermaid who gave up her voice so she could walk on land to be with the prince who never loved her. With each step the rough stones and concrete ripped my tights and feet to shreds like the mermaid's knives.

I slammed my front door behind me, forgetting how late it was and that I might wake my neighbours, and sprinted to my bathroom, sinking to my knees, throwing everything out of the sink cupboard on to the floor around me, desperately trying to find the stupid mouthwash, praying I hadn't chucked it away.

I found it and ripped the cap off, throwing it behind me. I heard it bounce off the wall tiles and land on the lino floor. I lifted the bottle to my mouth and took a glug, gargling like a woman possessed. It was helping. It stung. It stank. It was washing away the taste, but not the memory.

Why couldn't I stop him? How did it happen? Why did no one help me?

I ripped my clothes off, feeling where his arm had been across my shoulders, where his hand had touched my skin as he reached inside my dress. I wanted to wash him away. I got into my shower. I scrubbed. Hot water. I stood there for so long the water went cold.

I turned it off, wrapped myself in my towel and fell to my knees, facing my toilet, and the nut roast finally emptied itself into the bowl. I managed to wipe my mouth before I fell asleep, exhausted, wet, naked, cold and miserable on my bathroom floor.

13. An Ultimatum

It was the first Christmas since Dad had died and I was heading back to the cherry farm for a few days. I was going to be spending New Year in Milan with Luca's family and their friends and I had to work between Christmas and New Year, so it was going to be a flying visit. And one tainted with those painful 'first time since' moments that line up to greet you in the year after losing someone you love.

I drove over there on the afternoon of Christmas Eve. It was the earliest I could get off work. I was greeted by hugs and kisses and the smell of the big celebration dinner being prepared. The kitchen was chaotic, filled with people helping and hindering, as Nonna supervised the creation of a feast for fifteen of us that evening. I couldn't tell what she was cooking yet but I knew there would be my favourite: chocolate-coated panettone. It's not like the stuff you buy in the shops, which can be dried-out and crumbly, in comparison to Nonna's, and best turned into an eggy pudding. It's so light and fluffy that, as a child, I used to be surprised that it didn't take off and fly. Nonna bakes it with raisins and tiny chocolate drops and then, when it's cooled, she drizzles it in melted chocolate icing. Christmas wouldn't be Christmas without it.

The tree was up in the entrance hall, filling the house with its scent of pine needles. The candle decorations were lit despite the fire hazard; the baubles glinting and the space below it patiently waiting for Babbo Natale, our version of Father Christmas, to fill it with gifts while we are asleep tonight. A generous handful of Christmas cards sat on the table in the hallway, ready for me to read through, all tainted with memories of Dad and sympathy at our loss. The news had taken months to travel through the distant reaches of family and friends. I decided to read them later, if at all. Maybe I would just ask Nonna what they say instead. That would be less painful.

I spied one of Pietro's teenage daughters coming towards me with a tray of Christmas biscuits, decorated with, of course, our home-grown glacé cherries. And they tasted delicious. It was good to see her. I didn't risk telling her how much she had grown. I used to cringe when relatives did that to me, when I was her age. We chatted for a while about how school was going. It was quite a commute for her and her sisters – half an hour by bus – now that they were at the town's secondary school. But she was finished by 2 p.m. every day and then had the rest of the afternoon free for fun, once she had trawled through the piles of homework she had been given.

Nonna put me on vegetable-peeling duties. "A nice low-risk job that even a city boy could handle!" she teased, as I sipped the espresso I needed to keep me going beyond the midnight church service. "How have you been?" I hadn't seen her for a month. It was the longest I had stayed away from the farm in ages, but there wasn't much to do and Nonna was right: I needed to get grounded, back into 'normal' life for a while first. I updated her on learning to trampoline, though not mentioning the emotions, and gave her the briefest overview of the Denucci case.

"Be careful, *caro*," she warned. "They don't play nicely when you're in that game." She knows what she's talking about. One of her cousins dared to cross the Mafia down in Sicily and was never seen again. His family never found out what happened to him. The *Camorra* was no more forgiving.

"Don't worry, Nonna," I reassured her. "Most of what I'm doing is desk-based work, so it's invisible to them. And if anything I do involves people, I will be really, really careful."

She stroked my hair, like she used to when I was a boy, and I could see the love in her eyes. I gave her a massive bear hug and then she smiled, giving us both permission to get back to our dinner duties.

It was nearly 4 p.m. when Pietro walked into the kitchen, making a beeline for me. Hugs and back-slapping formed our greeting. Then, with no preamble, he reminded me, "It's time." We both knew what he was talking about. It was an annual event and it would be the first time I had done it as the man of the house – the owner of the farm. It still feels like a bucket of icy water when I think of it like that. All of this is mine. My responsibility.

There's a tradition in Italy called *tredicesima* – the thirteenth month's pay. It's a bonus that employees get in December. Thirteen – *tredici* – is a lucky number in Italy. For families in farming communities *la tredicesima* can be the difference between comfort and just 'survival'. For the farms they work for it can be the difference between comfort and just survival. Finding an extra month's salary at the poorest time of the year takes planning and budgeting that many farmers struggle with. When I took over running our farm's accounts about ten years ago, I insisted that Dad have a separate bank account where we put one-twelfth of the annual salaries each month, so we spread the cost across the year. He resisted at first, but was soon convinced once he realised he no longer had to take out a loan to cover it each winter.

Over the generations, the owners of our farm had developed

many traditions and today I was going to be carrying out the one that Dad created. I had asked Pietro to send me over a current list of farm employees last week so I could prepare. He was carrying the pile of envelopes I had given him.

Nonna gave me a nod and a smile as she followed me out of the house to the front courtyard at the end of the driveway. She knew this wasn't easy. This was Dad's job.

In front of me stood a huddle of our employees. They didn't know what to do or say either. I had been over and over this in my head over the past couple of weeks. My role was to reassure them, to help them feel okay with the changes that have happened this year, to know their jobs were still safe, which I prayed they are.

It felt strange to have them all staring at me expectantly. So I took a deep breath, hiding my apprehension, smiled and welcomed them. I gave them a short speech, acknowledging everything that has happened this year, and told them that I didn't plan for anything to change, unless they needed me to, in which case they should ask Pietro to tell me. It was important not to undermine his position in their eyes. They answer to him; he answers to me. Nonna keeps the peace.

They looked relieved, and cold. I needed to move on with this. Pietro handed me the first envelope. The *tredicesima* payment goes straight into their bank account, whereas twenty years ago it was paid in cash, which is where this tradition sprang from. Nowadays each envelope contains a handwritten thank you note and a twenty-euro note, as a token gesture. I called out the name on each envelope and the employee came forwards. Handshakes and hugs and thank yous were exchanged and they returned to their huddle. We went through each of them in turn, then I wished them all a happy Christmas and told them I looked forward to seeing them again in the New Year.

And we all headed off to our respective family celebrations.

We had a wonderful evening. Nonna had created a magical feast as usual, and it was good to catch up with family members I haven't seen for a while, as well as Pietro, his wife and their girls. It has been a tradition for years that we celebrate Christmas together, even though it is normally only reserved for family. It wouldn't feel right without them.

After the meal there were a few hours spare before we walked to the church in the next village for the midnight service. It's the one where Dad is buried. I didn't want to think about that just now. But I hoped that, in some way, it might mean he was with us tonight.

Pietro pulled out a rare cigar to smoke and gestured to me that he wanted me to come outside with him, while he smoked it. I agreed, pulling on a coat against the late-night cold. I had that sinking feeling that normally went with being caught out doing something naughty at school and hearing the teacher call your name.

"Don't look so worried!" he laughed at me. My expression was obvious. "But we do need to talk, Christof."

So the sinking feeling was right.

I followed him outside and we stood in silence for a while, looking up at the stars. "Christof," he started, "this isn't working."

"What's wrong?"

"Nothing yet. But it will be."

I gave him a curious look, feeling confused.

"When your Dad died," he scored a direct hit to the knot of tension in my stomach, "I was able to keep the farm running, while you got the financial stuff sorted, because the big decisions for the year had already been made. I was just carrying them out. That's my job."

I thanked him again. I knew we couldn't have done this without him.

"But in the next few months we'll be starting the cycle again and decisions will need to be made. I'm not going to be making them. That's not my role. It used to be your Dad's. And now it is yours. I need you to start acting like you understand that, Christof."

Blunt, but true. I thought I had been spending the months since Dad died doing my bit, but I hadn't. Not really. I have been hiding from the responsibility, even though it has been waking me up at 3 a.m. and yelling at me. I felt myself freeze. I don't want to do this. It's not the financial or practical side. I can do that. It's knowing that if I make the wrong decision I could destroy the crop – or make all of those families homeless – or lose the farm that has been in our family for more generations than we can remember.

Pietro has known me since before I could walk. I had to tell him how I was feeling about this, that I was scared. But I couldn't have him thinking I was weak. I needed him to know he could trust me.

"You watched your Dad running the farm for over thirty years, Christof. You know what to do."

He was right. The *what* is easy enough. It's having the conviction to do it that's hard. I needed to get practical on this, to shut out the emotions. Dad was here full-time. I have a job that barely leaves me space for a social life, let alone running a farm. It's not like Dad used to sit in the kitchen drinking coffee all day. I know that the employees have had to pick up the slack to cover the work he used to do. I'm not being fair on them.

I took my second scarily deep breath of the evening before I replied to Pietro.

"Pietro, I know you're right. Somehow I need to find a way

to juggle the farm and my work in Milan."

"So you're not quitting your city job? You're not coming back?" That was a question I hadn't expected. An urgency in his voice that told me how stressed he is. I hadn't realised that was what he had been hoping for.

God, no! I can't come back to live on the farm. I need to be in the city. I crave the challenges of my work. I wouldn't get that level of problem-solving on a cherry farm. I love the excitement too much. I get addicted to the adrenalin when we're close to a breakthrough.

"I can't come back to live here, Pietro. That's not my path. But I know we can work something out. We're going to need to do things differently. I'm not going to be here every time there's a decision to make, like Dad was. And sometimes you might not be able to get hold of me for a few days, if something comes up." I think about the trip I'll be making to the South soon for the Denucci case. There's no way I'll want to be distracted by cherries then.

"I'm here for a few days now. Could we go through the planning for next year's growing season and work out which decisions you'll need from me and when? If we've got that sorted, it means if anything urgent comes up I'll have more time to help."

Pietro gave me a look that told me that wasn't how it was done here. They go with the flow, with the seasons, with the moon, following nature's lead. Dad was always there to give the answers Pietro needed, at least twenty-four hours a day. But I knew he could also tell things were going to have to change. I was sensing he wasn't happy about it as he took a deep puff of his cigar.

"As you want it, boss. We'll make it work somehow. But you need to step up into your Dad's old shoes, before you lose the farm and we all lose our jobs. We're not playing at this. Those guys have got kids to feed. You can't forget about us when you're off partying in the city."

My jaw tensed with annoyance. *Is that how they really see me? As some city kid having fun and forgetting about them? They don't know about my 3 a.m. self-torture. I never asked for this.*

He was right about the stepping up, though. Of course he was. There are precious few jobs out here in the countryside and if I make a mistake the farm's employees will have to commute into the town to find work, or maybe even move out of the countryside entirely. I could end up splitting up families, if one of the parents has to move to Milan. And they're farm-workers, so any work they could get in the city wouldn't pay enough to cover the rent of a place in the city and the costs for their families. This isn't a game.

"Something's got to change, Christof."

January

Trees snore silently
Fallen leaves crinkle with frost
Snow weighs heavily

14. Stuart Makes His Mark

For the two days after the office Christmas party I blotted out the memory of what Stuart had done by keeping myself busy. Not difficult the weekend before Christmas, when I had barely started my present shopping and I still had my perfect brother, his perfect wife and their perfect children to buy for. I never get it right for them. Sometimes I even consider putting the receipt in with each present, under the wrapping paper, to save them hassle when they take them back.

I went out with Anna and the girls on Saturday, but I didn't say anything. I didn't want to relive those memories. It felt too disgusting, too slimy. Telling them would have forced me to keep going through it, to dissect it in minute detail, to remember bits my brain has blocked out. I wasn't prepared to do that. It was just a kiss and a grope. I convinced myself that it was no worse than snogging someone you didn't really want to, because you were drunk at a university gig night.

But it wasn't like that at all, really. Stuart is my boss.

I ended up spending the whole of the holiday week stressing about how he was going to behave when we were back in the office. Would he even remember it? Yes. I turned him down. That would have cut through the booze haze.

I didn't bother with any New Year Resolutions. I don't feel like I've got anything to aim for this year apart from surviving

Stuart and not getting fired. Achieving that will take all my energy, so I forgot about the usual 'give up chocolate' or 'go to the gym more often' guilt-inducing promises. I knew I'd have broken them by the end of the first week, so I cut myself some slack and didn't bother this year. I'd love to say it felt good, but it didn't. Nothing does.

Stuart was on holiday the Monday and Tuesday after the office Christmas party, so today was the first time I had seen him. I did my usual thing last night of keeping myself awake by telling myself stories about how today would be. The old 'what if' scenarios, where I second-guess what the other person will do or say, and let my Inner Drama Queen wind me up until the thought of going to work in the morning was worse than the idea of jumping out of a perfectly air-worthy aeroplane with a rucksack strapped to my back, hoping that the student who packed it remembered to put the parachute in.

I got in extra early this morning, mainly so I could sneak in my coffee from the coffee shop without Stuart laying into me again. He was already there, sitting in his office, his bulging Filofax in front of him, smirking, looking like he just spent the holidays with Claudia Schiffer.

"Good morning, Sophie!" he announced, as he walked past my desk, scowling at my coffee, but knowing he couldn't reasonably ban it. Not that that would stop him. "I want a run-through of tomorrow's pitch in my office at ten."

He walked off, without smiling, but that was nothing unusual. He acted as though nothing had happened at the party. Maybe he didn't remember.

Fortunately I had prepared for this pitch meeting before the holidays, or Stuart's request would have been unfair, as though he were trying to catch me out. We had until tomorrow afternoon to finalise it. When I turned up, on time, in his office, with my presentation in my hand, he looked disappointed. There was a flash of annoyance across his face before he told me to sit down and hand him the file.

The presentation will be the analysis of some research we did for a potential future client. We ran some interviews and two focus groups to find out where their proposed new product might fit in a crowded market, where the competitors have ten times their advertising budget. The company wants to launch a range of high-end artisan biscuits in supermarkets. Some of them have dried cherries in them, a particular favourite of mine, so I have a soft spot for the project.

We're up against another agency for the work and we know that we need a 'yes' from the potential client, otherwise they'll just take our ideas and pay someone else to implement them. This one's only a small company, so the project budget for them didn't justify us doing much more than this. But sometimes we invest a fortune in the research and initial advertising campaign concepts, only to get a 'thanks but no thanks' and then see our ideas in the media six months later. We used to get paid for these pitches, but the market has changed. And that's why my presentation tomorrow has to be compelling.

"Talk me through the results," demanded Stuart, reaching for his bulging Filofax and a stainless-steel biro. He scribbled furious notes as I went through the 'so what' for each PowerPoint slide, unless he was bored, in which case that pen tapped time on his desk, as though willing me to hurry up and get the run-through over with. I got to the end and he put his pen down. I was really pleased with my work on this, most of which was done before Stuart had arrived. I had already been through the outline presentation with Lucy, so I was confident of a positive response.

It knocked me over like a wobbly skittle in a bowling alley when Stuart told me he didn't agree with my recommendations and my analysis was sloppy. Then he dropped the bombshell. I won't be presenting it tomorrow. He will.

"But Lucy and I had agreed I would!" I protest. I didn't tell him that it was part of her plan to raise my profile in front of Harry, to get me promoted.

"You will sit at the back of the room. 'Room meat', I believe, is the American phrase. I can't have you presenting this. You'd lose us the contract, Sophie. You're out of your depth."

"But that's simply not true! Lucy said this was great work!" I blurted out, failing to keep a lid on my emotions. I didn't want to give him any more excuses for shutting me out of my projects. I wanted to explode and could feel the pressure building up inside, but I had to try to stay calm. Or he would win.

"At her advanced stage of pregnancy I hardly think we can rely on her judgement. It must have been clouded by her friendship with you. And it wouldn't be politically correct for me to mention the effect her hormones will have been having on her performance. Let's just agree that she screwed up by recommending you on this one. This is the standard I would expect from someone who is new to the industry, not a professional."

He waved my presentation at me, holding it by the very corner with his fingertips, as though picking up a dog turd from the pavement with one of those super-thin bags that I'm never really sure are waterproof. The look of revulsion in his face would have been comical under other circumstances.

I didn't know what to say. Indignation fought for podium position in my brain against the fear that Stuart might be right.

He can't be right, can he? I did a great job with this. And the potential client, I'm sure, will love my recommendations. It makes great use of their tiny budget.

I wanted to get us the work. Now I was going to have to sit

at the back of the room as Stuart took credit for my work, misinterpreted the results, made us look stupid and probably lost us the project.

"You're clearly not ready for client-facing presentations yet," he continued. I felt tears stinging. This wasn't fair. I had done them before! "But don't worry, I can take over. I think we might need to review the kind of work you're doing, maybe go back a few steps and lay better foundations? Going back to basics?"

I wanted to scream at him: *This isn't on! I'm really good at what I do.* He was telling me he was demoting me. I tried to defend myself but he wasn't interested. He waved a hand at me, dismissively, and ordered me to email him the presentation file so he could edit it. Yes, it was an order. I didn't trust myself to speak. I left the room, trying not to slam the door behind me, and spent the next hour festering at my desk. I couldn't think about anything other than how grossly unfair Stuart was being. It was so obvious that this was punishment for the Christmas party disaster. He wants me to know he's in control of me, even if I won't kiss him.

Then Harry walked past. He knew I should be busy, super-busy, getting ready for tomorrow. So when he found me rearranging my files in the filing cabinet he was less than impressed.

"Shouldn't you be prepping for tomorrow, Sophie? It's a big gig, you know, and I've gone out on a limb, trusting you to do this. Lucy persuaded me. Surely the filing will wait?"

I didn't know what to say. The knot in my stomach grew until it felt like an iron ball. Stuart is one of his best friends. I knew that if I told Harry what had happened, he wouldn't believe me. He would think Stuart had been right to decide I wasn't ready to present. It would make him less likely to trust me next time. And he'd never believe what happened at the office Christmas party.

I'm scared that tomorrow Harry will see that Stuart doesn't think I'm good enough, as Stuart messes up some of my best work and, no doubt, blames my incompetence for the fiasco that feels inevitable. But I don't see what I can do to stop him. I wish Lucy were here. But there was no way I could bother her about this. I was just going to have to find a way through it on my own.

Sure enough, the presentation was a nightmare. Stuart was so confident that it came across as bravado. He missed out most of the key research findings and his conclusions and recommendations didn't make sense. I barely recognised my own work in this.

I cringed all the way through, wishing my chair could protect me as Harry shot me glares from the front of the room, assuming that I was responsible for Stuart's mess. He had clearly decided that Stuart must have been forced to take over from me at the last moment, because I had made such a hash of the pitch, and that was why his presentation was bad. As for Stuart's client recommendations, which simply didn't make sense, Harry blamed me for those, too. By the end of the meeting, when we got to the 'questions' part, I could feel the daggers he was sending me, even without looking at him.

My Inner Drama Queen was chanting 'it's not fair' so loudly that I didn't hear the client address a question to me. I sat in silence, wondering why everyone was staring at me, before mumbling, "Sorry, did you say something?" More daggers from Harry and an audible sigh from Stuart.

The client repeated his question, looking irritated, "I asked what your hypothesis was before you carried out the research. I understand it was *you* who ran the interviews and the focus groups, before Stuart arrived at your firm? And how did the findings of that research match with your hypothesis."

It sounded complicated, as a question, but it was actually quite straightforward. They wanted to understand whether I had been open to having the industry assumptions challenged and how I had used the research data to do this. In other words, would our agency churn out yet another cookie-cutter (excuse the pun) advertising campaign or would we use evidence to create something unique, that would allow their business to fill a market gap, quickly and cost-effectively? Had I done the presentation, the answer would have been easy. In fact, the client would already have known it.

I was racking my brain for a way to tie my answer into the 'official company line' – in other words, into Stuart's conclusions, which were nothing like mine. I was pretty sure he had made them up. He never even asked me for the data. I felt the colour rising from my chest, through my neck and up into my face.

Great! So now I look like I can't handle pressure.

But it wasn't that at all. I was trying not to make Stuart look stupid, so I could save Harry's company's arse and find a way to rescue the contract. I couldn't think of a way to do that, not with everyone staring at me. All my brain would say was 'run!' which wasn't helpful.

I was too freaked out to think of a lie, but I had to give him an answer, so I went with the truth. I explained the journey the research had taken and the overview of my conclusions. The client, far from looking impressed, was looking confused. And curious.

"That's interesting. But that's different from what Stuart has just presented, isn't it?"

Harry stepped in. I could see he was siding with Stuart and no longer trusted me to defend his firm. "Stuart?" he grunted, gesturing towards him, to take the attention away from me. And suddenly I was invisible again, back to being room meat.

"What Sophie *meant* to say was ..."

I didn't hear the rest. My thoughts drowned out his nasal whining. All I could focus on was holding back the tears until I could get somewhere private to cry. This wouldn't have happened had Lucy still been here.

Suddenly I was pulled out of my thoughts by the sounds of chairs scraping, as people stood up, and the client's insincere platitudes about 'thank you for a thought-provoking morning and we'll be in touch'. It was over. We had all made massive fools of ourselves.

We sat in silence in the taxi back to the office. The air was thick with Harry's barely suppressed rage and Stuart's ego. The moment we got back to Reception, Harry gave me a look that would wilted a cactus and said two words:

"My office".

Stuart smirked.

I got roasted. It was all down to me. My research was flawed. How could he expect Stuart to pull off a good presentation when that was the material he had to work with? Lucy had 'carried' me and my career for far too long. It was a blessing that we had Stuart on the team for the coming year, to sort things out; that he agreed with Stuart's recommendation that I stop doing the qualitative, face-to-face research and went back to supervising surveys instead, where there was less room for misinterpretation. How could I expect him to keep his company running if I couldn't support my boss in client pitches?

The moment he let me leave his office, the tears came. Frustration. Rage. Unfairness. Fear.

I need this job. It feels like Stuart is out to get me fired.

How could I possibly persuade Harry to change his opinion

of me when Stuart was so determined to undermine me? But I couldn't prove any of it; even if we had anyone at the company I could complain to. Who would listen to me?

I feel empty. I can't lose this job. If I get demoted, I can't afford my flat.

I wasn't surprised to hear that we didn't get the contract. And Harry made it clear it was all my fault.

15. The Trail Reveals Itself

T he thing about stealing lots of money is that it's surprisingly easy to hide. Every year or so a story comes up in the news about some loner in a bank managing to defraud it of millions – or even a billion – by keeping their head down and hoping no one will notice. And they usually don't.

That's exactly what had been happening with this Denucci theft. No one noticed, until the MD did, and suddenly both the suspect and the MD were *disposed of*. The thing is, when someone was mining a rich seam, it was hard to stop mid-flow, even if *complications* came up. And that's why the company's anonymous owner was so convinced that the theft was still happening. Denucci's team would have found a new accomplice.

The late MD had found the *what* and the *who*, but not the *how*, so the inside man – or woman – could simply keep doing what had been done before and the money would keep rolling in.

Our job isn't to find out who killed the suspect or the MD. That is for the police, once they wake up and start taking this seriously. Our job is to find the 'how' and the new 'who', to collect enough evidence against them so that the police are forced to take action.

I still find it surprising how much information I can uncover by sitting at a desk. We have learned a lesson or twelve from the banks who had been through this over the years. Many of them brought in new rules saying that all employees who had anything to do with transferring funds must take a compulsory two-week holiday each year. Why? Because it's harder to cover your tracks if you're not in the office and you're forbidden from checking your emails or logging into secure financial systems.

Denucci's funding trail went cold for the few weeks after the inside man *disappeared*. It's hard to keep stealing if you're dead. And it will have taken Denucci a while to get someone new on board. We estimated there would be at least a month when the theft stopped, when the patterns of financial data went back to *normal*, and we knew roughly when that would be.

By number-crunching until my head hurt, looking for patterns that repeated and then stopped, I was sure I was getting close to knowing which department the new inside man is working in. Or at least which section's security ID he is using – no competent fraudster would log in as himself to steal funds from his boss.

We still couldn't find the link with Denucci and we couldn't prove where the money was going yet. The closest we had come was a Swiss bank account, but that would be too obvious and the sums didn't match with what the owner felt was missing.

But we do have evidence of money disappearing, as though it falls off a cliff into a ravine, never to be seen again.

"We need to catch them in the act, Christof," said Luca, as I updated him. I knew we did. Isabella was sitting next to me in his office. I was far from impressed. She would soon be coming back to the Milan team and was visiting from Paris for a few days, to help on another project. Luca had agreed to her request to sit in on all of our update meetings, so she could get up to speed as quickly as possible, ready for when she returned.

"Do we know *when* the money disappears?" she asked, "I mean, is there a weekly pattern; a time of day when systems are accessed unusually?"

I nodded. I showed her the clues in the data, like a Native-American Indian tracking prey in the dried-up mud: hard to see, nothing but dust if you didn't know what you were looking for, but plain as day to someone who had spent years practising.

"We need to get you down there, Christof, to catch them in the act," replied Luca, looking me straight in the eye to see if I was up for this. "We need to see how they're doing it and, ideally, get a good look at who it is."

So that meant a trip down to Naples and some undercover work. It had been a long time; since before Dad died. But I felt that familiar blend of excitement and fear bubbling away inside me. Luca smiled, letting me know this was the reaction he had been hoping for.

We have good-quality photographs of all the key employees who might have access to the systems that would enable the theft, so if I can see who it is, I'll be able to identify them.

"I could go with you," volunteered Isabella, fluttering her eyelashes like a finalist in a beauty pageant, having a drink with the judge.

"Thanks, but I work better on my own on this kind of thing." I replied dismissively. She took the hint. Luca raised an eyebrow but then agreed.

"Not this time, Isabella. You've got too much to do back in Paris and it's not the kind of stake-out where we've got space for extra bodies."

She stuck out her lower lip like a sulky child considering whether it was worth throwing a tantrum and then seemed to reconsider, flashing her perfect smile at Luca and agreeing that he was right.

"Christof," Luca continued, "remember, this is *not* a murder enquiry. We just need to prove who is taking the money, how and where it is going, and – ideally – to link it to Denucci."

It might still be a few weeks before I headed down to Naples. We needed a stronger indication of when would be the best time, as I was going to be hanging around outside the buildings, waiting for our suspect, for hours, potentially all night. I wanted to be certain I was going to see them before I put in that kind of effort. So Luca and I agreed to meet again next week – without Isabella this time – to finalise our timing and discuss strategies.

It felt great to be back on the road again. I hated being stuck in the office. I realised I was smiling, as I headed back to my desk. It was about time.

February

Early bulbs' spring songs
The cherry trees stretch and yawn
Buds break on branches

16. A Team-Building Day To Remember

H arry had decided it would be a great idea to have a team-building away-day, to help us all work more closely together and to help him make more money. He didn't mention that bit. But knowing him the way I do, he wasn't doing this for our benefit. I'm guessing some contact of his did one and raved about it and so now we all get to do it. We're on a budget though, so there are no overnight stays and we'll all be home for dinner. But we're going to the seaside. In February.

Growing up in Essex, my childhood memories of the seaside involved mainly Southend Pier, sunshine, the distant smell of sewage and being placated with ice cream when the sea swept away my sandcastle's bucket and spade. As I turned into a teenager nothing much changed, except the ice cream was replaced with cider and sunstroke and hangovers. I once managed a holiday in Gran Canaria, where the weather was fantastic, the booze came without being measured, secret skinny-dipping in the hotel pool was a compulsory activity and I had a nightly routine of killing cockroaches the size of my palm in the hinges of the bathroom door.

But Eastbourne in February?

With a 'team-building' company? I suspected it would be writing a new chapter in my seaside experiences and I was right.

Firstly, as a kid, I never had to be out of the house by 6 a.m.

to get to the beach. Even the Germans don't get their beach towels on the sun loungers that early. I also never went to the seaside unless there was something bright, yellow, shiny and hot in the sky. I never had to wear my ski jacket, my thickest woollen scarf and a chunky hat. And I never went with Stuart. That wasn't on my bucket list.

He is still being a shit. Things have improved since the failed client pitch, but only because I have given in and am doing his dirge-work, while I try to figure out a plan to get him fired. If he taps his pen on his desk while I'm talking one more time, I might have to grab it and ram it up his nose. He sighs and tuts when I speak. He scribbles in bright red ink over anything I send him, even if I email it. He prints it out, covers it in angry graffiti, scans it in and emails it back. Where does he get the time? Oh, that will be because I'm doing all the boring bits of his job, as well as mine.

I arrived in Eastbourne soon after nine, having left Victoria Railway Station far too early to mention and changed trains at Brighton. Why couldn't we spend the day *there*, instead? I reluctantly lugged myself the twenty minutes on foot from the station to the hotel we were meeting at. Harry had made it clear that any taxis were to be self-funded. "The exercise will do you good!" he had said when Gary objected.

I found myself sitting on my own, having arrived before everyone else, in the café bar of a hotel that looked like it had once been grand. I could picture it overflowing with ladies in their finery, with their influential husbands, come to stroll along the promenade and 'take the sea air'. If I closed my eyes and concentrated, I could almost hear their conversations about unreliable butlers and housemaids who got themselves 'in the family way'. I lost myself in my murky grey-brown coffee, wishing I could speed up time and get back home. The barman, baggy-eyed and scruffy-haired, looked like he felt the same way as he lazily polished already clean glasses and arranged them on dusty shelves. I wondered if he had become immune to the stench of stale beer that wafted up from the carpets with each step he took. It felt like a very long time since anyone showed this place any love and attention.

I was brought back to earth by someone obnoxious tapping a spoon on a beer glass (previously full of tap water) and announcing in far too jolly a voice for 10 a.m. that it was time to begin! To save costs, Harry hadn't even hired a meeting room at the hotel, so the mortification that masquerades as 'team-building' was to happen in public, in the café bar. Joy of joys.

We started with the usual ice-breakers: tell the person next to you something they don't know about you. Well, I now know that one of our creatives has toenail fungus and that Freddie from reprographics is convinced he once snogged Marc Almond from Soft Cell at a night club and has never found anyone who lives up to him in the past fifteen years.

We moved on, with a flourish, to sharing our hopes and dreams with someone we 'don't know very well' from the team. For everyone except Harry that would have been Stuart, but we were all understandably reluctant to pick him. The choice of person to talk managed to waste at least ten minutes, as most of us have worked together for years. We hovered and mingled and pretended to ask each other how well we knew each other. I was happy to see that I wasn't the only one who thought that sending up the whole 'team away-day' idea was a sensible coping strategy.

"Well, maybe someone you don't know as well as the others?" suggested the facilitator, with a pleading tone. More shuffling and mingling, and pretending to check who we knew best and least. No, that still didn't fix it. We were starting to laugh – at him – but he didn't seem to realise.

"Okay then, with someone you haven't spoken to yet today?" He was sounding desperate. That wasn't going to work either. All of us had now spoken to everyone, with the possible exception of Stuart, and Gary had valiantly taken one for the team on that one, agreeing to be his partner.

Mr Facilitator eventually settled for 'someone who doesn't have a partner yet!' and we finally agreed who to sit with.

My hopes and dreams include settling down with someone drop-dead gorgeous, intelligent enough to keep me amused, but not so much that I feel inferior, and running my own market research agency. I ended up partnered with Harry, so number three wasn't something I could discuss without risking being fired for fear of stealing his clients, or him wetting himself with laughter, given my recent performances. And I didn't want to talk about the total absence of my love life since Jamie. So, instead, I opted for *feeling happy and doing something to help towards world peace*. Harry's only comment? "You're not taking this very seriously, are you, Sophie?" I protested just enough to cast doubt over the obvious truth. His dream was the one we all know about: he mentions it every time one of us messes up and threatens the future of his business – his baby. He wants to sell the business, buy a tiny island in the Caribbean and spend the rest of his life being fed tropical fruit by beautiful people who hang on his every word. Woe betide any of us who gets in the way of that.

Ever-more tedious variations on the embarrassing over-sharing theme took us up to lunch which, of course, being by the seaside, had to be fish and chips. But we didn't get to stay in the warmth of the hotel bar for this. No. Mr Over-Enthusiastic-Facilitator insisted that we had to wrap up warm, looking like extras on an abominable snowman movie, to enjoy the traditional version of fish and chips, wrapped in paper with too much vinegar making it go soggy, stinging our eyes and noses, huddling in a shop doorway to escape the bitter, howling wind as we watched the waves batter the shoreline. I found myself stumped by the choices offered to me for eating my lunch: eat the now-lukewarm chips with my gloves on and have to throw them away because I would never get the vinegar smell out of them; or take my gloves off and lose my fingertips to frostbite.

We were permitted a five-minute toilet break back at the hotel before "It's time!" according to Mr Über-Happy. We headed back down to the beach. "We'll be down there, soon!" he said with a level of enthusiasm that would have been subject to a drugs test if he were an athlete. I caught myself wondering how his wife puts up with him, before noticing the nasal hair and the beyond-bushy eyebrows and deciding there probably wasn't one.

"We're going to play games!" he announced, as though it were the highlight of our year. The thought of my year peaking already, in early February, in the wind and cold on a beach with Stuart and Harry, filed me with despair. I crammed the idea back into a corner of my mind and willed the clocks to speed up.

We yomped in step, with Mr Über-Happy swinging his arms with the sheer pleasure of the day and I was almost surprised he didn't have us singing, call and response style, like US marines on a march. I sang a suitably lame version in my head instead, as a form of distracting self-torture, in my best comedy American accent.

> Team-building, that is our aim!
> Growing business ain't a game!
> Get to know each other well
> And the future will be swell.

I cringed at my utter lack of creativity, but at least it cheered me up and took my mind off the cold and from worrying about what awful things we were going to be forced to do next. I briefly debated sharing it with Mr Über-Happy, but I was concerned he might get so excited he would risk peeing his pants.

The beach reached out into the distance, a mass of pebbles and shingle, held back by big black posts and fences, to stop it from washing away. I caught sight of the pier in the distance, about 300 metres long with a low white building at either end, pavilion-style. There was clear evidence of the recent fire but, as Mr Über-Happy told us, visibly relieved, the Council plans to repair the damage so it will all look as good as new before any of us could say *flibbertigibbet*.

This nutcase, who Harry had presumably paid to torture us – though there was a strong possibility he was doing it for free as he seemed to love it so much – then got us started building a human pyramid, in the wind, on the shingle beach where it was hard to stand upright on your own, let alone bending forwards with your hands on your knees, trying to support the weight of other humans on your back. He wouldn't accept failure as an option and, being the girls and the smallest, Susie-from-Reception and I got to clamber over the others, to balance on the top. We discussed strategy as a team, and it was agreed that anyone not standing on the beach should take their shoes off. I could understand why, but it was freezing. I was wishing I had been able to find my hiking socks this morning, but it had boiled down to a choice between hunting for them in my overflowing underwear drawer/the laundry basket, or consuming enough coffee to be able to make it out of the door and onto the train. I noticed, to my horror, that the big toe on my left sock had a hole in it. Stuart saw it too. He grinned, his nose dripping disgustingly with the cold and the wind, making sure I knew how superior he was to me. He might be ugly and horrible, and sexist and a lying shit, but he would never, ever wear socks with a hole in them. Every cell in my body wished I had been able to keep my boots on and had used his head as a step.

It took one of the slowest, coldest hours of my life for us to meet the arbitrary requirement of balancing as a pyramid for thirty seconds. The first seven attempts all failed too soon. It struck me as strange that we were all going along with this, doing what Mr Über-Happy told us, not telling him to stuff off. Surely five seconds were ample proof that we could do it and please could we go back in the warm now? Was that what team-building was meant to be about? Doing what some unelected leader ordered us to, without questioning, even if we all knew it was stupid? While our hands went numb and we pretended we were enjoying ourselves?

We were allowed a hot coffee before the final team-building exercise. But we weren't allowed to go inside, in the warm, to drink them. Warmth was for wimps. Freddie and Susie, our willing volunteers, balanced cardboard trays of milky everyone-except-Stuart-gets-the-same-drink-because-it's-easier coffee over the pebbles and rocks. Mr Über-Happy insisted that we gave them a cheer, as though they were Stone-Age hunter-gatherers dragging a dead wildebeest behind them, rescuing us from certain starvation.

And that was when my favourite event of the day happened – totally unexpectedly – and one that will make me laugh for the rest of my life. In fact, it's possibly the only memory I expect to have of Stuart that will ever make me happy. His Filofax never leaves his side and he point-blank refused to leave it in the hotel safe when we came to the beach. He brought it with him instead. What kind of idiot takes a leather folder that is bulging with loose papers with them onto a windy seafront?

We soon found out.

During the pyramid scheme, his Filofax had been on the floor, with the toes of his right foot keeping it safe. In fact, it was his refusal to shift position, in order to protect his Filofax-baby, that caused so many of our pyramid attempts to fail. But then Harry asked Stuart to pass round one of the trays of non-descript coffees. This tray-passing required the use of both hands: one to hold his hot chocolate and one to pass the coffees, with his face turned away in disgust at the smell. The shingle was too uneven to safely hold a cardboard cup so he held his hot chocolate – he had to prove how special he was – in his left hand and his Filofax got tucked neatly, lovingly, under the right arm of his dirty beige raincoat, one of those baggy ones you imagine flashers wearing in London parks late at night when it hasn't been raining.

He passed on the tray and lost his footing on the stones as he leaned forwards, instinctively putting his right hand out in front of him to break his fall. That happened to be the arm that was nestling the Filofax, which tumbled to the ground. In slow motion, Stuart threw his hot chocolate (what a waste!) away and fell to his knees to grab his beloved papers, which were ruffling dangerously in the wind. Too late.

Between us, we spent the next fifteen minutes sprinting round the beach (not easy when it's made of loose cobbles), while Stuart screamed at us to catch every piece of flying paper. Even Mr Über-Happy joined in, congratulating Stuart on bringing us all together as a team, as he leapt and dived to catch yellow Post-it notes, crumpled envelopes and folded, dog-eared pieces of scribbled-on paper, as though this were one of his planned exercises. Stuart seemed too traumatised to help, or perhaps he was enjoying having us all run around after him.

Freddie managed to rescue a piece of roughly folded A4 from the waves, as it fluttered like a child's badly made paper aeroplane and flew further and further away from the rest of its squadron with each gust of wind. Stuart nursed its dripping limpness with the tenderness of a mother whose baby had narrowly escaped a tumble down the stairs.

We were nearly finished when a final piece of paper landed at my feet, bright red with determined writing on it in thick black ink. It stopped moving. Stuart unfroze, his face filled with panic, and he sprinted as fast as his tiny legs would take him across the uneven, loose stones, falling down just in front of me, clutching at the piece of paper that was now in my hands. Everyone stopped their chasing and turned to see what was going on. Some dared to laugh. It must have looked like he was paying homage at my feet.

I looked down at Stuart's bright red face and then at the paper, which was an almost matching shade. In writing so angry that the pen had almost torn the paper it said just four little words under the heading 'to do':

Get that bitch fired!

I felt rage welling up from the soles of my feet, spreading through my body and getting ready to drown out the February cold with its white hot heat. But I refused to give him the satisfaction of seeing me react. With all the dignity I could manage I looked down at him.

"Is this one for me?" I asked, innocently. The others were assuming it was something he had wanted to remind himself to tell me. The hardness in his eyes told me my assumption was right. Well, it was either me or Susie and I wasn't aware of her having offended him, so it was an easy guess.

"Thank you!" I said, giving the impression to our audience that it was something work-related, then making a fuss of slowly and deliberately folding it in four, before tucking it into the inside pocket of my down jacket and doing up the zip. I walked off towards the coffee tray – cold by now, the way Stuart thinks they should be – leaving him sprawled on the stones like a four-legged starfish, washed up by ungrateful waves.

I got home exhausted from commuter trains. Harry had refused to give us dinner, which meant I was so hungry that I soon made the most of the tub of cherry ice cream that had been waiting in the freezer with my name on it.

I felt a determination inside, now I knew what I knew. It was time for *me* to get rid of *him*. This meant war. And now that I was back at home, I was going to treat myself to a lovely long bubble bath while I plotted my revenge.

17. No One To Talk To

I couldn't believe it was February already. The last few weeks had gone far too fast. It was time to do the final preparation at the farm, before the spring blossom arrived on the cherry trees. In fact, there were only a few short weeks before the earliest blossom was due, so it was our last chance for pruning and fertilising at the end of the winter. It was also our last chance to replace any trees that were past their best. I always find it hard, taking out a healthy-looking tree, but there's no space for sentiment in farming. Lowering crop levels is something we can forgive, but if anything happens to a tree to affect its flavour or quality, it has to go. We can't risk those cherries tainting the quality of the rest of the crop.

I thought back to Pietro's warning at Christmas: "Decisions will need to be made. I'm not going to be making them. That's not my role. It used to be your Dad's. And now it is yours. I need you to start acting like you understand that, Christof."

I had avoided the farm since Christmas – the longest I have ever been away since my six-month university placement as an intern in a management consulting firm in New York, over a decade ago. That had been one of the perks of having an English mother, even though she left when I was ten: I speak fluent English. It has opened many doors for me.

But there was no more putting it off - I had to get down

there for the weekend to agree this spring's strategy with Pietro.

Although I knew that finances were already tight, we were going to have to hire someone to fill the gap that Dad left when it came to working on the orchards. There's no way I'm leaving Milan and Pietro couldn't take on all of that extra work. Nonna had offered – she had done it often enough in the past – but the manual work would be too much for her now. I needed to persuade Pietro to do the hiring. I couldn't handle that from Milan and I wouldn't know what kind of person to recruit. So that was my main goal for my visit: convincing him to accept help and to seeing if he knew anyone who would be a good fit to work with him.

Late on Friday evening I pulled onto the courtyard in front of the farmhouse and prepared to explain, yet again, to Nonna and Pietro why I was choosing to juggle my city job with my responsibilities at the farm. They still didn't understand why I wouldn't move back home.

I also needed to get on top of the accounts, which I had let slip for a few months. Pietro had been handling the payment of invoices, as he and I agreed at Christmas. There was no point in me slowing things down by having everything sent to Milan and risking invoices going missing in the post. And no one at the farm was ready to scan and email things to me. So I had got Pietro added as a signatory at the bank: a simple process that Italian bureaucracy manages to complicate to the point of extreme frustration, but we did it.

It was just me and Nonna for dinner, which made a lovely change. It was almost the first time we had been alone since Dad died. There have always been people staying or visiting at the farmhouse – another reason I craved my Milan life; being able to shut the door on my apartment and enjoy my own company, with no obligations or forced socialising.

I could tell Nonna was worried about me. She wants me to find a girlfriend, hates the idea of me being 'on my own' in a city of over a million people.

"We could look after you, if you came back to the farm, *caro*," she said again as we were eating. She had made fresh ravioli with last-season's sundried tomatoes, fresh local goats' cheese and her secret recipe pesto sauce. It felt like bribery.

"It's what your Dad would have wanted." *Is it? How can any of us know what he would have wanted? He was Nonna's son. My father. Pietro's best friend.*

Dad and I never discussed the future. There had seemed to be all the time in the world, so there was no need. We had decades to decide anything that was important: decades for me to get 'office work' out of my system before I came home to take over my role. He was happy that I went to university. I was the first person in my family ever to do so. You didn't need a degree to run the farm, you needed to know about things that university couldn't teach you. But was he happy about me taking up what he saw as a 'desk job'? I didn't think so. He couldn't understand why I wouldn't want to live on the land. He saw it as a passing phase, living in the city, buying my flat, earning money 'just for fun'.

I suddenly realised that Dad was born and raised with the responsibility of the farm running through his veins, but he and Mum, before she left, had encouraged me to open my options to include the whole world, not just this little patch of Italian countryside. And now that it was mine, I felt tied to it. The responsibility of it weighed heavily round my neck, threatening to drown me.

I distracted Nonna from asking me questions I didn't want to answer by talking about the practical side of things, like agreeing that, although the farm was legally mine, she would remain as the principal occupant, not me. Otherwise it would count as my 'second home' and one of Italy's many 'rich taxes' would kick in –increased utility bills for a second house. The farm could ill afford any of its costs to rise.

And I asked her what kinds of things Dad would normally have been doing at this time of year. She had been an essential part of the farm for so long that its seasons were second nature to her. I find it weird how I can't remember what needs doing when, despite having lived on the farm for two decades, while I ignored its seasonal routines: the curse of youth, thinking time is eternal and there was no rush. Nonna's list was longer than I wanted to hear. Pietro was right. There was no way he could manage it all himself, but there was no way I was going to leave Milan to come and do it.

"How are you getting on with selling the crop?" Nonna asked at a carefully chosen point in the conversation. My heart sank. My leads had come to nothing and I knew time was running out. I had been trying to blot it out, half hoping that ignoring it might make a buyer appear. There was no point in lying to Nonna who I knew could see the answer she expected in my face.

"Have you considered going back in with the local cooperative? It might make things easier for you?"

I shook my head. We both knew that would mean the lowest prices, losing our premium for being organic, and struggling to harvest the cherries to someone else's timeframe. There were good reasons why Dad had left the cooperative and after twenty years it was unlikely they would want us back, no matter how desperate we were. The farm has been run organically and biodynamically for as long as anyone can remember and each farm in the area has its own unique methods for looking after their trees, passed down for generations, carefully guarded secrets. Going in with the cooperative would mean losing our individuality – our competitive advantage.

"I've got leads I'm working with. It'll be fine, I promise." But we both knew I needed to get it sorted soon. It felt strange, selling the crop before the blossom had set, when we had no idea how good or large the harvest might be. I didn't want to tell Nonna that last year's buyers had pulled out, refusing to give a reason, and that it felt like every door I knocked on got slammed in my face. I had been so busy at work I hadn't had time to find a new buyer, even though it should have been my absolute priority.

"I'm here to help if you need me, caro," Nonna soothed. "Promise you'll let me know if you need help?" She wasn't used to being shut out of the process. It usually all happened in front of her at that very kitchen table, under her watchful eye, so she could be part of it. But I could sense she was trying to show me she trusted me.

I lay in bed that night thinking about all the conversations Dad and I should have had. I never agreed to be a farmer. I wondered if Dad ever did? Did he fight it? Did he want to see more of the world? Did he rebel? Did he ever lie awake at night, dreading the responsibility? Not knowing how he would pay the wages of the families who relied on him, whose children needed him to make good decisions, so that they would have enough to eat? Did he ever worry about surprise, late frosts threatening to kill the blossom before the fruit could set? About summer downpours just before the harvest, with no way to dry the fruit before packing? About bugs and diseases blown in on winds that could weaken the trees and devastate the crops?

I never asked for any of this. I want a career that uses my brain, not my brawn. I love intellectual challenges. If I want to get physical, I've got mountain-biking and rock-climbing, not tree-pruning and mulching and crop-harvesting and tractor-driving.

There wasn't space in my life for both, but I couldn't leave the farm without selling it, making Nonna homeless, and it was unlikely a new owner would want to keep our staff on. They would have their own ways of doing things. I couldn't betray the memories and generations of hard work that went into creating this place. Sometimes the feeling of being trapped hit me like a tsunami of panic, making it hard to breathe, urging me somehow to claw my way free.

Am I the man my Dad wanted me to be? I don't know. He would have wanted me to take over the farm, to step into the role he created, but he also taught me to be free and to dream of other things. So why is it I feel like I'm letting him down?

I wished I had someone to talk to about this. I could talk to Nonna. She would be devastated if she knew the truth about how I felt about the farm and not wanting to come back. She wouldn't understand. She has lived here since she became Nonno's bride – my grandfather, who inherited the farm from his father, who inherited it from his father before him. Luca is already worried that I might leave work. He has been dropping hints that I'm too distracted as it is. None of my old friends would understand, not now that they're settled with their jobs and their families and their routines.

With a pang so heavy it hurt in my chest, I realised that I didn't want to be alone. I wished I had someone I loved and trusted to talk to about all of these decisions, to help me get clarity about what I wanted and how to handle everything. I'm going to be thirty-six next week and I never imagined I'd still be single. On my own.

It felt like being in a tiny boat, bobbing around in the ocean with no sight of land or of anyone else in the world. No one to talk to. No one to trust. No one to fall asleep with. To share breakfast with. To curl up on the sofa with. I surprised myself at how much I wanted all of this. Just being 'normal' with someone special. Having someone to come home to after a long day at work or a few days away. Someone who knew me so well they understood my hopes and dreams, and could calm my fears.

It struck me again that with the life I have been leading there's no way I'm going to meet anyone special. It's not like I've put much effort in, in the past. I mentally scanned back through the last decade of girlfriends and realised that, with the exception of the ill-fated romance with Isabella, I hadn't been ready to settle down, not with any of them. I hadn't fully committed to the relationships, even though I pretended to myself that I had. They were just distractions, albeit great fun at the time. I felt a surge of guilt as I suddenly wondered if that was how they saw it. Did they lie awake at night wishing I would commit? Did they want more than just fun? Were they wondering why I never let them get closer to me? Why was that? Why did I keep them at arm's length? What was it I was scared of? Would I have settled down by now, had I let them in?

I knew I only had myself to blame for the fact that I was careering towards forty, on my own, with a job that took all my energy and now a farm to run, too. I couldn't see how to make space for the love of my life to find me. Then, without warning, it hit me: what if this was it? If the next fifty years were going to be about me juggling my two separate lives, on my own, never letting anyone in? Never meeting that 'someone special'?

What I wouldn't give to have her wrapped in my arms right now, listening to the gentle sound of her breathing, feeling her skin against my skin, smelling the scent of her hair, seeing the smile on her face as she falls asleep, both of us happily exhausted from making love, knowing we're there for each other, no matter what.

18. A Career-Trashing Mistake

I couldn't wait to see Anna and the girls, to tell them about Stuart's note, and how great it had felt to make him look stupid at the team-building day when he landed at my feet. He has been unbearable since then. That's the thing with war: you don't want the enemy knowing your strategy, so now I feel like I've got the upper hand. And, if he ever tries it on again, I've got evidence to give to Harry. He would recognise Stuart's handwriting.

Thank God for weekends. The girls and I had a raging night out and a hangover to match. But it was fun. We started with cocktails in our favourite bar in Soho, the kind of place you go to be seen, rather than heard. We had to yell to have any kind of conversation.

Then we moved on to dinner, which we barely noticed ourselves eating, because we were so busy catching up with each other's news and gossip. And finally we made it to a club, where we danced like crazy, forgetting about anything in the world apart from the music, until they threw us all out at 2 a.m., by which point my feet were screaming at me for wearing high heels and my head was pounding like Morse code, telling me I should have stopped drinking three hours before. I could barely walk, I was so tired and tipsy, and I crashed out at Anna's, because it was closer than my place. She had the sofa bed made up already, just in case. She knows me too well.

But over a bleary-eyed breakfast she went all *serious* on me; trying to convince me I needed to tone things down a bit, to focus on my work, that I was going out too much and drinking too much. Well, who wouldn't, with Stuart as a boss?

The way she sees it, I have to keep my nose clean until Lucy is back, so there's nothing Stuart can do to get me fired, to carry out his plan. Turning up with a hangover or sleep-deprived would be a great way to guarantee I'd make mistakes that would give him the ammunition he needs.

But I know I can handle it. She doesn't believe me. I'm used to late nights and travel and working hard, when I'm running interviews and focus groups across the country. Now that Stuart has taken all of that off me, I've got to fill the void somehow. And socialising is working fine. I wonder if she's just jealous because that 'socialising' doesn't always include her.

"Why do you think he has taken all of that off you, Sophie, *really*?" asked Anna, as she made the second round of coffee.

"Because he's a shit!" I replied.

"Obviously. But I wonder if there's more to it than that?" I gave her my depth-interview, quizzical eyebrow raise that says 'do tell more', without interrupting the interviewee's conversational flow. "It's a good little earner, isn't it? What would he be getting, as a manager doing all that travelling?"

I considered it for a moment. I used to be able to supplement my income quite nicely from my expenses. Harry is generous with them and managers would get even more. For a late-night focus group we get dinner and an extra payment for the inconvenience. If I have to travel and stay away from home overnight, I get my direct expenses and the inconvenience payment is higher. Lucy and I used to split the work between us. But with just one manager doing it all himself, with a little bit of rounding up on bills, it could easily come to a significant portion of his monthly salary.

"Think about it, Sophie, he has a financial interest in you being gone, as well as an ego one. If you're not there, he can take on even more responsibility, argue for a pay rise and even engineer himself to be Lucy's boss when she gets back from maternity leave."

"Do you really think he'd want to stay on?" I asked. I was surprised. I had thought he was happy with short-term assignments – flexibility, freedom.

"Think about it, Sophie. He was able to drop whatever his other commitments were at short notice, at his age." He must be in his fifties. She waited for my nod. "To take on a senior role for just twelve months? It doesn't add up. He isn't running an agency of his own and he wasn't a manager in anyone else's. Why not? I think there's something he's not telling you all."

My instincts told me she could be onto something. It didn't add up. How could someone in Stuart's position take a year out of his life to help Harry? It wasn't like he was into travelling or anything else that he might move on to after Lucy's maternity leave. I wondered if there might be more of a story there than he was letting on.

"Just watch your back, will you, Sophie?" added Anna, "He's got a lot to lose if you make him look stupid and it sounds, from what he has done so far, that he doesn't play by the rules. It feels like you're standing in the way of what he wants and his note proves he's happy to take you down as collateral damage to get to his goals. Don't play into his hands."

"What do you mean? How am I doing that?" I felt my hackles rising, my cactus spikes growing defensively.

"All this late-night partying and drinking. It will be affecting your performance at work. Yes, it might drown out the pain of what he has been doing, but don't give him any excuses to get you fired."

"Will you just get over this?" I yelled back at her. She just had an attack of the green-eyed monster because I get to go out more than she does. "I'm not drinking too much and I've got a right to go out. It's none of your business. And it's not affecting my work."

"Whatever…" she responded, seeing there was no point in arguing with me. "I'm just trying to help. To be a good friend."

I was grumpy with her after that and I left as soon as we had finished breakfast. I didn't need another opinionated bully in my life. I dragged myself home and slept off the rest of my hangover in my super-comfy bed, one of the best investments I ever made, with the blackout blinds drawn behind the curtains and my duvet over my head, so I could pretend it wasn't lunchtime. What would Anna know, anyway?

Stuart and I both knew it was war and everyone else in the office was fully aware, apart from Harry, who still seems to think that the proverbial sun shines out of Stuart's arse and the atmosphere is all down to my sour grapes at not being allowed to cover for Lucy's maternity leave. Yes, I am pissed off about that, but it's driving me crazy that Harry can't see how incompetent Stuart is. The blindness of a lifelong friendship. And, of course, it helps to have the boss's ear down the pub.

"These figures need to go over to the eco cosmetics account, as soon as possible."

I took a look at them. They didn't look right, but then again, I wasn't in the loop as much as I used to be. They were for the costs of the extra focus groups the client had asked for, to test out an alternative ad concept for their new launch, in addition to the research we had already agreed in the contract. "Are you sure?" I asked, by implication questioning his judgement. But something was off with these. They didn't seem to fit for the work we will be doing for that client.

"Are you daring to question me?" he whispered so quietly and with so much malice that it felt more unnerving and threatening than if had he shouted it. "Just send them. Or leave. It's up to you."

I humphed out of his office, his scribbled notes in my hand and dutifully typed an email to Ben, our contact at the eco cosmetics client, telling him that Stuart asked me to send the figures through. Something in my gut was telling me I should double-check them, but frankly I was too tired after last night's dancing and I couldn't be bothered to go back and ask, risking more flak from my boss.

I pressed 'send' and headed out to lunch with the guys. Something was still niggling, but I didn't care. I blotted it out. It wasn't my problem. Stuart had made it clear that it wasn't my job to double-check his work. It was his to check mine. I smiled as I thought it made a welcome change to get home after midnight due to having a social life, rather than being buried under research group work. Maybe Stuart has been doing me a favour, after all.

Our team doesn't often get time to go out together for lunch, but we had just finished a massive contract for a client and this week was bringing us a bit of calm, a chance to catch up with things we don't get time for when we're racing to deliver deadlines. It was just me and the advertising guys – no Stuart. They managed to 'forget' to invite him. They were dragging me along as a member of their team, for old time's sake. We slipped out of the office while Stuart was away from his desk so he couldn't invite himself. We were heading out for a pizza – and a couple of glasses – and taking an unauthorised, slightly extended lunch break. It felt like a celebration. Harry has never objected to this kind of thing. He knows we put in many more hours than he pays us for normally. So it was a shock when we got back and found him pacing the office, with thunder in his eyes and steam coming out of his ears.

"There you are!" he hissed, looking right at me. I turned round, just in case I was misreading his gaze, but I knew I wasn't. I felt the heaviness of the pizza and the wine in my stomach as it processed the fear that always springs up when Harry is about to blow his top.

He was waving an email printout at me. I had no idea what it was. Or what I had done. But then it hit me. Those figures were wrong. In my head I ran through them again, totting them up as best my brain could after half a bottle of Chianti. Shit! I knew it was wrong. I was finding it hard to breathe. Those numbers were for the costs of running the extra research for the *deodorant* project, not the *eco cosmetics* work. It made sense now. I had known something was up. Stuart gave me the wrong client's figures.

Stuart watched this realisation as it spread over my face and he smiled the knowing smile of someone who could see he had caught his prey. Harry's face turned beetroot purple and I longed to cover my ears with my hands because I knew he was about to let loose and scream at me in front of everyone.

"So was it stupidity or are you trying to ruin me?" he yelled. I feigned innocence, about sixty seconds too late. "Don't pretend you don't know. You sent the deodorant research quote to the eco cosmetics client. And that email is part of a legally binding contract. Unsurprisingly they've come back accepting the quote, sounding utterly delighted at the bargain they're getting, and now we're going to have to run that research at less than half what it is going to cost us. These are real costs, Sophie. It's not a game of Monopoly. What were you thinking?"

"But Stuart …" I tried to defend myself.

Stuart was standing next to Harry and he shook his head, smiling. He mouthed 'I don't think so' at me. The bastard! He planned this!

"Stuart warned me you would try to blame him. That won't wash with me, Sophie. He made it clear to you this morning who to send these to and you picked the wrong email address. You have let me down."

My heart sank. There was nothing I could say to convince Harry that this was Stuart's fault. Was Stuart incompetent? Or did he do it deliberately? I quickly decided, from the look on his face and the way he reacted when I questioned him, that this had been deliberate. His face contorted into a grin that looked like the Cheshire Cat on a day when the local farm was giving surplus cream away for free.

I felt a wave of hatred welling up inside, but did my best not to explode, to keep my dignity … and my job.

"You sent the wrong quote to the wrong client and you dare to try to place the blame for your sloppiness on Stuart? Honestly, Sophie? Stuart has told me how he's been having to cover for you ever since Christmas, how you let him – and me – down with the client pitch presentation you did in January and things have gone downhill since then. He's carrying you. Like Lucy must have been before. But she was too close a friend of yours to tell me the truth."

I felt my knees threatening to crumple. This guy had been thorough. Tears strung my eyes and I still wanted to scream, to defend myself. But I couldn't. There was no way Harry would believe me. I couldn't prove anything. And he had already been poisoned against me by Stuart's lies.

I looked at Stuart, his complacency making his usually unattractive face even more ugly. I wanted to gouge his eyes out. I felt my fingers tensing, longing for the thrill of hurting him as much as he has been hurting me. But there were laws against that and I wouldn't give him the satisfaction of seeing me behind bars.

March

Winds threaten branches
Blossom blows like confetti
Fearful of late frosts

19. An Unexpected Find

I had put the morning aside today to go through the past few months' accounts for the farm. I haven't done much on them since Dad died. And I got a shock. Things were much worse than I realised.

I have been doing the accounts since I graduated from university. I'm not an accountant, though Dad refused to see it that way, but my business studies degree taught me enough to be able to do the accounts to the level we needed, so all our accountant has to do is sign them off. It has saved us a fortune in fees and, more importantly, it has meant I have been able to keep a regular eye on the business, making sure Dad moved from hand-to-mouth to planning ahead more for expenses, so that we didn't get caught out every time big contracts came up for renewal, drowning in our temporary overdraft that far too often threatened to become permanent.

I had grabbed a pile of papers and post when I was at the farm last weekend and this weekend was the first chance I have had to go through it. I started by sorting things out into monthly piles, to try to create a sense of order. Some of the invoices went back to months before Dad died. They needed to be paid urgently. I was surprised by how much of a backlog there was. I had thought that Pietro would have handled them. Maybe he's not keen on the banking side. But why hadn't he told me?

And we've got accounts owing to us that no one has chased up for half a year or more. They are also a priority. It all means that the figures in our bank accounts are meaningless as a guide to tell me whether or not the farm, now my business – that feels weird! – is solvent or not. This side of things I can handle, if Pietro can keep the practical side sorted.

But the more I looked through the piles of paperwork, the more worried I felt. Things weren't looking good. I was on my third espresso of the morning by the time I had got my spreadsheets updated and I could see the full extent of the damage. By my calculations, we're about three months from going bust. And if we can't get a good price for the cherry harvest this year, that will be the inevitable outcome.

The overdue invoices and next month's wages alone will wipe out the bank funds, excluding the emergency account, which we all agreed was not to be touched under any circumstances. But I couldn't find any statements for that one. I was going to have to chase the bank on Monday.

And with no one hassling for payment of the invoices we have sent out, we're owed six months' worth of cash from key customers, but there's no guarantee we'll ever get those payments. Many of the businesses who owe us money will be taking the attitude that our lack of chasing means we are their bottom priority for payment. So much business is done on gentlemen's agreements that I can't evidence most of the debts with contracts. Dad will have agreed them verbally in many cases. That's something I will have to change.

I have to chase the debts before I can pay our invoices, so I spent the rest of the day writing letters asking for immediate payment and making a note to chase them weekly, until the money comes in. And for the invoices we owe, I paid the oldest ones and then wrote to the more recent companies to ask for a few more weeks, explaining about Dad and promising to pay them by the end of the month. I know I may have to do this out of my own savings to honour my word, though mixing private and company money is a place I never wanted to go to. But we can't risk our suppliers pulling the plug on their services without warning.

After a quick lunch I went for a walk around the grounds of the Castle Sforza in the centre of the city to clear my head. I love the way this 600-year-old place gives me back my perspective. As I looked up at its old towers and huge arches and gates I imagined generations of people with their own struggles or worries and it reminded me that I'm not alone in all of this. Shit happens to each of us and, most of the time, we find a way to get through it. The gardens were full of families making the most of the early spring sunshine, going for walks and playing. There was a sense of freedom and fun in the air that lifted my spirits, as long as I blocked out the fact that I seemed to be the only person meandering these old footpaths on my own. Everyone else was either with someone special or had at least brought a dog with them.

I walked back to my flat and went through the invoices with a more pragmatic eye. Who were we paying, for what, and why?

And it just didn't add up. Some of the invoices seemed crazily high and I couldn't understand what we could possibly be getting from these companies to justify the costs. I made a note of those, so I could look through the paperwork next time I was back at the farm. Were there contracts that needed renegotiating? Did we need to at least threaten to change suppliers? They were all names I remembered from my childhood – local firms – people Dad knew and trusted, but that didn't mean they were giving us a fair price. I could hear Nonna's anger already if I dared to suggest leaving any of them. But the state of the farm's finances means I need to take decisive action, or we'll close and everyone will lose their homes and I'll be responsible. I guess this is the kind of decision that Pietro told me he didn't want to make. But it seems that Dad didn't either.

It was late afternoon by the time I reached the pile of 'general correspondence'. I had left it until last because it didn't have an impact on the accounts, so felt less urgent.

I grabbed a chilled beer from the fridge to reward myself for all the hard work, and to try to ease some of the stress I felt mounting up inside. I'm usually good at bottling it back down, but this was different. The state of outgoings versus incoming cash meant it felt like the farm was perched on a sea cliff-top, with erosion threatening to make it collapse into the waves, to be destroyed by the jagged rocks that are patiently waiting below.

Most of the letters were unimportant – marketing from potential suppliers (I kept those on one side in case I needed quotes from any of them to bring costs down) – and yet more condolence messages I didn't want to read, from firms who had worked with Dad for over thirty years. Then I came to one from a bank we don't use. I nearly threw it away, assuming it was just a mailshot, touting for business. It was addressed to Dad and then our business name.

A quick scan showed it wasn't junk mail. It was a letter from the 'Debt Manager' at the bank's branch in our local town, asking Dad to contact them urgently. But there was no hint as to what it could be about. It didn't make sense. We don't bank with them, so why do they want to talk with Dad? I hadn't sent them the required paperwork about his death – I didn't know I needed to – so they wouldn't talk with me in his place until that was done. But this letter was dated from four weeks ago. Whatever it was they needed to talk to him about would be much more serious now, and it could take weeks for them to process the documents, signed in triplicate by notaries and officials, needed for them to agree to talk to me instead. God knows what state things might be in by then.

I was starting to panic. There was only one reason why a bank's Debt Manager would ask someone to contact them urgently and they would now think Dad had been ignoring them. By the time I can get the paperwork together to convince them I've taken over his estate, a month could have passed since they sent the letter, which is bound to be an important deadline for them. I felt sick, a cold dread creeping over me. It was looking likely that Dad had taken out a loan he hadn't told me about, which was hidden from the farm's accounts and, being dead, he was now in default. I was really hoping it was small, but I was worried it wasn't. Why would he have used a bank we don't normally work with, unless he was hiding something? I couldn't see where the money could have gone: there had been no sudden cash injection to the business and we hadn't had any work done on the house or farm buildings. When he died I had to go through his bank statements for tax, and there wasn't anything obvious there either. And there was no evidence of any repayments being made on the loan.

How much did he borrow? What for? Why didn't he tell me? We're already on the edge as it is. The business can't take a hidden debt.

20. It's Not Fair

We have finally finished the work with our deodorant client and they invited me out for dinner with them to celebrate last night. I was feeling a bit the worse for wear this morning. Some of the team went clubbing after dinner and I haven't been to bed yet. I had time to take a very long shower and drink a bucketful of coffee (not literally) and throw on enough make-up to give the illusion of having slept, so I hoped I would get away with it. It was due to be a quiet day today, after a few really busy weeks and maybe being in so early – not having bothered with the traditional going-to-bed thing – I might earn some brownie points.

I defied Stuart's coffee ban on the way into the office and arrived with a takeaway cup from the coffee house on the corner, plus a treat of a large slice of apricot *frangipane* tart – they didn't have any with cherry – hoping the almonds and pastry would help to soak up some of last night's booze. I plonked my coffee on my desk and booted up my geriatric laptop. It always takes ages to wake up so I wandered over to the mail trays, to see if there was anything interesting in there.

As I was leafing through the letters I heard Stuart on the phone. I hadn't realised he was in yet. I was just round the corner from his desk, so he couldn't see me. In fact, he's not used to me being in so early, so I didn't think he had seen me at all today. He probably thought he was in the office on his own.

I paused with the post and listened in. It was sounding interesting. Stuart was getting cross with someone else for a change. It was nice to know he didn't just single me out for his attacks.

"When will I see a return on my investment?" I heard him demand, sounding really frustrated. This was followed by a few moments of silence, with the occasional *hmmm* … and *uh-huh*.

"You promised me it would be a fast turnaround. I'm relying on you." He was sounding more stressed now. "Look! I've already trusted you. The last time you promised it wouldn't be long, and that was over a year ago."

Hmm … Uh-huh …

"No! I don't have any more funds to invest! I'm already going to be grinding my fingers to the bone well past retirement age as it is!"

Hmm … Hmm …

"You told me this was a sure-fire investment. *Hmm*." *Tap tap tap* went his pen on his desk. I wondered if the person talking to him could feel the danger they were in. The early warning sign might not be carrying down a phone line.

Woah! He was yelling now!

"I told you! I don't have anything left. And no, I can't wangle more out of my expenses. This isn't like the last place. They keep a much tighter log of things here."

Wow! So he *has* been trying to fiddle his expenses. Anna guessed right. Was that why he left his old job and was so suddenly *available* to help us with Lucy's maternity cover?

"Look, if I don't see a return by the end of this month, I'm stuffed. I've borrowed money, you know."

Sounded dodgy. This was too good to miss.

"No, not from the bank. That's the problem. The interest

rates are *painfully* high."

Emphasis on the *painfully*. Loan sharks? Big guys with bats? Baseball, not flappy-winged. Interesting visual. Not his granny from the panic in his voice.

"I need to see a return on my investment by the end of the month. I've told you that!"

He was cranking up the stress levels now. He really meant this.

"I've told you! I don't have any way of getting more money – not yet, anyway. You promised me two years ago this would set me up for life and I've not seen anything back yet. I'm not giving you another penny. I don't care what the contract said. I don't have any more to give you."

I was rooted to the spot. I knew I shouldn't be eavesdropping, but I couldn't help it. This was compulsive listening. He had lost the anger and was now sounding desperate. Stuart is broke. And some dodgy get-rich-quick scheme isn't working for him.

"Morning, Sophie!" yelled Susie as she walked in to the office. I was visible from the door, but not from Stuart's desk.

"Shit! I've got to go," said Stuart, abruptly ending his call.

"Morning, Susie!" I replied, with an obviously false lightness in my voice. I scurried back to my desk, clutching my post to my chest, almost ducking as I passed Stuart, as though avoiding machine-gun fire.

I stupidly glanced in his direction. I had never seen him so angry, white-faced with fury. "Wait, Sophie!" he commanded. I stopped dead in my tracks. "Were you listening in to my private conversation?" he continued, with obvious malice in his tone.

How to handle this one? Don't panic. That would be a good start.

"I was just collecting my post." I replied, stating the only truth I was prepared to give him, starting to move back towards my desk.

Stuart knew I had heard every word. And I knew that he knew I knew. That didn't bode well for cessation of hostilities. But it did give me extra ammunition. I now knew that Stuart has been pushing his expense account to the limit, I strongly suspect he had to leave his last job for fiddling his expenses and he must be so heavily in debt that getting me fired so he can take on my responsibilities and negotiate a pay rise would be hugely motivating for him.

The rest of the morning passed uneventfully, though propped up with near-intravenous caffeine. Stuart seemed quieter than usual. Lunch was a festival of carbs and fats, trying to mop up the residual alcohol from last night. I was really glad it was Friday and I could sleep all weekend. I've been going out a lot lately, but it doesn't feel like there's much else to do. And going out drowns out how crap the last three months have been at work.

I wasn't expecting anything in particular when Harry called me into his office after lunch. He doesn't do it as often now that Lucy isn't here, but it's not unheard of and it's usually to pass on positive feedback or thanks from a client. When we do well, clients know that the best way to keep us on the team for their next project is to tell Harry, so we feel appreciated and maybe even get a bonus, to make us less likely to leave. So I was in a good mood as I knocked on his office door, stepped inside and took the seat he ushered me towards. No doubt it was some praise from last night's client, now their project is finished.

Someone once told me that Catherine the Great's motto was to 'praise loudly and blame softly'. Harry is wired the other way round. If we screw up, half the population of the south-east of England will hear him yelling at us. If we do well, it's a quiet one-to-one meeting in his office with the door closed. After a while we get used to it.

Stuart was sitting next to Harry, behind the desk, the pair of them facing me like an interview panel, which surprised me. Then I saw the look in Harry's face and my heart stopped.

"What's wrong?" I asked, nervously.

"Oh, I think you know that one, Sophie."

I shook my head. I was clueless. I really couldn't think of anything I had screwed up recently.

"Don't come over all innocent with me, Sophie. Or don't you remember what you said at dinner last night?"

Harry hadn't been there. It was just for their research team and our research team: me, while Lucy is away. They didn't know Stuart yet. I was still confused.

"The discussion you had with Malcolm?"

Malcolm is the client's Head of Market Research. I racked my brain and shook my head again, still with no idea what I might have done wrong. There were lots of conversations last night and, once the wine had been flowing for a while, they all tended to blend into one.

"Let me make it a bit easier for you. He says it was around 3 a.m. this morning in the little Italian coffee place opposite Liverpool Street station?"

I still didn't know what he was talking about, but that familiar sense of did-I-put-my-foot-in-it dread was creeping up on me.

"Malcolm's boss and I have just had a very interesting conversation. Malcolm wanted him to pass on to me how impressed they have been with you and how you're worth your weight in gold. However, they also wanted to pass on their concern that you won't be available to do any more research for them until next year, when Lucy returns from maternity leave, because Stuart is – and I quote," he looked down at his notepad, "keeping you imprisoned like Cinderella not allowed to go to the ball. Feeling familiar yet?"

My heart was racing and my breathing sounded like I had just run up a hill. I could feel a wave of red the brightness of a police helicopter searchlight moving its way up my neck and covering my face.

"I thought you might," continued Harry. "But that's not all, is it?"

I shook my head – again – but this time because I knew what was coming next. I stared at the carpet.

"Do you know what Malcolm's boss has decided, as a result of last night's conversation, Sophie?"

More head-shaking. My mind tried to distract me with the thought that it might fall off if I shook it much more. I was too slow to stop the smile. I prayed Harry hadn't seen it.

But he did. His face turned a dangerous shade of crimson. That bit in my brain that likes to make me smile at inappropriate moments was telling me to grab the Dulux app on my phone to get a picture of it. It would look great in my bathroom as a feature wall, if only I could convince my landlord.

"What the FUCK are you smirking about, Sophie? I've got a good mind to fire you for gross incompetence, but our HR prat told me I can't. And I'm sick of you showing up here half-cut, exhausted and too busy partying to put any effort into your job anymore."

Shit! This was much worse than I had thought.

"Malcolm's boss has told me they won't be placing any more business with us until after Lucy is back because they can't trust their research to – I'm quoting again – 'someone as incompetent, chauvinistic and power-crazed as Stuart'. Do you have anything to say for yourself?"

I risked a microsecond's glance at his face and caught Stuart's smirk out of the corner of my eye. I was frozen. I couldn't reply. I remembered the conversation. Malcolm had been horrified to hear I had been taken off all qualitative research work – that's the depth-interview stuff, rather than the box-ticking surveys – and said he'd do his best to sort things out, like a knight in shining armour. I had felt grateful to him at the time. I hadn't thought he would do something like this. I hadn't thought, full stop. It was just chatting. Surely everyone knows that anything said after the first bottle of wine is confidential? It's like Chatham House rules. Apparently not.

"Do you know what this means? If they need any more advertising this year, they'll go somewhere else. And they'll probably stick with them for whatever work they need in the future, regardless of whether Lucy is back or not. You have cost my business millions with your drunken, unfounded gossip."

I wasn't drunk and it wasn't unfounded! It was true! But the words wouldn't come out. One look at Stuart's glee and Harry's rage and they froze in my throat.

"Stuart and I have had a long talk and we both agree that there is only one option."

I felt the ground tumbling away beneath me, leaving me stranded in a rickety rowing boat that with no oars, plummeting over Niagara Falls after heavy flooding. Stuart's grin looked like it wanted to explode with childish glee. If Stuart was that happy with whatever Harry was going to say, then I was done for. A vision of having to hand in my notice on my beautiful flat flashed across my mind, because there's no way I could pay the rent without this job. I imagined myself having to sell off anything of value, which wasn't much. Or sitting on a street corner with a piece of cardboard and a message in marker pen: *Half-decent market researcher available to hire.*

"I'm not going to fire you," continued Harry. Whew! A wave of relief. I started to relax.

"But only because it would be illegal."

*Oh my God, so he **wants** to fire me!*

"I have taken advice from our HR consultant and she says that what you have done does not count as gross incompetence or a clear breach of your contract. I don't agree with her. But the only other option I have is performance management."

I was shrivelling under his angry stare. I felt like I was trying to melt into the chair, to make this go away.

"Stuart has been explaining to me how much he has had to support you over the last three months. It's not good enough, Sophie."

"But that's just not true!" I yelled. It wasn't.

Harry shook his head, as though with disappointment. "As of today you are on one month's performance management. Unless we see a marked improvement in your work – and your attitude – then we will have to begin formal disciplinary proceedings," he started reading from notes on his desk, "with a view to terminating your contract with us without a reference. It would all be documented in your HR file, which would be passed to any future employer who requested it."

I gasped audibly. This was bad. Really bad. Stuart was loving every moment.

"For the next month, you will show every email you send, every report you write, every tiny piece of research you want to do, to Stuart, for feedback and approval. You will listen to that feedback politely. You will take it on board. You will learn from his experience. And if you can't do that, you will leave. And if I ever hear of you bad-mouthing anyone at my company again, either in public or in the loos here, you will be instantly dismissed, without notice. Do I make myself clear?"

I still couldn't speak. I struggled to nod.

"Now get out of my sight!" he spat and I ran out of his office as quickly as I could.

"Oh, and one more thing," he yelled after me, as I looked back at him, "don't expect to be getting your bonus this year. I've got a good mind to give it to Stuart, to compensate him for the extra work and responsibility he's going to have to take on to train you."

My feet felt so heavy I could barely walk. I had been relying on that bonus to pay for my holiday in Italy this summer. I haven't been away for years and since Jamie's extravagances emptied my savings account, my bonus is the only way I can afford to get a break. And God knows I need one. I couldn't afford to lose it. But there was nothing I could do. As I turned away, I saw the biggest, ugliest, rotten-tooth-filled grin on Stuart's face. His smug, flabby features told me I had played right into his hands. And he was right. He had been waiting for an opportunity like this.

Unfair didn't begin to describe it. I was sure I was going to vomit, to collapse in a heap on the floor. Susie spotted me staggering towards my desk and came running over to help me. I was piling my stuff into my bag. For once I decided to leave my laptop. I was pulling on my coat. My arm got stuck in the sleeve. She helped me. "What the hell is wrong, Sophie?" she implored, shaken by my behaviour.

"I've got to get home. Tell Harry my period just started."

She understood. *Women's problems* – a great way to make sure a male boss doesn't ask awkward questions.

I ran out of the office, my head swimming with fear and uncertainty. Did Stuart just win the war? I didn't think so. Not yet. But he came damn close. I'm going to have to up my game if I want any chance of winning.

21. Luca's Final Demand

I went to see Luca this morning to ask if I could take some time off to sort out some things at the farm. I didn't want to tell him what – he would just worry and he might even think it would have an impact on my work here. He wasn't impressed.

Things have been busy at the office. I'm juggling four cases at the moment, of which the Denucci case is the biggest. We've done all we can for now from a desk-based point of view. We need to wait for my stake-out before we can move forwards. We're building up a strong case and soon the evidence will be compelling enough that the police won't be able to ignore it. Then our work will be done, until it goes to Court.

But Luca wants me on standby for more fieldwork. Being single with no kids, I'm the one in the team that can most easily drop everything and travel around the country – or further – in pursuit of a hot lead.

"Christof, how committed are you to this job?" he asked, as I requested flexibility on leave. Given how stressed I have been feeling about Dad's hidden debts and the possibility of losing the farm, it took all my self-control not to snap back. For years, Luca has had my undivided attention on this job, to the exclusion of a social life and I rarely use up even half of my annual leave entitlement. If he needs someone to be there for him, with zero notice, it's me every time.

"I need a couple of days this week to sort out some urgent paperwork I missed when Dad died. You know how it is with bureaucracy." I couldn't read his face. Being unreadable is one of our most important skills. But I knew this request would count against me long term. Unscheduled leave isn't something we do. We plan our time off at the start of the year and it only moves in absolute emergencies – usually dictated by work, rather than our personal circumstances. "Do I have any choice, Christof? Or have you already decided?"

"I need to do this, Luca. I wouldn't ask if I didn't." He grudgingly agreed but I could tell he was cross with me. I won't get away with this again in a hurry.

So it took me by surprise when he called me into his office again at the end of the day, far from poker-faced, and said we needed to talk. It turned out to be him needing to talk and me having to listen.

Nonna always said you can't take responsibility for the stories people tell themselves about you in their heads. She loves reading Mark Twain and one of her favourite quotes from him is the one about how some of the worst things in his life never actually happened. In other words, he would tell himself stories about what might happen, or he would embellish what had taken place until it was unrecognisable from reality. And it was clear that Luca had been doing this today.

When I reached Luca's office, he was sitting stiffly in his chair; tension showing around his eyes and his jaw clenched. He was fiddling with a pen in a way I was sure the pen wasn't appreciating. It looked like it would feel seasick.

"I'm not going to beat around the bush on this, Christof. I need you 100 per cent in this job, or not at all. And since you took over running the farm, I feel we have lost your 100 per cent."

Wham! That hit hard. Dad died less than six months ago, and since I came back from bereavement leave, I've worked every hour available and haven't taken a single day off. Yet Luca is questioning my commitment to the business? Before I could defend myself, he continued.

"There isn't space in this team for someone who's only half in. I have agreed to you taking the leave you need this week, but you need to change the way things are running. You need to make a decision. We don't need a part-time farmer here. You either get yourself someone to run the farm for you, properly, so you can be fully back on board here, or you leave us and do it yourself. That is all I have to say on the matter." And he looked at his desk, starting to pack his things into his bag; making it clear our conversation was over.

An ultimatum. So now I get to add to the list of things that keep me up at 3 a.m., not just the fear not being able to pay the farm-workers, or even losing the farm, but also letting down Luca.

I don't want to be a full-time farmer. I love the city life too much, along with the sense of achievement I get when we solve a client's conundrum, which has foxed their team. I can't see myself getting that from cherries. But on the other hand, I have a choice to make with the farm: I either do it properly and make it work, or I'm going to have to sell it. I never asked to inherit this responsibility. Just because I am the only child, it doesn't mean I should have to take on the family business, no matter how long it has been run by us all. I feel trapped by the obligations on all sides.

And what do *I* want? Where do *I* want to be in ten years' time? What do *I* want my life to look like? Who do *I* want to be with? What do *I* want to be doing? Why does no one seem to care about that? Why is it all about what *they* need and want from me? I don't normally do 'it's not fair', but it's how I feel tonight. Something needs to change, and I need to decide whether it will be me making those changes, or if I'm going to leave them to everyone else to decide for me.

22. Home Sweet Home

I spent most of the weekend under a duvet, feeling sorry for myself. The one time I managed to drag myself out of my flat, I was in my pyjamas, hidden under a long winter coat, scurrying to the corner shop to buy comfort food. The cherry tree I usually love walking past, in front of the obligatory Big House on my road, had the audacity to be in blossom, celebrating the spring, as though it didn't have a care in the world. I'm not sure I want to be its friend any more, with that kind of selfish behaviour.

Going back into work today was hard. Thank God Stuart was out on the road for a client meeting, so he couldn't look over my shoulder physically, with full smirk in operation, but that didn't stop him from calling me every ninety minutes to vet any emails I had drafted and to check up on me. What is it going to be like, once he gets back in the office?

Harry was quiet today, making a point of ignoring me. I guessed he was still angry about what I said to Malcolm. But I had only told him the truth! Stuart *has* taken me off all qualitative research work and it will stay that way until Lucy is back, so if Malcolm wants to work with me, he'll have to wait until then. But Harry was right. I probably shouldn't have told him in the way I did. Certainly not half-drunk at 3 a.m. while trying to drown myself in an Americano.

Even so, I can't begin to imagine the lies that Stuart must have told Harry to get him to come down on me so hard. Friday was the proverbial last straw that broke the camel's back. That was clear. Stuart has been mounting quite a campaign against me. It's easy to do, when you're the boss's best mate.

Susie was embarrassingly sympathetic this morning, wanting to know how I was. She seems to genuinely care. I made a mental note to put in more effort to be friendly with her in future. But for now my absolute priority is getting off performance management, so I can escape from being slimed over by Stuart every few minutes. I know I can't bear that. I really have no clue how I'm going to get through this.

It was clear that the crew at work had been gossiping on Friday after I left, with thinly veiled questions wanting to know more from me about what actually happened. I'm not telling any of them. I know they'd be on my side, but that would make things harder. I know they would think it's crazy too, not just me. But I don't want to add their righteous indignation to my inner seething rage at this unfairness. None of them likes Stuart either. Anyone who wasn't his best mate could see he's all bravado and no substance, that he used other people's work to make himself look good, and that his morals made Attila the Hun look like a saint.

I had texted Anna over the weekend, to let her know what was going on. She agreed that Stuart and Harry were behaving like idiots. She invited me over to dinner tonight, but I decided I was going to go home and grab something out of the freezer, instead. I need to get a plan of action together about how to handle the rest of my probation, before Stuart gets back in the office tomorrow. At least Easter will take up four days of it and other weekends will account for eight more, so there are only nineteen days to get through, including today. I visualise a calendar with bright red crosses smothering out the full month and wish with every bone in my body I could press the 'fast-forward' button.

I trudged home, carrying the weight of the mess I'm in, and let myself in through my gorgeous deep red front door. I kicked my shoes in the direction of my shoe rack as a token gesture towards tidying and found my slippers. My floors are too cold for bare feet at this time of year. I hung my coat up on the spare hook and ditched my bag on the hall floor, where it could stay until the morning. One thing I definitely wasn't doing for Harry any more was working evenings unpaid.

I bent over to pick up my post, feeling the painful tension in my lower back and wishing I could afford to book myself in for a massage. The thought of someone running well-oiled, practised hands over my aching muscles while surrounded by the scent of aromatherapy oils and easy-to-ignore elevator music would be blissful. I leafed through the letters. Electricity bill. A mailer offering me yet another instant-approval credit card. It's no wonder people get so heavily into debt. A handwritten white envelope. Curious.

I shuffled towards my sofa and wrapped myself up in my favourite blanket. The heating was doing one of its 'I'm not sure I'm going to bother' impressions this evening. I aimed the credit card application towards my open-topped recycling bin. I'd love to say I hit it like a basketball pro, but that would be a lie. It was close enough to remind me to chuck it in there the next time I was walking past. It's not like it's a long way to go in my tiny flat. But even so, I love this place. It's all mine; no one to share it with; no one to argue with about washing up or who stole the last piece of cheese from the fridge. And I have a big, old Victorian roll top bath – a rare luxury in a rented flat – that I can soak in for as long as I want after a stressful day at work, with no one yelling at me, legs crossed, behind the bathroom door because they need the loo.

I decided the electricity bill could wait. It gets paid on direct debit anyway, and it doesn't need me to give it attention to make it feel good. If it's too high, it will only make me feel worse. So I moved my attention to the hand-addressed envelope.

I didn't recognise the writing. It's not my birthday and it didn't feel like a card. And it had a real stamp on it, so it wasn't a machine pretending to be a person, like some charity mailers use.

I tore it open along the long edge and pulled out the contents: a single piece of A4, folded into three. Good quality paper. I unfolded it and looked for a sender's address. Printed along the top, centred, was my landlord's business address. I felt a slight disappointment. I had hoped it might be something exciting, something to lift my day, but it was probably just him telling me when my next inspection will be. Time to tidy like a crazy lady and move the rug to hide the scratch on the lounge floor again.

I scanned down for the signature: Mary Williamson, his secretary. It couldn't be that important if he hadn't signed it himself. Clause numbers from my tenancy contract were blended like a failed British Bake Off cake with phrases like 'consolidate his portfolio' and 'given the current market conditions' and 'with deepest regret' and 'you are obliged to give the agent access for viewings' and 'vacant possession'. My head was swimming. It thought it had understood what this meant, but it was running too fast in the opposite direction to admit it. It was the final sentence that finally woke me up, like a clown's custard pie in the face, straight from the fridge, but really not funny: "Your tenancy will end two months from the date of this letter." Last Friday.

I read through the letter more carefully and the bottom fell out of my world.

23. The Answer I Didn't Want

I had to take two days off work to speed up the paperwork with the bank, traipsing round offices to get documents stamped and approved before they would agree to see me. It was nerve-wracking, waiting for the meeting, not knowing how much the debt might be or where the money had gone. My imagination filled the time well.

Eventually I had all the documentation I needed to prove that I had inherited Dad's estate, including any debts, and the Debt Manager agreed to meet me at the end of the week, Friday afternoon, so I didn't have to take the full day off work.

The bank is in our local town and its facade shows how seriously it takes its business. It is one of the oldest buildings in the town; ornate carvings surrounding the stern, heavy oak doors, letting you know that there is no laughter or fun inside these walls. The once cream stonework is now dyed sooty black from the pollution of the busy street it stands on, where traffic crawls nose to tail for most of the day. I walked inside, wearing my best suit, with a file full of paperwork under my arm and just one question in my head: Why?

The 'how much' is almost irrelevant until I can find out where the money went – what it was used for.

The Debt Manager is a portly man in his late fifties with the air of an official who is counting the days to retirement on a wall calendar that gains a new marker pen cross each time he hits 5 p.m. Bored but officious, and well-practised at sniffing out excuses and lies.

He shook my hand, sensing my nerves and walked me to a meeting room. He didn't offer me a coffee or make pleasantries or offer condolences for my father's passing. None of that would move him closer to his goal: to get the debt repaid to his employer.

He spent much longer than necessary going through the raft of documents that proved he is allowed to talk to me, even though he had already seen them. For one heart-stopping moment he decided a single piece of paper was missing, one that would have instantly drawn our meeting to a close. He made a phone call. I wondered if he secretly wanted to disappear back to his back-office desk, to while away the final hour of the day, rather than having to deal with a defaulting customer.

A few minutes later he nodded. "*Certo. Grazie.*" He hung up the phone, finally making eye contact with me.

"You have questions about your late father's loan with this bank. What do you want to know? And when can we expect you to make good the missed repayments?"

I had been holding back the stress and worry, so as soon as I had permission to speak, I blurted out the whole emotional saga of how I had found the letter in a pile at the house and how there were no records whatsoever of the loan. The Debt Manager held up a hand as though to stop traffic and silenced me.

"I don't need to hear the sob story. Believe me, I get them every day and they never change anything. I repeat my questions. What do you want to know? And when will you make good the missing repayments?"

"I need to know how much the loan was for and where the money went," I reply meekly.

He showed me the figures and Dad's original contract. My mind had been telling me stories over the past week, but none of them had been this bad. I swallowed the wave of alarm that threatened to drown out my attempts at thinking rationally. The debt was more than €200,000. It was a short-term loan with a high interest rate and there were already months' worth of penalty fees for failing to keep up with the payments. Each monthly payment should have been nearly €4,000 and there was no way the farm business had surplus to cover a fraction of that. What was Dad thinking of?

I took a deep breath to tried to calm down.

"Did he say what he wanted the money for?"

"To repair the old barn, according to our notes."

The loan was double what Dad and I were going to ask our regular bank for when we drove to meet them, the day he died. This simply didn't make sense. The loan had been taken out over a year ago and definitely hadn't been used for repairs.

"And his collateral?"

"The farm and its buildings, including the house."

"Which account was the loan transferred to?"

"I can find that out for you, but it will take me until Monday. You'll have to bear with me. But that's not my priority at the moment. The loan has defaulted. This is serious."

"And when was the last repayment made?"

He confirmed what I had suspected. Dad had stopped making payments several months before he died. In fact, only the first two monthly repayments were made, but from the bank statements that wasn't done by Dad. The bank had been sending him chasing letters, but I had no idea where they'd gone. I was amazed they had let the non-payment go on for so long. The Debt Manager said it was their policy not to foreclose for twelve months, especially when the debt was owed by a local farmer;

they are too important to the region. This seemed extremely generous and I was grateful to them, but it didn't fix the mess we were in.

To bring the account up to date would cost ten months' payments, plus penalty fees, and they wanted it within two weeks. I had to find over €40,000 by the end of the month.

I thanked the Debt Manager and assured him I would do something to make good the missing payments by their deadline. We both knew it was a promise I might struggle to keep. We shook hands and as we said goodbye I detected the smallest hint of sympathy in his eyes. He had to play the tough guy, but he could see how hard it had been for me to discover Dad's hidden mountain of debt.

The only hope I had was the emergency funds account. We always kept €100,000 in there, in case of disasters or emergency repairs on buildings or equipment. I walked the short distance to our regular bank, to find out how quickly funds could be transferred to pay the €40,000 to bring our loan account up to date while I found out where the money had gone and figured out a sustainable plan. We couldn't sell equipment and this would take more than 'cost-cutting'. And I still haven't sold this year's harvest, as Pietro reminded me on the phone yesterday. I haven't mentioned any of this to him yet. I need answers first.

I barely touched my espresso as I waited half an hour for the Bank Manager to see me. I didn't want to deal with this at the public counter. He has known our family since before I was born and he started by telling me how sad he was about Dad's accident. Then he asked me why I needed to see him.

I explained the outline of the situation. His initial response was indignation that Dad had gone to one of his competitors for the loan. Then he realised the implications of the figures. I saw a shadow of worry pass over his face. His sympathetic eyes betrayed his shock at the news. He knew as well as I did how out of character this had been for Dad. And it was clear from his expression that he knew nothing about this.

"So how are you going to clear this debt, Christof? From what I know of the business's finances it's not going to be easy. Do you have any good ideas?"

I reminded him about our emergency funds account. I passed the account number over the desk to him. "I wanted to check the balance on this account and see if we can transfer the first €40,000 over today."

He typed in the numbers and the friendly smile faded from his eyes. "Christof, you need to see this," he said, quietly, turning the computer screen to face me across the other side of his desk. The last few transactions on the account were displayed for us. It hadn't been touched since before Dad died. And it was empty. Zero. Nothing left. The account had been closed a month before Dad died, and the closing statement wasn't in the paperwork I went through afterwards. He must have got rid of it, to hide his actions from me.

"But how can this be?" I was almost shouting with the shock that another €100,000 was missing. "We haven't touched this account in years! Where did the money go?"

There were two payments for €50,000 each, made a month apart, at the same time as Dad took out the loan. The bank manager printed out the transaction list for me. I could see the bank details for the recipient – the same for both payments – but there was no other information.

"I can tell you the bank name from the sort code," said my Bank Manager, apologetically, "but that is all. I can't tell you who owns the account or what the money might have been used for."

I managed to keep a lid on my emotions as we said our goodbyes. But I needed to get into the hills, before I drove back to the farm for the weekend. I needed to be somewhere where only the grass and the trees would hear what I needed to scream at Dad. How could he do this? He had endangered the farm and its workers. And why? Where did the money go? Why hadn't he told me? Why did he work so hard to hide the paper trail? As if my job weren't hard enough already!

I was well into a little-used hiking trail in the hills before I finally let the tears join the anger, oblivious to the purple-tinged beauty of the hills as the sun prepared to set. I sat, like a ten-year-old boy, hugging my knees, letting my rage out at Dad for his lies, missing him so much that I could hardly breathe, and with no idea how to fix the mess he left behind.

24. A Once In A Lifetime Offer

E very year, on the anniversary of Harry founding his company, he throws a party for all of his employees. I didn't want to go this year, but it's a tradition and Harry made it clear it wasn't optional. I was feeling really low and I would rather have hidden at home for the evening. Going out has lost its appeal. I'm at risk of losing my job and I lose my home in just seven weeks now.

I phoned the landlord to beg for longer. He agreed it would take more than two months to sell the house and to go through the paperwork to complete the sale, but he needs to offer the flat as a 'vacant possession', so the buyer will want me out as soon as possible in the process. And he was contractually obliged to give me two months' notice, so that is what he has done.

I cried myself to sleep the night the 'for sale' sign appeared outside my front door. I've already had a talking-to from the agent, dressed in a cheap suit with too much aftershave, and he didn't even offer to take his shoes off before traipsing the dirt from the street around my lovely home. "You're going to have to put in a bit more effort on tidying and cleaning, dear, if we're going to sell the place."

Great. I'll turn it into a hovel and then it will never sell!

"But don't think you can block the sale. Your tenancy runs out towards the end of May, whether it gets sold or not. Your job is making sure you get your deposit back in full. Helping your landlord with this will make that more likely."

I hate it when they do viewings. They want me to turn the place into a show home for them and then put up with strangers going through my stuff, on the pretext of checking the size of the inside of the wardrobes or the bathroom cupboard. Sometimes I get home after work to find there was a viewing they forgot to tell me about. "Sorry, we tried to contact you!" Really? And things have moved; just little things, like mugs or jewellery or clothes from the bathroom floor. I hate the thought of Mr Aftershave touching my stuff. It makes me cringe and recoil. It reminds me of the night at the Christmas party with Stuart.

At work, Harry isn't really talking to me any more. At times, I wonder if there's something sheepish in his look. Does he realise he overreacted? It wasn't my fault the client pulled their future work. I had only told them the truth. It has been hellish having Stuart check everything. And he isn't letting up. We're halfway through my probation and I've been counting – I have nine working days of it left - and Stuart has been true to his word. Every email I send, every summary I write, each piece of strategy I dream up has to be approved by him. He loves reminding me of this each time I walk into his office, waving his podgy hand at me in a 'please don't interrupt' movement as he pretends to be busy and makes me wait for the attention I don't want anyway, standing like an idiot in his doorway for the whole company to see.

The guys from graphics are on my side, but they also know what it's like to get on the wrong side of Harry and their advice is just to grit my teeth and get through it. The thing is they don't have my sixth sense – that Stuart will have something else up his sleeve for once my probation is over. He isn't going to let this be the end of the fight.

I haven't told Lucy yet. Her baby is only a couple of months old and the last time I spoke to her, she was holding the phone to her ear with a shoulder while rocking Emma, trying to soothe her out of a colic screaming fit, more obsessed with breastfeeding than business. I can't add to her stress levels. This is my problem, not hers, and I don't want her risking her job by annoying Harry to help me. I don't think it would help anyway. I'm due to see her for dinner next week. Her husband is going to babysit Emma for the first time. It's hard to imagine that Lucy hasn't had even an hour off for over two months. She's excited, but nervous that he will mess up and she'll go home to a disaster. I really want to talk to her about Stuart, to find out what she would recommend. I promise myself I'll break it to her by phone before we go out for dinner. And I'll make sure I don't say anything that would stress her.

Our company dinner was in a lovely restaurant near our office and I should have been excited at the prospect of someone else picking up the bill. It's not a place I could normally afford to go to, as the maître d' made clear with his snooty look as we all pushed our way through the door to their 'party room', set slightly back from the main restaurant, so we didn't upset their 'real' customers. Harry was greeted with enthusiasm as a valued customer, but it was clear to see that they wished he hadn't brought the 'rabble' with him this time.

I managed to bag a seat as far as possible away from Harry and Stuart, so maybe I could pretend for the evening that they weren't there and do my best to have a good time. The guys were great. They refused to talk about work outside of the office, so we were having fun. They were slowly reminding me that I knew how to laugh. It wasn't illegal. But it hurt. It clashed so heavily with the frustration and anger that set the tone for my Inner Drama Queen's monologues most days. She loves reminding me how it's not fair that Stuart has won with Harry, that he is destroying my career, and that my *bastard* landlord is making me homeless. But she hasn't yet managed to kick my arse into gear on flat hunting. I'm firmly in denial on that one.

The wine was flowing freely and it wasn't long before I needed to pop to the ladies. Susie had just been so we couldn't do that 'girl thing' of going together. The loos were up a corridor and they were individual toilets, each with their own sink, with no distinction made between men and women, rather than rooms with separate cubicles. I looked in the mirror as I washed my hands. The worries of the past few months were wearing heavily on my face. I looked older than my thirty-three years. My skin was looking grey. I hoped it was just the lighting. Why do so many hotels, restaurants and pubs – and changing rooms for that matter – put in lights that make customers look ill? Surely they'd make more money if they could invent magic mirrors that made us feel great about ourselves?

I shut the door behind me as I left to go back to our table, lost in imagining myself looking like I'm sixty by the end of the year, if my stress levels carry on like this.

I collided with Stuart.

My entire body wanted to leap back through the wall, flooding me with memories of Christmas and falling asleep on my bathroom floor because of this guy. He was wearing that same look. No. It couldn't be. Not after everything he's done. He couldn't still think I'd be interested, could he?

Without noticing, I'm backed up against the wall and he puts one hand either side of my head, leaning towards me as though wanting a lover's kiss. I want to push him away, paralysed by the horror of his watery eyes, just inches from mine. I can see every single one of his blocked pores. I can smell his breath, the wine failing to mask its foul stench.

"*Get away from me!*" *I manage to hiss, starting to struggle, trying to duck under his arms. He places his hands on my shoulders to hold me in place. I can feel the weight of him pushing me into the wall. Where are the rest of the team? Why is no one else in this corridor? Why won't someone help me?*

"*Sophie,*" *he murmurs, as though he loves saying my name. I feel my starter curdling with the acid in my stomach, ready to revisit.* "*You know I'm only just getting started with getting rid of you, don't you? You've seen what I can do already, haven't you? You know you're not going to win this one.*"

He's asking me questions, but he doesn't want answers. I just want this over. No. I want Harry to see Stuart for who he really is. This isn't okay.

"*I think we both agree it's better if you leave, don't we? Before you force me to take action you'll regret.*"

I can't speak. So I was right. That is what he wants. This has gone beyond his position and money. He wants me gone. I try to shout. He places a hand over my mouth. My body has shut down. I gag at the taste of his clammy palm. I struggle. He pushes me harder against the wall. I can feel him bruising me. I want to kick him. To scream. But I can't. I can't believe this is happening.

"*With your track record this year you're going to need a really good reference to get you out of this mess. Do you want to do a deal?*"

He raises a bushy eyebrow that sends dried-out wrinkles shooting up his forehead. He's repulsive. His eyes are gleaming and he gives me a smile that sends another waft of bad breath in my direction. I recoil.

"*I'm prepared to give you a glowing reference,*" *he continues, as though we were chatting in the office and he didn't have me pinned against a wall with his hand over my mouth,* "*if you'll have sex with me.*"

What? How can this guy even begin to think that might happen? Disgust forces me into action. I have to escape. I start to force myself free from his grip, but he isn't letting me go.

"One blink for yes, two for no?"

How about one bite for fuck off? I sink my teeth into his hand as hard as I can. In his shock he loosens his grip. I wrench myself free and sprint back to our table.

I was sobbing, creating the very scene that the maître d' had feared 'people like us' would cause. I didn't care. I couldn't stop shaking. I ran to our table and grabbed my bag and coat and managed to say 'got to go' before I sprinted to the door. I heard Harry in the background, loud enough for everyone to hear, telling the team that Stuart had just given me a 'pep talk' and it looked like I hadn't taken it very well.

No. The guy was trying to use blackmail to force me to prostitute myself.

I didn't remember how I got home. I collapsed on my sofa, sobbing, unable to think straight. I had no one to turn to. I wished Jem were in the country. She would have known what to do. But one thing I did know: there was no way I was going to let Stuart win. I had had three months of hell from him, and I was sure this counted as sexual harassment. I had to stop being such a doormat. It was time for drastic action.

25. A Meeting With Pietro

I left the hills at sunset. I was putting off going back to the farm. I had to talk to Pietro about the loan and the disappearance of the emergency account funds. I knew that he was going squirm. He was Dad's closest friend. I don't believe Dad would have kept him in the dark about such a large amount of money. But why hadn't Pietro told me something about this before?

Nonna greeted me with her usual love and enthusiasm and dinner was on the table almost before I had taken my coat off. Pietro wasn't joining us. I felt disappointed. I had wanted to have it out with him. But I also knew that the best way to get answers from him was if I could find a way to be calm about it. Tonight I felt too full of anger, and if he thought I was accusing him of something, he'd have clammed up.

Nonna and I managed small talk for the evening. She knew something was up, but also knew not to press me for what was wrong. Maybe she had to do that with Dad too? The only time things got awkward was when she raised the question of the cherry harvest again. I had had so much on my mind that I had let finding a buyer slip.

"How are things going with selling the harvest, *caro*?" she asked gently, as she served me a generous slice of the plum tart she had made that afternoon, using up the remains of last year's harvest. We were about to hit that *hungry gap* fruitless time of year. I had half-expected her question, so I managed to compose my face into what I hoped she would read as *calm and confident*.

"I think things will be fine. All on track," I lied.

"That's great news! Who do you have in mind?"

I hadn't expected to have to deceive her in this much detail, "Oh, I'd rather not say until it's all signed, if that's okay?" Nonna shrugged and smiled, tousling my hair like she used to when I was a boy.

"However you want it, *caro*. It's lovely not to have to nag you, the way I did your father. But remember I'm here if you need help." I struggled to eat my dessert. I felt awful about misleading her, but the truth would have hurt even more.

Back in my teenage bed it took me hours to fall asleep; in the bedroom that hadn't changed since I had left for university, frozen in time, paying homage to a phase of my life when I didn't really know what stress and worries were, but still managed to dive into the drama whenever the urge took me. The more my brain searched for answers to the 'why, Dad?' question, the more dead ends it found in its reasoning, until I gave up, exhausted and empty, and waited for the sun to rise.

On Saturday morning I was the last one up, unsurprisingly. I was due to meet Pietro at ten to agree the start of spring work in the orchards. He was friendly enough when I came down to see him and I managed to hide my frustrations, my desperation to ask him questions that I knew would silence him faster than Usain Bolt at the sound of a starter pistol. We walked round the farm and discussed the work that would normally be done at this time of year. We talked about pruning and mulching, which trees were past their best and needed to be replaced, and where to plant the new variety that Pietro wanted to try out, to fill a gap that sometimes happened in the season if the weather was too hot in late June. I agreed to his recommendations and he seemed satisfied that I was making the right decisions.

We went back to the kitchen for a coffee, which Nonna delivered to us complete with home-made cherry tarts, made with some cherry sauce left over from last year, carefully stored in glass jars in the dark of our cold room. The aroma was wonderful. I chuckled to myself about how food-free my kitchen is in Milan, how rarely it smells of genuine 'cooking', and I wondered if Nonna realised or if she thought I cooked like her all the time. She has never visited me in Milan; she won't leave the countryside. I decided not to shatter any illusions she might have.

She sensed that Pietro and I still had things to talk about so she disappeared off somewhere, leaving us in peace. I took a sip of my espresso and a bite of my tart and then raised the subject of Dad's loan. There was no point in softening it. I told him about the letter from the bank and what had happened over the past week.

I studied Pietro's face, watching for any sign of recognition or surprise. I saw a glint of darkness pass over his eyes, as though he were trying to decide how much to open up, whether or not to tell me the truth. It finished with a sheepish look as he stared at his old black boots. His heavy eyebrows were furrowed, betraying the emotions driving his thoughts. I sensed he was weighing up what to tell me. He was processing carefully, working out how much I might know and how much to tell me – how much I might guess for myself.

"Couldn't say," was the only reply I got, when I asked him what the money had been used for, whether Dad was in trouble. He was playing it safe and didn't realise how strange it was that he hadn't made any comment about what a terrible situation we were in, or surprise at Dad suddenly wanting so much money, but never mentioning it to either of us. He didn't realise that what he was *not* saying told me more than what he *was*.

I let silence work its magic and nodded, continuing with my coffee and cherries. After a few minutes, Pietro shuffled in his seat and I seized my chance.

"Pietro, you do realise how astronomical this debt is, don't you? We can't repay the overdue instalments, let alone make good, if the bank forecloses on us. We could lose the farm. Please tell me anything you know."

He was still fascinated by his boots, but his 'tell' – fidgeting with the cuff of his shirt – told me he wasn't being honest with me. He knew what had happened to the money.

"Christof," he eventually replied, not making eye contact, "I have nothing to tell you. I didn't get involved with the money side of things. I ran the farm. I can't help you."

I could tell he was lying, but I've known him for long enough that I could see there was no point in pushing him today. It would backfire. He would dig his heels in to defend his lie. So I let our meeting end with pleasantries and kept my cards close to my chest.

If he knows where the money is – which I think he does – I don't want to tip him off about what I'm going to do next. He might warn someone and it could disappear forever. I'm sure he's mixed up in this somehow. I'm also sure that Dad trusted him with whatever his plans were. I can find out what I need using the systems we have at work. It's the slow way round, but it will collect evidence that Pietro can't deny. And it looks like the only way I'll find out whether or not we can get any of the money back.

26. The Formal Complaint

I woke up this morning, having struggled to get to sleep, with my head throbbing and my body aching. Pneumatic drills were keeping pace with my heartbeat in my brain, pulsating behind my eyes. My joints were complaining as though a single night's sleep had aged them by forty years. Every bone in my body wanted me to spend the day in bed. But I had made myself a promise last night and I was determined to keep it.

So I slowly eased my way through my pre-work routine and somehow made it to my desk. On time.

My stomach was heavy with worry about seeing Stuart again, until I remembered he was visiting a client today and it relaxed a little. But not much. It was still knotted like a 1980s macramé plant pot holder at the thought of Stuart's 'proposition' last night. Once I had got over the shock, I had spent for hours lying awake, applying my market research head to dissect his words.

"I think we both agree it's better if you leave, don't we? Before you force me to take action you'll regret." In other words, he would stop at nothing to get me out of Harry's company. He hadn't finished his nastiness. There was still further to go. And he was making it clear he wanted to win on this one. He had the upper hand.

"With your track record this year you're going to need a

really good reference to get you out of this mess." The track record that was solely down to Stuart, his bullying, his lies.

"I'm prepared to give you a glowing reference, if..." I couldn't bear to even think the rest of the words. The implicit threat from this worm of a man was that my refusal to comply meant he would give me a terrible reference that would make any job offer fall through.

But it didn't make sense. From what I had overheard of Stuart's phone conversation, he wants to get me out so he could take on my work and get a pay rise. So why would he want to make it hard for me to find work elsewhere? Surely he should be helping me? Then I remembered: I had rejected him – twice now – hurting his ego. He wants to leave me unemployed. That is going to be his revenge.

So he is going to force me to job hunt and make it impossible for me to succeed, unless I... I can't even think about it!

I hate the way I feel about work now; the negative thoughts that get stuck in my head. I used to love my job. I used to jump out of bed in the morning. Okay, maybe that's a slight exaggeration, but I did used to look forward to the projects we were working on. I miss running focus groups terribly. I loved meeting so many new people and figuring out how they ticked, what motivated them, what they were looking for in life.

More and more lately, I find myself waking up in the middle of the night with my heart racing, drenched in sweat, worrying about how to get myself out of this mess, how to fix things. I feel powerless. I can't talk to Harry, because he would never believe me. I don't trust him anymore. He would help me against his friend. After all, he and Stuart have been drinking buddies and best mates since not long after I was born.

But I had to do something. I had to find a way to drag

myself out of this blackness; the emptiness that threatens to take over when I'm lying in bed, awake, with no one to turn to.

I promised myself this morning, around 4 a.m., that I would make a formal complaint about Stuart's behaviour. Not to Harry. He wouldn't trust me. That probation fiasco was the final straw, proving he'll never side with me. He and Stuart go back too far. I'd have to be impossibly convincing to overcome the lies and prejudices that Stuart has been selling him since December. I want to talk to Sally, our Human Resources consultant. She would listen to me. She doesn't have the agenda that Harry does. She would be able to help. I can't do this on my own. I don't want to leave this job; at least not the job I used to have. I can't face house-hunting as well as job-hunting. And without Stuart, I love this job. I love working with the team, I enjoy our clients and their projects and Lucy and I had a strategy to get me promoted, when she gets back. I can't let Stuart take all of that away from me.

So that's my plan: to get Sally to help me make sure Stuart stops all of this. To find a way to keep my job. To have someone who can mediate for me with Harry, so he can see me for who I really am, rather than through the slime-tinted glasses he always puts on when I'm in the room.

But I don't know when Sally is next due in. She works for us as a consultant because Harry doesn't need HR support very often, so there has never been a need to have someone full-time in the role. She is usually in at least once a month but the last time was only a week ago and I don't want to wait another three weeks before I can do something about this. The thought of that brought back last night's panic and nausea. So I spent my travel time this morning trying to come up with a plan to convince Harry to call her in.

I stopped by my favourite coffee shop to grab my early

morning Americano and then headed over to the office. I was only just in on time, so everyone else was already at their desk. Susie saw me coming through the door and ran over to hug me and see how I was. I had forgotten that I had run out on the company dinner before the main course had arrived. I had become Major Gossip. Suddenly the whole team was around me, smothering me in hugs and 'how are you?' and friendly curiosity. At least, everyone apart from Harry, who stood in the doorway to his office, staring coldly at me. I wanted to blame a 'dodgy prawn' in the starter, but they all know I've been vegetarian for years. I still blamed a 'stomach bug' and told them I had thrown up in the loos and decided it was better to leave than to provide an extra condiment for their meals.

"So why are you in today?" asked Freddie confused. Great question. Why was I? Because stewing for a full day at home would have made things worse. I had to take action. I mumbled something about having too much to do and untangled myself from their caring concern, heading over to my desk.

They were all turning their attention back to their work when I saw the note. Written on pale blue Filofax paper was a single sentence in handwriting I instantly recognised, impossible to miss, lying on top of my keyboard.

Think about my suggestion.

The wave of revulsion I had been suppressing since the Christmas party took over and I ran to the toilets, just in time to be sick. So it wasn't a drunk joke. I had been hoping it was. The thought of him being in the office before me this morning and standing behind my desk, perhaps even sitting in my chair, to write this note, touching my things… I could still feel his filthy skin as his hand had covered my mouth last night. I remembered the violation of December's kiss. I couldn't escape from the powerlessness that had paralysed me not once, but twice, as he tried to force his desires on me. And I knew I could never see him again.

I rinsed my mouth out and washed my face, patting it dry with one of those horrible grey-green, folded paper towels that have such a horrible smell that most people prefer to dry their hands on their trousers, rather than use them.

I stood up and looked in the mirror. My mascara needed attention. The tears that had come with the vomit meant I was doing a panda impression. And my hair looked like I had been driven along the French Riviera in a 1960s soft top with no head scarf. The practicality of fixing what I was seeing in the mirror helped to ground me and allowed me to regain some composure. I wished I had my bag with me, hairbrush and tissues, to avoid having to try to scrape stray mascara blobs away with those wretched paper towels. But that would have meant going back into the office in this state. So I did my best with loo roll and water.

I knew what I had to do. I was breaking it down into simple steps to help my brain cope with it, to give myself the courage. Once I was half-decent again, I needed to walk into Harry's office and ask to make an appointment with Sally. I wasn't legally required to tell him why, so I wouldn't. I didn't think I could right now. The thought of Harry refusing to believe me – doubting my story – almost made me lose my resolve. I couldn't let those worries in. I had to be strong on this. But the likelihood of him believing me was close to zero. That's why I couldn't tell him. I couldn't take the risk that he might make me doubt myself – what was reasonable – what was acceptable. I needed to talk to Sally. I wanted to make a formal complaint about Stuart, before I changed my mind.

And once Harry had agreed to the meeting, I would tell him I had a vomiting bug and go home.

I took a few deep breaths to psych myself up for what I knew was going to be a difficult discussion with Harry and drew myself up to my full height, for what it was, with my shoulders back and my chin high. I needed to appear calm and confident.

Leaving the ladies' loos I felt strength I didn't realise I had. I was going to find a way through this. I shouldn't have to give up my job, just because Stuart had old debts and was into sexual harassment. Each step towards Harry's office door felt like I was wearing lead boots, trying to climb uphill through a river of treacle. But I did it. I reached the closed door. For once Janet wasn't there guarding it. I listened. He wasn't on the phone. So I knocked. Two firm but calm knocks.

"Come in!"

I closed the door behind me.

April

Cherries hanging green
Basking in hopeful sunshine
Newborn leaves emerge

27. The Stake-Out

I took the train to Naples and headed straight for my hotel. I needed to grab a few hours' sleep before heading to the stake-out at our client's premises, once their office had closed for the night. We were pretty sure the inside man would be heading back into the office tonight after everyone else had gone home, based on previous patterns, but it could be at any time and the last thing I wanted to do was to miss him because I was dozing. My hotel room was comfortable, with a generously sized double bed, but I was too excited to sleep. So I closed my eyes and tried to relax my mind. I couldn't rely on caffeine to get me through tonight. It makes me jittery if I have too much of it and I need to be calm and focused for the work ahead. I can't afford to make a single mistake.

I ran through my early morning conversation with Luca again.

"You're there to watch, not to interfere. Under no circumstances should you let the inside man see you. You are not to stop him. Just watch. Take photos – preferably videos – if you can," I have a night-vision video camera, "and make sure you are not seen by anyone, even the security guards."

Yes, I know, Luca, all the usual procedures. He saw my thoughts in my face. "I know you know all of this already, Christof, but it has been a while since you were last out in the field and it doesn't hurt to remind ourselves of the rules. We are *not* the police. We are *not* private investigators."

"I know. You can trust me, Luca. I'm just there to watch. To notice. To track. Everything."

He smiled. "You've got the security codes and your all-areas ID pass?"

I showed them to him.

"Good. Now, there are CCTV cameras at all the entrances and in the car parks. You'll have to do your best not to be noticed by the one at the door, but inside the building there is no additional security. So once you're in, you're clear."

I nodded.

"The owner agreed to your request not to warn the security team, in case they're in on this, so that means they would see you as breaking and entering if they catch you. And the security guys will be looking for anything unusual. They won't be reassured by you having all the access codes and an ID pass, quite the opposite. They will know you're not an employee and I don't want to have to explain to the police what you were doing there, if they decide to give you a bed for the night. Understood?"

"Yes."

"It would blow our case. The police could consider it entrapment, so it is absolutely vital that no one sees you there."

I mentally ran through the security access process, based on the photos and videos the company's owner had sent us, until it felt like second nature. I have committed the layout of the building to memory. I will be waiting in the main employee car park – the other one is reserved only for senior managers and the security staff – and as soon as I see someone enter the building, my brief is to follow them in, a minute later, guided by their footsteps and looking for the light of their computer screen. I need to get photos of them, for the company owner to identify, to note which computer they're using and to capture the exact time, so we can trace any transactions it carried out.

I was dressed from head to toe in black, like a penguin Goth, and with my secret weapon – silent shoes. It took me years to find them. I know it sounds stupid, but most shoes make some sort of noise. They squeak. They creak. They shuffle. They stomp. One of the women who used to work with us would wear ballet pumps for this kind of job: silent and non-slip. But my inner Italian male won't let me go there. Then, a few years ago, I found a pair that fitted the bill: 'normal' enough to wear with standard clothes if someone sees you, but soft, supple and silent. They're such an important part of my kit – and took so long to discover – that I never use them anywhere apart from on a stake-out. I don't want to wear them out.

I wore normal shoes to get to the car park and then dug my special shoes out of my bag, handling them with the reverence they deserved, before grabbing my camera and then hiding the bag under a conveniently thorny bush, which would also give me cover as I waited.

Although it's now April, the end of the March winds put a chill in the air, even as far south as here. I pulled my jacket tightly around me and buried my hands in my pockets, wishing the inside man would hurry up.

Time ticked on by excruciatingly slowly. It was surprisingly hard to sit and wait and stay focused. If I let myself get distracted, then I might miss the crucial moment of arrival. If I let myself get tense, I'd risk jumping and cracking twigs or even speaking, without realising, in surprise at the person being there. The years have given me plenty of practice in mindful awareness: being fully present, in this moment, without engaging with my thoughts; being here, relaxed and alert.

I focused on my breathing, to stop the adrenalin taking over and exhausting me or causing me to make a stupid mistake. It was hard work, but I had to stay calm. If I let myself get stressed then the survival part of my brain would kick in: the ancient bit that evolved to keep me safe from sabre-toothed tigers and the like and doesn't care what happens afterwards, so I might make stupid, short-term decisions that could ruin the stake-out. By staying calm it would be easier for me to think logically, to foresee the consequences of the actions I took. I would be more likely to get a positive result.

I was feeling curious – excited – to find out who has been committing these thefts. What did he look like? How was he doing it? Tonight was going to help us to move forwards. We might have got an answer through desk research, but that would have required a massive dose of luck on our part and a mistake or three on theirs. This way we take months out of the investigation and potentially save the client millions. But even if we find our man, there's no way the company owner will get back his missing money. That was long gone. The best he can hope for is to stem the flow of more losses, and to make sure none of his other employees meets a nasty end. I sense revenge against Denucci was motivating him more than money.

It was shortly after 10 p.m. when I saw a movement at the far corner of the building. No car. Someone on foot, walking close to the wall of the building, no doubt out of reach of the cameras. They were creeping, rather than walking, as though scared that any movement might attract the attention of the night watchman. I didn't move. Peripheral vision is heightened at night, especially if someone is already tense and scared, and I didn't want to do anything that might make them think they were being watched, scaring them off. They were far too far away for me to see their face or do anything useful with the camera yet.

So I watched, impatiently.

I saw them use their security codes to open a side door. I heard it close behind them. *Wait. Don't move. Give them time to be well away from the door before I use it.* The one thing the owner couldn't turn off was the beep that the codes make. I couldn't risk the inside man hearing that.

I mentally checked the map of the building in my head. I wasn't going to use the door that they did. I would use the next one along. But first I had to get close enough to the building to see which way they had gone. The fastest way would be to run across the car park, bringing security after me, so instead I went round its perimeter and then crouched down, skimming the edge of the building, below window height.

My heart was racing. I was remembering why I love this.

Suddenly I was distracted by a glint of light, maybe some kind of reflection of the security lights on something shiny, back near the bush where I was waiting? I froze and crouched down as low as I could in a shadow. I waited to see if there was more. My heart was pounding. I tried to calm it with my breathing. My nerves were on high alert. I waited for what felt like an infinitely long minute and there was nothing; no more movement. It could have been an animal or just my imagination. I had to keep going.

Shit. I had lost the inside man. I couldn't tell which way he went. He wasn't using a torch. I was going to have to go in and look for signs. I came to the door I wanted to use and held my breath as I typed in the well-rehearsed ten-digit code. The beep was so loud I was sure half the city must have heard it. I needed our inside man to be far enough away from this door not to have noticed it.

I crept inside and listened, with my ears and my instincts. No sounds. No signs. I was going to have to go on patrol.

Luca and I had agreed that it was unlikely this person would be using their own computer for their dirty work, or even one in their department, unless they had a colleague they wanted to frame. It would be too close to home, too easy to trace. So our fallback plan, if I lost track, was to start in the less likely departments; those that don't normally have access to the company's finances, such as Human Resources and the sales team.

After five minutes of silently creeping through empty offices, using desks and filing cabinets for cover, I struck lucky. They were using a computer in the marketing department. That made me pretty sure it wasn't anyone in the marketing team committing this crime. In the distance I could see the glimmer of a computer screen. I strained my ears, trying to drown out the noise of my heart, breathing silently, and I caught the distant tapping of a keyboard. This person was stressed. The tapping was frantic. They were not doing anything to keep the noise down, so they had no idea that I was here. Good news.

I eased my way closer to them, one desk at a time, and pulled on my balaclava. I only use it when absolutely necessary: it's much harder to claim innocence if security catches you with your face covered, rather than in relatively normal clothes. Hiding your face outside of a Siberian snowstorm or masked ball generally implies guilt.

I was just a few desks away and slightly off to the side, looking at the back of their computer screen. I made a note of the time on my watch and the location of the desk they were using. The light of the screen would make the darkness behind it even more black, hiding me well, but even so, I had to move in super-slow motion as I reached for my camera to capture their face. I couldn't let any lights glint off the lens or I would give myself away. And I had to be prepared for the risk that they might be armed – and scared.

I could make out their face clearly, though it was ghostly pale in the grey light of their screen. I got the photos and video I needed and then sat and waited until they were done. Watching. Listening. Gathering evidence. Scarcely breathing, for fear of being caught and scaring them off, making the trail go cold again. I took a couple of shots with my phone, as back-up. Its camera isn't good enough for night videos, but it can manage a pixelated photo in low light, which would probably be good enough if we end up having to rely on it. *Never trust tech* was one of the many lessons this job had taught me; always have back-up.

I was crouching under a desk that gave me a view of the inside man and after ten minutes I got terrible cramp in my left calf. The muscle spasm was such a shock I nearly shouted out in pain. An involuntary movement meant I nearly hit my head on the underneath of the desk. That could have been a disaster. I held my breath. I wasn't sure if I had done something to give myself away. But the inside man carried on typing. He noticed nothing.

I massaged my calf as silently as I could and tried to move my ankle and foot to ease the cramp. Nothing worked. I had to sit and take it. *God, I hope they're done soon.* I wasn't sure how long I could last before my body insisted that I stood up. My senses were screaming and the effort was draining me.

As though hearing my prayer, after another minute the inside man shut down the computer, put a piece of paper back into his pocket and stood up, looking around him to make sure he was still alone, and then left the office.

I waited until the door had closed behind him and then slowly uncurled myself. My calf was screaming and it took me a full minute to restore normal movement. I limped over to the desk he had been using, made a note of the name of the owner – kindly placed on the in-tray beside the computer screen – and checked in case the inside man had left anything. That would have be great. But it didn't look like he did. I took some extra video, just in case.

I left the room, closing the door silently behind me, and headed to the exit at the furthest corner of the building, as far away from the security teams as possible. One of the two of us could have aroused their attention tonight and I wanted to be able to run, the moment I had got my bag back.

I stood and listened intently, trying to figure out which way the inside man might have gone. He was just over a minute ahead of me. I couldn't hear anything. I hoped that was a good sign. I jumped at the beep of the door as I flashed my security pass at it, to be allowed to leave, and held the handle tightly, easing it closed behind me as slowly as possible, as silently as I could.

I was standing in the car park and finally gave myself permission to take a deep breath. I could hear the sound of the road in the distance, late-night cars and taxis going about their business on what was, for them, a perfectly normal evening. I couldn't see anyone or anything moving. The inside man was likely to have gone back the way he came, meaning he had probably left the car park by now. But, just in case, I crept around the furthest edges, hiding in shadows, making my way slowly back to the bush where I had left my bag.

I must have gone back to the wrong bush, because when I got back there, my bag wasn't there. I stood up and looked around. There was no one in sight. I looked at the other bushes. My heart raced again as I realised this was definitely the right one. I chose it specially because it was wide and squat with the remnants of a young tree, long since died off, poking out of the middle of it. It was easy to find again, even in the near-dark.

Someone had taken my bag.

Who? How? Local kids? Drunks? Was someone else here tonight? This place is off the beaten track and surely security would have seen them and done something? I felt like I was going mad. I risked detection by scrabbling further under the bush. And my hand found the strap of my bag. The wave of relief was almost too much for me. It was dark now and my bag is black, which made it hard to find. I must have pushed it further under the bush than I remembered. It's funny how my imagination can play tricks on me. Luca often tells me I'm paranoid.

I double-checked what was in the bag: my shoes, emergency snacks and water, emergency cash, batteries and an empty notebook with a pen. It was all still there. I never store anything traceable in my bag when I'm on a stake-out, in case someone finds it. Anything important is either on me or in my hotel safe: not desperately secure but better than it being found under a bush.

I walked back to my hotel, grateful for the exercise and the fresh air, feeling light-hearted, promising myself a stiff drink at the bar once I was changed out of my stake-out-blacks. It was a couple of kilometres, but it's harder to trace walking in dark side streets than the CCTV on public transport or someone asking a taxi driver. I was playing extra safe with this, given Denucci's track record. A couple of times I had that eerie sense of being followed, but I couldn't see anyone there. I put it down to my nerves, having had the shock of thinking someone else had been at the stake-out tonight, when I couldn't find my bag. I shuddered at the thought of what might have happened had I been followed this evening. I remembered the two bodies this case has already claimed.

When I got back to my hotel, I went straight to my room and got changed back into jeans and a shirt, and then headed downstairs to the bar. Normally I would have backed up the photo and video files to our secure server at the office – they're too big to email – but I had checked the hotel's internet connection before I went out and that wasn't an option. The phone data signal here was so slow it took thirty seconds to load a web page and the Wi-Fi was unsecured, and almost as slow as the data network. It would have been too big a risk. So I was using our plan B of keeping the phone and camera on me at all times and locking them in the safe in my room while I was asleep. I patted my jacket pocket to reassure myself they were still there, even though I could feel their weight. I allowed myself to start to let go, to unwind. The stake-out had gone incredibly well. There had been no guarantee that the inside man would even show up. But now I had evidence of him in action; the proof the client needs.

I made my way to the restaurant to see if they were still doing food. The stress had made me ravenous. Not just tonight's stress, but that of the past few weeks, what with the farm finances and work. The restaurant had stopped serving for the night. It was empty apart from one guest, finishing her meal. The waiters could barely keep their eyes off her and I could see why. They were making no effort to be discreet. She was beautiful. She reminded me a little of Isabella. She looked up and caught me staring at her. She smiled a smile that made my insides jump. I smiled back, feeling like a gawky teenager at a school disco, then hurried off to the bar.

I picked a small table in a corner, somewhere easy for people to ignore. The evening's bar menu had finished half an hour ago. Damn! The waiter came over and politely asked me what I wanted. I ordered a double whisky, not my usual drink, but I felt I needed something of medicinal strength this evening, and three packets of whatever bar snacks they did. *Salted nuts* was his reply. I nodded.

The first whisky didn't take long to go down and a second soon followed it. I knew I shouldn't – that it would go straight to my head – but I ordered a third, wanting to numb the adrenalin I had been swimming in today. It was working. I could feel it soothing my thoughts, calming my mind, and I felt grateful. I had worked hard. It was okay to let go, to relax. My brain was starting to feel fuzzy. One more double and I would be ready to sleep.

It must have been past midnight when I noticed the woman from the restaurant walk up to the bar, wearing an ankle-length, deep blue silk dress with spaghetti straps and a long split up to the thigh of her left leg. I smiled in approval. Her long dark brown hair curled lazily over her shoulders and back and she held herself with the confidence of a woman who was used to being stared at. The barman was spellbound by her and struggled to pour the glass of red wine she had ordered. She paid him in cash, rather than putting it on her room account, and then turned round, her eyes surveying the near-empty room to decide where to sit.

She caught my eye and I quickly looked back at my whisky. I could feel her walking towards me, towards the empty chair opposite me.

"May I?" she asked, her southern accent gently softened by studying somewhere expensive.

I couldn't say no. She took her seat before I could reply, crossing her left leg over her right to make the most of the view her skirt gave me.

"Where are you from?" she asked. Was it that obvious that I wasn't local? Then I realised it was the whiskies going to my head: of course I wasn't local or I'd be staying at home, not here.

"Milan," I replied automatically.

"I'm curious. Why are you in Naples tonight?"

I wasn't going to win any prizes for communication this evening. "Work. How about you?" I managed.

"Oh, you know, this and that."

We chatted politely about nothing in particular. I was tired. But she was so beautiful it would have seemed rude to desert her. She didn't tell me much about herself. But she was easy to talk with. She didn't mind the silences either. And sitting with her made me smile.

She sipped her wine. I suddenly found myself longing to be that wine glass, to have her hold me, her lips caress me. I shook myself out of her spell. I needed to go.

She stared at me as I finished my whisky and ordered a fourth to take up to my room. The waiter gave me a knowing smile, assuming the nameless beauty would be going with me.

I wanted to run and stay in equal measure, but most of all I knew I wanted her. There had been no one since Isabella. Far too long.

She leaned over to put her drink down on the table between us, slowly and deliberately. The soft fabric of her dress fell forwards and I had a glimpse of a naked breast in the dim light of the bar. She heard my involuntary gasp, looked up at my face and smiled at me, convincing me her movement had been intentional – testing the waters.

"Do you like the view?" she asked teasingly. She took my silence as a yes. My body was reminding me how long it had been since I last saw a naked woman, let alone got to hold one in my arms. I felt a blush of embarrassment threatening to give me away, hoping she couldn't see it. I didn't notice myself closing my eyes, imagining what the rest of her might look like, under that deep blue silk dress, longing to slip the straps from her shoulders and have it fall to the floor, hungry to find out what was waiting for me underneath. I opened my eyes to find her staring at me, intently, as though reading my mind. I tried to tell myself I was exhausted from the adrenalin of the evening and that the whisky had gone straight to my head – that I wanted sleep – but most of me knew exactly what I wanted.

"Your room or mine?" she asked. I was shocked. And excited. "I only have a single bed," she said, "I'm guessing you would have booked a double?"

I could hardly believe I was doing this as we walked to my room, me carrying a whisky I would never finish. She had left her wine in the bar. I was surprised at how easy this felt.

Under the dress she was every bit as beautiful as I had imagined. The softness of her curves, the passion in her kiss, the firmness of her breasts. I had forgotten how good this could be. It was sex, not making love, and it was the first time I had ever had a one-night stand. I didn't care. I wanted her. It was clear she wanted me. It felt great, being with her. Cathartic. Freeing. Releasing the pent-up tension of the stake-out, and even the past few months. She had a self-assured confidence about her body and how she liked to use it that I had only ever seen in Isabella.

As we dozed off, exhausted and satisfied, I realised I didn't know her name. I wanted to ask her, but she was already sleeping, looking peaceful, her beauty intensified, if that were possible, with her hair resting on the pillow next to me and a soft smile on her face. I didn't want to wake her.

The next morning I looked over at her, wondering if she'd like some more of what we did last night before we both had to leave, but all that was left was a dent in the pillow. I called out to her, in case she was in the bathroom, having to stick with a lame 'buongiorno', feeling stupid that I didn't have a name to call.

I rolled over to check the time on my phone, but it wasn't

there. I was confused. I sat up to look for it. I'm a creature of habit. I always leave my phone in the same place on the bedside table, wherever I travel. I shook my head to try to wake myself up. Then I remembered I had locked it in the safe, with the video camera, as per protocol, while my mystery lover was in the bathroom. I must have been lost in the moment, too busy breaking my personal rules to remember my routines.

I took a long shower to clear my head and try to wash away some of the hangover that I knew I would be treating myself to this morning, before heading down to the restaurant for breakfast. Maybe she would be there? I already know she wouldn't be. She had gone. And I was surprised that I was okay with that. I smiled at the memories of the night. It was fantastic.

I wanted to take the camera and phone down to breakfast with me. It was still in the safe, tucked away in the wardrobe. I was glad the safe wasn't one of those combination lock ones. I have a good head for numbers but ask me to type in a 4-digit code when I'm in a hurry and something I need is behind that door and I'll fumble until it tells me I have to call Reception because I've got it wrong too many times. This was one you swiped with your room key.

It beeped as it opened and I reached inside for where I had left my kit. It wasn't there. *Please, God, no.* I bent down to look into the blackness inside. *Please don't let anything have happened to it! Luca would kill me.*

I rummaged around inside, fumbling for the corners of the safe that now felt cavernous in its emptiness. And there were the phone and camera. Relief forced me to sit down. I was stressed and distracted last night. I must have pushed them right to the back of the safe when in my hurry to lock it last night.

I gave Luca a quick call, leaving him a voicemail to let him know the stake-out had been a success and told him I would update him when I got back to Milan later today. Then I zipped the phone and camera into the inside pocket of my jacket with my phone. I wasn't taking any risks with them.

Sure enough she wasn't in the restaurant. It felt better that way. It might have been awkward, seeing each other again. I went back to my room and packed what was left of my things into my compact suitcase.

I took the lift down to Reception to settle my bill and was hit by curiosity. I wanted to know the name of the beautiful woman I had just spent the night with, even though I knew I'd never see her again. I couldn't believe I had spent the night with her without asking her name. As the receptionist printed out my invoice I asked her, as casually as I could, about a tall woman, mid-thirties, with long black hair who was staying in a single room last night. The girl looked blankly at me.

"We don't have any single rooms, sir," she replied. "They're all doubles."

Maybe I had misheard her last night. Or maybe it was just a ploy to save me having to make a decision about which of our rooms to use? The need to find out her name overrode any caution I should have been showing.

"My mistake. I wonder if you could tell me her name though?"

The receptionist shook her head. "I'm sorry, sir. That information is confidential. We can't share guest details with anyone else. But I can tell you that we didn't have many guests last night. We had some businessmen, like you, and two couples. But the women with both of them were over sixty. No one matching that description was a guest here last night. I'm sorry."

28. Sage Advice

"He won't let me see Sally, Lucy." I was sitting in her living room, munching on a juicy early season Turkish cherry from the packet I had brought with me, surrounded by baby clutter. I didn't envy the bags under her eyes and I was pretending not to notice the fact that her roots were now four months old, but I was grateful to her for sending her husband, Sam, out for a breezy walk with the baby, so we could spend some quality time with each other. It was so good to see her.

"Why on earth didn't you tell me about all of this?" demanded Lucy. She was cross. She had every right to be. Great question. Why didn't I? Why hadn't I told anyone?

"I didn't want to stress you, with the baby," I started. Then I realised that wasn't all. It wasn't the truth. "I thought it would all go away, that I could handle it on my own, but it kept getting worse and worse." And that still wasn't the truth. Every time I think about what has happened, I feel ashamed. I feel like it's somehow my fault – like I should have done something differently and then none of this wouldn't have happened. But I'm not ready to admit that yet. Then, other times, I feel like none of it is my fault: I'm the innocent victim of Stuart's schemes, that he's the crazy one, that it's not fair. I felt hatred welling up inside me and pushed it back down, fast. It makes me do and say things I regret later.

Lucy nodded, sympathetically. "So you're like the horrible experiment where they put a frog in cold water and it doesn't notice it's getting too hot until it's too late?"

Yes.

"Is it too late for you yet, Sophie, or can you still get yourself out of the pot over the fire?"

"Leave, you mean?"

"No. But get out of this mess?"

"That's why I want to see Sally. I need her help."

"So why won't Harry let you see her? What's his view on all of this?"

"That's the problem. I haven't told Harry." I fidgeted with a baby vest that was on the coffee table in front of me. "After the probation thing, he'd just think I was trying to get back at Stuart. I don't trust him – either of them – anymore. Harry won't authorise Sally coming in for an extra visit unless I tell him exactly why I need to see her. He says that if it's too important to wait then I have to tell him first, so he can justify the cost. But that's the point: I need to see her because I can't talk to Harry about this. He'd just do one of his emotional outbursts and tell me I can't prove anything."

Lucy moved over to hug me. I surprised myself by pulling away. She gave me a confused look.

"Please don't hug me yet," I said, my voice starting to shake, "I'm scared that if you do, I'll start crying and I won't be able to stop."

She hugged me anyway. She could see how much I needed it. I started to cry. It hit me how much I had been bottling all of this up, how I hadn't talked with anyone about it, how I hadn't allowed myself to experience these emotions. It felt good to have someone who wanted to help me.

"Sophie," Lucy said as my crying subsided, pulling slightly

away from our hug, so she could look at me, "have you considered going to the police on this?"

Wow! Does she think it's that serious? Actually, it probably is. "No, I haven't! That would feel really formal. And I don't have any evidence, no witnesses. And both times I had been drinking. He's been clever."

She was right though. That was how bad Stuart's behaviour has been. If I had any way of proving it, it was sexual harassment, sexual assault and intimidation, all of which were criminal offences. And here I was, putting up with it and hoping it would just go away, which both Lucy and I knew it wouldn't.

"Do you want me to talk to Harry?"

"God, no!" I slammed back. The thought of how Harry would react if I got Lucy involved to do my 'dirty work' for me didn't bear thinking about.

"Why not?" I had a sudden vision of Lucy in full armour on a white horse, baby Emma strapped to her front in an ethnic-print baby wrap, with a lance big enough to span our entire office and a dirty nappy bag attached to the end of it (poo, obviously), riding up the stairs and demanding justice for me. In this scenario, Harry would be cowering under his desk, grovelling an apology, terrified that baby Emma might empty the nappy bag's contents over his head. I was sure that Freud or Jung would have something to say about my imagination.

I realised I was smiling The muscle movements felt strange, alien. It had been too long. Then I realised that Lucy's horse wouldn't fit up the stairs and she'd hate wearing armour and that the more likely outcome to her 'interfering', as Harry would see it, would be him turning against Lucy, as well as me. The smile vanished from my face like cleaning a white board in a business meeting.

There's a classic problem called the 'backfire effect'; a major issue in the market research world. When the research data contradicts the client's assumptions or pet theory, they tend to dig their heels in even more deeply, doing everything in their power to defend what they have already chosen to believe – or paid someone else to tell them to believe. Lucy's involvement would make Harry side even more strongly with Stuart, to defend his friendship and his own behaviour. After all, which boss would be brave enough to admit that not only had they hired someone capable of sexual assault as maternity leave cover, but they had been friends with them for twenty years without realising what a shit they were? Harry isn't that kind of boss.

"Penny for them?" interrupted Lucy.

"I don't think I can stay, Lucy. To be honest, I'm ready to quit, whether or not I have a job to go to." She gave me a look that reminded me how stupid that would be. It's a small industry and everyone knows everybody else's business. It wouldn't take long for Stuart to put the word round that I was 'politely asked' to leave. That would be playing right into his hands. "Don't worry. I'm going to start job-hunting next week. There will be plenty of adverts in the back of our trade magazines, so I'll start there."

Lucy's face dropped. "Please don't go, Sophie," I could see she meant it. "It wouldn't be the same there without you."

"I know," I gave her a hug this time. She looked like she wanted to cry. "I'm going to have to take a risk with the reference. There's no way I'm agreeing to Stuart's terms." We both shuddered at the thought.

"Look, I can see you feel that leaving is the only option," Lucy said gently. I looked up from my lap, not realising I had been avoiding her eyes. "I wish I could convince you that you're strong enough to get through this. I wish you would let me talk to Harry. I'm sure I could help."

I shook my head violently, glad I wasn't wearing chunky

earrings or they would have just knocked someone out. "I can't do it, Lucy! I'm only a quarter of the way through the year of working with Stuart and I'm already in pieces – on probation – with zero confidence, and he's stolen all the bits of my job that I used to love. I can't do another nine months of this. Remember how long your pregnancy felt?" She reached over for one of Emma's tiny dresses, smoothing down the fabric. Motherhood is suiting her so far. "And who knows what Stuart will do next? He's not playing fair and he has told me he wants me gone. He has already shown me how low he will stoop. Surely it's better for me to jump ship, quickly and quietly, rather than wait until he has an audience together, to watch me walk the plank."

We both sat in silence for a while. I could see Lucy processing all of this, looking for solutions. She's an expert problem-solver, which is one of the many reasons why she's such a great Planner. We were both processing the new reality that would be waiting for her when she came back from maternity leave: she would be there without me and I would be somewhere else, without her. That wasn't what either of us wanted. But I could see she understood that I couldn't stay, just to be there when she got back.

"I've got an idea, though, Sophie!" Lucy looked excited. A lightbulb had gone on somewhere. "Legally, I am still your boss. Stuart is only temporary cover and he has known you for just three months. Put me down as your referee, using my home address. It's easy to explain why you're doing it. I'm still there on the company website as your boss, so it's completely legit, and we get to bypass both Stuart and Harry!"

I couldn't believe we were both working on plans for me to leave a job I used to love, with clients I had spent years building relationships with, all because of a few months with a psychotic pervert as my boss. But I really didn't see what else I could do.

29. Reporting Back To Luca

"How did it go?" Luca was itching for news, so I headed straight back to the office after my train got into Milan, despite being entitled to the afternoon off to compensate for my late night. Company policy is applied more loosely in our team.

"Great! I saw him. Watched him in action. I got the videos. The Client will be able to tell who it was and we should be able to trace the transactions to that computer terminal, now we know when it was used."

Luca grinned. "A complete success!" he laughed, looking happy and relieved, "I knew I could rely on you, Christof."

His smile dropped as he looked at my face. He knew there was something I wasn't telling him.

"What is it? What went wrong, Christof? Were you seen?"

"Maybe." I conceded, trying not to let my nerves show by fidgeting.

"Walk me through exactly what happened. Don't miss out a thing."

I took him through the whole evening, up to the point where I thought my bag was missing, but it wasn't, and then got back to the hotel, following procedure by keeping the camera on me, before treating myself to a nerve-calming whisky or three. He didn't mind that bit.

"So what's the problem?" I wished I knew the answer to that

question. I had been racking my brain on it for the whole 4½ hours on the train. Something didn't feel right.

"I don't know. Nothing, most likely. Just something feels *off*. I was even more cautious than usual for the stake-out, given the raised stakes on this project," we both knew I was talking about the corpse count. I must have sounded defensive, because Luca rushed to reassure me.

"I know you were careful, Christof. It's just that we can't afford to take any risks. I don't want to blow this project and I don't want you hurt." Genuine concern showed in his face.

"Let's look at the videos," he said, changing the subject and giving us both something practical to focus on.

I pulled out the camera that had been untouched, safe in my jacket pocket for the whole of the journey. I couldn't risk watching the videos on the train. It's always exciting – that moment of slight stress as you hope the camera did its job and wonder what you'll see.

I pressed the play button but nothing happened. I wanted to shake it; like a child frustrated that a Christmas toy doesn't work without its batteries. I resisted. The screen was telling me that the memory card was empty. There were no videos on the camera.

"Shit! The stupid thing didn't work?" Luca was almost yelling with frustration.

"No, that can't be right. I did the usual test video before I left the hotel. *That* should be there. I watched it last night before I went out, to make sure the camera was working." I pulled the camera back from him and desperately searched for at least the test video. It wasn't there.

"So the memory card wiped itself while you were asleep? You must have messed up the settings."

Luca tends to accuse without thinking when he's stressed. I was half a step ahead as I pulled my phone out of my pocket to find the back-up photos.

"Don't worry. I took the back-up shots on my phone, as per procedure. They won't be as good but they should still be enough to identify our inside man."

I used my thumb to unlock the phone and scrolled through the recent photos in the viewing app. I'm careful to delete old photos as soon as they have been backed up. They can munch up storage space and I never knew when I might need to record something important. The last thing I wanted was for my phone to tell me it was full at a critical moment.

So the only photos in there should have been from last night's stake-out, plus one of a weird pattern I saw in the lighting over my platform at Milano Centrale station yesterday, which appealed to my love of abstract designs. I quickly found that, but it was the only photo on my camera.

That couldn't be right, could it?

Luca saw the dread in my eyes and instantly jumped to the right conclusion.

"Gone, too?"

I nodded, silently.

"Not even you, distracted as you are these days, would screw up both cameras. What else happened last night that you haven't told me about?"

I knew I had no choice. I told him the briefest overview I dared of what happened in the bar, but not about the events back in my room. They were private.

"Yes," I said, thinking back, scene by scene through my evening, "I checked the videos had worked last night, before I locked the camera and the phone in my safe. I didn't watch them, but the camera had worked."

"What aren't you telling me about last night, Christof?"

Reluctantly I gave in and told him.

"For fuck's sake, Christof! That's the oldest trick in the book! How did you fall for it?" I felt really stupid. A prize idiot. He was right. How did I manage to miss it? It should have been so obvious.

"I've never done anything like that before," I mumbled. It didn't help. Luca was on a steam train with his anger by this point. Rightly so.

"So you were so drunk and tired that you slept through the beep of your safe being opened by the room key you no doubt left on your bedside table? And you left your thumb print lying around, so she could get into your phone?"

I stared at my feet.

"And she followed you to your hotel, without you noticing?" Yes, probably.

"How am I going to break this one to the client?"

I shook my head, glad that wasn't my job.

"Look, it's not all lost. You'll be able to identify the person from the personnel records and you can still remember the name of the person whose desk they used?"

I nodded, still not knowing what to say.

"So we'll have our man and we'll be able to trace the transactions, but we've lost our evidence. We can't prove anything, unless you testify in Court, which means Denucci will link you with the case and you would be at risk of taking a swim in a cement bath. Didn't you *think*?" He was spitting with rage. I had no answers to give him. "We had to show them doing it, otherwise they could claim that someone stole their work ID. And you and I both know that's the last time he'll use the pattern he's followed for the past few months. Whoever that woman was will have tipped him off. There's no chance of another stake-out."

I couldn't believe I had been so stupid. Luca pointed out what I already knew: "We've missed our chance to catch him in the act. And that means we've missed our chance to convince the police to take this seriously. Denucci is likely to get away with it – again! – all because you let your guard down. I'm disappointed in you, Christof. I hope she was worth it."

30. The Job Interview

I failed another job interview this afternoon. I keep telling myself I didn't really want it – and that's probably right – but it was a disaster. I was easily qualified for it, but I kept messing up. This Stuart thing has hit my confidence, hard.

I was wearing my favourite suit – a long pencil skirt and matching cropped jacket in navy blue with a pale silver fleck. This I combined with a beautifully ironed (I'm normally allergic to the job) white blouse that didn't need to be tucked in, making it very forgiving on 'fat days', except it was a shock to realise that the skirt barely fits any more. The zip complained loudly as I tried to yank it into position. I haven't worn this since last year, but I seem to be getting bigger. I haven't had the energy to get to the gym much, not since Stuart arrived, and I guess I've been picking up treats more often with my coffee run, but surely that couldn't be enough to make this much difference? I pulled the blouse down as low as I could, hoping it would hide the creases as the fabric strained over my midriff. I laddered the first pair of 'ladder-resistant' tights I tried to put on, swearing at them and chucking them in the bin, digging through my drawer to see if I could find another pair. There was one, right at the back, with a ladder in the thigh, but a quick blob of nail varnish would stop the run, so it couldn't reach anywhere visible by the end of the interview. Why is it that the manufacturers of tights think it's okay to charge so much per pair for tights, but only have them last one day – or none at all? I must be single-handedly keeping these firms afloat.

It wasn't a great start, feeling hot and sweaty in clothes that were too small, knowing I was wearing laddered tights, feeling the dried nail varnish rubbing and catching the skin on my thigh with each step. Everyone else in the Reception area looked cool, calm and confident. I felt like a flustered old bag lady who didn't really belong there. What happened to my self-belief? I suddenly realised I hadn't checked my nails. I looked down at them as I was waiting to be called. Clean, but they were far from 'tidy'. They were all different lengths and some showed obvious signs of biting. If I were doing a depth interview with someone whose nails looked like mine I'd assume they were suffering from anxiety at some level. In my case, I'd be right. Needing to find a new job and a new home at the same time has been taking its toll. *Too late to fix them now.* I tried to have a surreptitious nibble of the worst of the nails, in a desperate attempt to tidy them up and make a better first impression, but the receptionist looked over at just the wrong moment. Great! I wished I could be like the Queen and get away with wearing gloves anywhere. I bet she never has to worry about how her nails look.

The man who collected me in Reception greeted me politely. He wasn't part of the interview, apparently. He would be my predecessor, if I got the job. I wanted to ask him what it was like to work there and why he was leaving, but I just couldn't find the enthusiasm. He passed me over to the interview panel, all three of them sitting behind a stern-looking conference table in a meeting room, with files of notes in front of them, no doubt containing the applications for all of us who were getting interviews today.

"Ah, Sophie, welcome," said another polite face, without

smiling. Handshakes all round. "How are you today?" *What am I supposed to say? I'm so nervous I've been to the loo ten times already? That I need this job – ideally at a higher pay scale than you're offering – or I'm going to be homeless by the end of May? That my boss is trying to harass me and get me to sleep with him, but he's pig-ugly, so I don't want to?* I managed a half-mumbled 'fine thanks' and realised, too late, I should have returned the question. That wasn't a great first impression.

The rest of it didn't go well either. I was finished long before my allotted hour.

Every time they asked me for examples of being able to, say, run a focus group, all I could think of was how I'm not *allowed* to do that anymore. *How did my last client presentation go?* I couldn't admit it was December and that I nearly nuked them all with that can of deodorant. *Tell us about a time when you took a risk at work that paid off.* The male models - but that's not interview material, either. They'd need to get to trust me first, before they would understand why it was such a great idea. *Why are you leaving?* Why didn't I come up with a decent answer on this before? 'Fresh challenges and new horizons' made their faces drop, as though they were imagining me taking all their training and then dumping them in a couple of years' time because I was bored again. They knew this would be a sideways move for me, if not a slight demotion.

All of my examples were either from last year, making them curious about why I wasn't doing it any more, or they were so bland that no one would feel inspired by them. I was being so dull that even *I* wanted to stop listening to my answers. My mind kept going blank. I don't think I can ever remember saying 'um' or 'errr' this often in a single hour.

I could feel the 'thanks, but no thanks' in the farewell handshake, with its dismissive, sympathetic smile. They were already looking at the details for the next candidate, even before I had closed the door behind me. I didn't need to wait for the polite rejection email that will arrive in the next few days.

Back to the drawing board. Most of our industry magazines come out weekly, so there will always be a fresh supply of jobs to be rejected for. *Hmm*. That's probably not how I should be thinking right now. 'Positive thinking' and all that. What is it that book said – *The Secret*, or something – that your thoughts create your reality? I can't be bothered to figure out how that works just now, but if it's true, I'm buggered.

31. Cologne

I had taken a 'work-from-home' afternoon for my interview, telling Stuart I had a sofa being delivered. It was a safe bet, because I'll never invite him round to my flat, so he will never know the old sofa hasn't changed. After the interview fiasco, I spent the rest of the evening scouring the internet and magazines for more opportunities to be turned down for jobs I know I don't really want, before drowning my sorrows with too many glasses of a bottle of cherry brandy Jem gave me a few Christmases ago, that I had forgotten was hiding in the back of the kitchen cupboard.

I was working from home this morning because there was no point in me going into the office for just a few hours before I headed to St Pancras to get the train to Cologne this afternoon, to supervise some focus groups. It was the second phase of the eco laundry detergent research and, following the success of the Paris research (despite François!) the client insisted it be me and not Stuart who travelled to Germany to supervise the next stage.

I love Cologne, with a passion. The cathedral – the Kölner Dom – is one of my favourite places on the planet. And I haven't been for so long. I did a full year of my degree in Germany and got quite fluent. Being a student out there got me cheap train travel – bonus! – so most weekends my fellow foreign students and I would explore the country, discovering the unique beers for each region and trying to decipher the enormous variety of accents. It was a brilliant year. And the next few days would feel like a much-needed holiday, getting away from Stuart's suffocating supervision. I have missed this kind of work so much. He hasn't asked me if I have made a decision on his offer yet, but I know it's only because he hasn't had a private opportunity. There have always been too many people around. I have made sure of that.

He didn't want to come to Germany. He wouldn't say why. Looking back, it was strange. I know he wouldn't have understood a word anyone was saying, but you can still supervise a focus group by watching the body language, to make sure it's going well, and the agency we are using – friends of Katja's – had offered to book an interpreter for him. So I got sent, despite my recent probation, because somebody needed to go and Stuart couldn't find a reason to overrule the client's request. I made sure I didn't appear too keen, or Stuart would have sabotaged it, just to spite me. As I raised imaginary objections to the trip it earned me yet more criticism from Harry. "Hardly the can-do attitude I expect from my team, Sophie!" A good dose of reverse psychology paid off well. It was worth taking that slap to escape from Stuart and get a chance to remind myself that I *can* do this. I *am* good at my job.

I hopped onto the Eurostar at St Pancras leaving for Brussels mid-morning, which took a couple of hours, and then changed to the Thalys train for another couple of hours to Kölner Hauptbahnhof, the main station in Cologne, arriving shortly after 3:30 p.m. It's right in the centre of the city, unlike the Köln-Bonn airport, and my transfer to my hotel was three minutes – on foot. Once you factor in security waits and transfer times, the train is faster than flying. As my train pulled in to its final destination I craned my neck to get a quick view of the Dom. I could see the people around me calling me a *bloody tourist* in their heads, but I didn't care. Three days at work without Stuart in one of my favourite cities in the world was like winning the jackpot in a contest I didn't know I had entered. I dumped my suitcase at my hotel. I had blagged a discounted room at the Domhotel on the main square directly opposite the cathedral, because Harry and Susie, who booked it, didn't know there are cheaper places, but I got a good deal for them. Then I called the hotel a few days ago and told them my sob story about how much I have missed the city and asked if I could have a room with a '*Domblick*': a view of the cathedral. These are normally super-premium rooms, but somehow they agreed. Result! My beautiful room has a gorgeous view of the gothic splendour of this beautiful building, with its chequered history.

I quickly changed out of my work clothes and almost ran out of the hotel to hang out with my favourite building in the world.

Luca was still livid with me over the stake-out. We have identified the employee and the data fits but, as Luca pointed out every time he saw me, we've lost the evidence, unless I testify, which would be incredibly high-risk.

So I was relieved when he told me he was sending me to Germany for the week. I think he wanted me out of the office. And, to be honest, I'm grateful for a few days where I'm not looking over my shoulder, paranoid that repercussions from the stake-out disaster might be following me around Milan.

It's time for another one of those international team

training courses and this time we're in Germany. When most of the rest of the country's businesses moved their Headquarters from Bonn to Berlin after the Wall came down and Germany's capital city and government moved, for some reason our company stayed put. They have a fantastic building in the centre of this city and the staff raised merry hell about relocating. So I get a full week here. I need the break. This isn't a holiday, but it feels like one, being somewhere completely different where there are fewer demands on my attention. And it's my first time in Cologne, a city I have always wanted to visit.

I flew in this afternoon, the night before the course starts. It's being held in a conference hotel, over the river from the cathedral. None of the meeting rooms at our German HQ were big enough to accommodate us all.

After all the waiting and sitting around that flying inevitably brings I needed to stretch my legs. The flight itself was only 1½ hours, but it took 7 hours, door to door. Looking across the river, I felt strangely drawn to the cathedral. It was the first time I had ever seen it in the flesh. I remembered reading about how the Allied Forces in World War II didn't bomb it, because it was too important a landmark for them. While Londoners huddled in the city's Tube stations to escape the bombings, the people of Cologne would often flock to the cathedral, believing themselves to be safest there. They usually were.

The city around the cathedral had been devastated, but the cathedral itself was left standing.

I wanted to experience the famous peace inside this incredible building and let go of the stresses and worries I have been dragging around with me for months. I felt pulled to go there. I planned to light a candle for Dad.

My view of the cathedral from the other side of the river gave a sense of its enormous size and height. I walked slowly over a river bridge to enjoy the views of it, with its black bulk and spindly looking spires, with intricate stonework looking like dirty lace. Then I get lost in the tumble of tall buildings that crowd around the old market square of Heumarkt, those that survived World War II dating back hundreds of years. I would glimpse the cathedral's spires between the buildings' irregular rooftops, but then it would disappear again. When I eventually found my way through the warren of side streets, the full impact of the cathedral's grandeur took me by surprise. If I hadn't known it was there, its unexpected arrival would have stopped me in my tracks. I saw huddles of Japanese tourists experiencing exactly this as they stopped in the middle of the main thoroughfare, selfie sticks at the ready. Locals dodged, clearly used to this, ignoring them apart from the occasional 'tut' if a tourist rucksack gave them a whack when someone turned round excitedly, forgetting they were carrying a bulky weapon on their back.

I craned my neck to take in the sheer size of the building. The foundation stone was laid in 1248 and it took over 600 years to complete the build: the final spire wasn't finished until 1880. All of this was done with scaffolding and manual labour. To give visitors an impression of how much hard work it was, there is a life-sized replica of a flower shape from the top of the spires in the courtyard in front of the building. It is about 8 metres tall and weighs around 20 tons – about the same as ten family-sized cars. Somehow they got this to the top of the 150-metre spire. I stood there staring at it for ages, trying to get my head round how on earth they managed to winch something this big and heavy up to the top of such a spindly looking spire, without modern cranes or helicopters. It was incredible.

The clock tower struck four and I decided to go inside and sit for a while and light that candle for Dad.

I love standing in the cathedral square, staring up at it like the tourist that I am. It always takes my breath away. There's a massive 'flower' in the square. It's a replica of the finials at the top of the cathedral's two spires. Most people ignore it, but I find it mesmerising. I stood, staring at it, losing track of time. I still can't believe how big and heavy it looks and I have absolutely no idea how they got it up on top of the spires. Magic?

Everyone seemed so busy, running around, not noticing the immense beauty and the achievement of over 600 years of planning, dedication and hard work that created the building in front of them. Most of them ignore the finial completely, racing to get inside the building and take yet more photos. I sensed someone was standing next to me, also lost in the wonder of this lump of stone. He felt familiar, somehow. Shivers of déjà vu scuttled up my spine. He walked off as the cathedral bells struck 4 p.m., jolting me back into practical mode. My meeting with our focus group manager wasn't until 7 p.m. and he was coming to my hotel, so I would have time to go up the tower, to exhaust myself with its relentless 533 steps, and then get back and showered before my meeting. I could still make it up and back down, before the tower closed. I couldn't remember if that was at five or six at this time of year, so I didn't want to hang around. If I headed up the tower now, I might even get some time to sit in the cathedral and get my breath back before tonight's meeting. And I'm determined to make sure I have time to pop into the café I saw on the way from the station that said it was selling Pfannkuchen mit Sauerkirschrumtopf – pancakes with sour cherries that have been stored in rum and sugar all winter. It's something I haven't had since my student days. It's going to be a real treat to get to eat it again.

The inside of the cathedral made me catch my breath. It was enormous, and somehow it felt larger inside than the outside should permit. Looking up towards the underneath of the bell tower spires gave me inverse vertigo, as my mind played tricks on me, worrying that I could fall upwards. I quickly moved my gaze back to the ground, before I could fall over backwards and take out unsuspecting tourists.

Most people were there for the photos and the guided tours, but I just wanted to sit. I chose an empty pew and let myself arrive, to become fully present to the magnificence of this space, its peace, its history, the love and commitment that went into creating it. The incense from the daily services hung heavy in the air, calming my thoughts. I felt myself start to rest for the first time in months. Time stood still.

After a while, I wandered over to the candles, finding a set in an alcove where most of them had gone out. I made my donation in the wooden box that has held the hopes and prayers of many thousands over the years, and chose a nightlight to light for Dad, in his memory. I needed to talk to him. I had made a decision and I needed to know he was okay with it. I knew, in my rational brain, that lighting a candle for him wouldn't change anything, but at some deeper level I hoped it might mean I could connect with him while I sat and chatted.

So I did it anyway and moved back to sit on a nearby bench, looking over at the candle, and started talking to Dad – but only in my head, or who knows where I might have ended up spending the night.

I told Dad that I had made some decisions – two of them – and I needed to know that he approved, so I could take action. Sitting in the cathedral's sacred space I felt safe – supported – somehow more confident in my choices. I had decided I have to let go of the guilt: the guilt of surviving; the guilt of not being as good as he was at running the farm; the guilt at not having supported him more, so he could have told me about the loans. I can't carry those emotions any more. They're not helping.

I told him about my decision to find ways to prioritise the farm, while also still keeping my job in Milan. I love my work too much, even when I screw up. I was never meant to be a farmer. But things have to change. I can't step into Dad's shoes and be like him. I have to do it my way. Living in his shadow and comparing myself to him with each thought and action is suffocating me – and I'm failing. Somehow I'll find a way to keep the farm going, but I need to find my own way, not keep repeating the past. After all, that can't have been working so well for Dad if he needed to rack up all of that debt, can it?

I felt a wave of peace flow through me as I thanked Dad for listening. At some level, I knew he had heard me. And having told him what I have decided, I sensed he'd be okay with it. There was a chink of light in the darkness I had wrapped myself in. It tasted like hope.

I chuckled to myself as I got up to leave the Kölner Dom, to head back to my hotel. It's funny how I had to travel nearly 1,000 km to be ready to have this conversation with Dad – how I couldn't have done this at the Duomo in Milan, just minutes from my office. But somehow it felt right here. Neutral territory. No baggage or personal history. It felt safe to leave the past here. I'm ready for the next step now.

32. Buying Time

C ologne was a good break. The course was useful and the local beer – Kölsch – was a refreshing way to enhance our networking between the international team members. I owe the cathedral a debt of gratitude, for the heavy load it helped me to release. The city will always have a soft spot in my heart.

I returned to Milan, where Luca seemed to have calmed down a bit. The client was happy to have stopped the fraud, having now fired the person responsible, which would hopefully make Denucci give up. There were no signs of the police wanting to press charges, though, which was mainly down to my stupidity. So I was back on the case trying to collect hard evidence from within the client's systems that this person committed the theft. It was a slow and tedious job and Luca knew it was teaching me a lesson.

I have also been going through the business receipts for the farm with a fine-toothed comb, trying to understand exactly what money is going where and why. I have to find a way to make those monthly loan repayments, while I find out where Dad sent that money. I didn't hear anything from the bank while I was away, so I was having to use work systems to try to trace the account.

Although I have done the accounts for years, I had always taken Dad's word for it that we were getting a good deal with our suppliers, but now I'm looking into it my way, instead of his, I have realised that assumption was wrong. The figures don't add up. They're certainly not good value for money. I have to find ways to save costs – to take out a major portion of our expenses, without making anyone redundant, and that will mean renegotiating contracts.

Pietro wasn't impressed. "That's not how we do it, Christof." Maybe not – at least not before – but this was me finding *my* way of running the farm … and saving its neck. If that meant we would upset a few people, then so be it. He keeps making it clear that the buck stops with me when it comes to decisions, and these are decisions for which I am taking full responsibility. This is a business, not a charity, and I intend to find a way to turn it around.

He was looking tired when I saw him – and older – as though he was struggling to sleep. He wasn't the only one. His dark brown hair was fast turning grey, the 'salt and pepper' sprinkles having become the predominant shade in this past year. He shifted nervously, as I asked him about each contract in turn: what they were doing for us and why he thought it was a good price to be paying.

I'm not out to ditch our loyal, long-term suppliers, but I am getting comparable quotes from other firms, to prove whether we're paying more than we should, and then giving our current suppliers the opportunity to match those quotes. Those who can come close will stay as part of our team. Those who can't, probably won't. Some contracts were charging us more than double what we would pay elsewhere.

I know it breaks with tradition and upsets some of Dad's old friends when I give notice that we'll be moving some services elsewhere, but we can't keep paying over the odds – risking losing the farm – out of sympathy. If they can't move towards the lower prices, then they have to go.

"It's the only way I can see to save the farm, Pietro," I explained when, yet again, Pietro complained about what his drinking pals see as some *city whizz kid* coming in and changing everything for the sake of change, being tight-fisted and devastating local firms.

Is that really how they see me? I grew up here! I was born here. Okay, so I happen to work in Milan, but I own this farm and it's my home. I'm not an outsider. Except that I am. I don't do things their way. I can't afford to. I have to renegotiate where we're over-paying. And if that upsets a few people in the process, then I'm sorry, but we can't keep spending what we have been spending and expect the farm to still be here next year.

There's no way it will be enough though.

I've been trying to renegotiate our payment terms with the bank too, but that's not enough either. I have no way of paying the €40,000 in overdue payments. We simply don't have cash reserves like that. I had another meeting with the bank's Debt Manager this week and explained it to him, but he wasn't sympathetic. He has extended the deadline, but he made it clear we risk losing the farm. I tried to buy more time by offering my apartment in Milan as collateral. It was a really tough decision – high risk – so I was shocked when he laughed at me.

"The bank wants to see cash, not promises." It wasn't the answer I had expected, "If, on the other hand, you were to sell your Milan flat, you could pay off the full loan. And then we would be interested in talking."

I thanked him for his time and I left, feeling deflated. He was suggesting something that I had already been considering. But selling a city-centre apartment can take months, and we don't have the time. I felt a pang of selfishness as I admitted to myself that I wasn't prepared to sell the home for which I have slaved for the past decade in order to rescue Dad's mess. That just didn't feel fair. Was I saying I'd rather sell the farm? It's Nonna's home, and it's the livelihood for all of those families. Everyone would see me as a failure, even though it wasn't my fault that it needed selling.

I have got to the stage where I feel I have saved as much as I sensibly can on the farm's outgoings, which would allow us to make the monthly loan repayments in the future. But there was no way I could make instant repayment of the backlog.

My gut instincts still tell me that Pietro knows more than he is telling me. There is no way Dad would have taken out this much money without Pietro knowing why. So I made myself a promise. When I go home to the farm next weekend I'm going to have it out with Pietro. I haven't told him the full extent of the debt yet. It's time. He needs to know how bad this is and then he might finally agree to help me – to give me a clue – anything I can use to find out where the money went and whether we can get any of it back. I need to go in heavily with him. He needs to see what I'm made of.

May

Hints of red appear
Nature flushed with excitement
Promise of bounty

33. Needle In A Haystack

I got back from supervising the focus groups in Cologne to another pile of rejection letters. I'm not even making it to interviews any more. I find it hard to believe. At least Cologne gave me something recent to add to my CV, to prove I know what I'm doing, but will it be enough? It's not like I'm applying for promotions. I'm only going for jobs I already know I can do; for which it's obvious I'm qualified. I don't understand why I have only managed to get two interviews so far – and both were disasters. I've got one more, scheduled for later this week. I told Stuart that the new sofa was faulty and had to go back, so I've got to work from home again. He smiled a knowing smile.

I flopped onto my bed and stared up at the ceiling, willing it to share the answers I so desperately needed. How was I going to find a new job? Where would I find a new flat? There has been nothing in my budget so far. I haven't even been doing viewings because I can't afford any of the places being advertised. It's not as simple as cutting back on other expenses to increase my budget: the agents will do referencing checks, including one on 'affordability'. It's a sausage machine that looks at little other than my salary and the rent and decides whether I'm earning enough to be trusted to rent the flat - and I would fail it. I'm adamant that I don't want to flat-share. I'm not giving up my bubble baths and morning singing to appease a housemate. Not that I've been singing much lately. The agent who is selling my flat feels sorry for me. He keeps leaving details of rental properties whenever he does a sales viewing, but most of them are too far out of town for me to be interested, or look like the previous tenant was breeding wild rats as part of a social experiment in contagious diseases.

Needles are easier to find in haystacks. At least you know they're in there. I'm not convinced my new home exists. It's hard, searching for something you don't really believe in.

Time is flying.

There is nothing in the local paper each time I look and the alerts I had set up on the property websites have been curiously silent. It seems that rents have gone up by at least 20 per cent since I signed the contract on this place. I need a promotion – a big one – not a sideways move.

I just can't be bothered any more. I've got no energy these days. Cologne perked me up for a bit, but it's over now and the client was so pleased with the results of the research that they have decided not to go ahead with the final groups in Brussels. They don't think they need them. So I won't get that jolly. There's nothing fun like that in the pipeline for months now, if at all. I haven't been able to book my holiday in Italy because I need to keep the tiny savings I have for a deposit on my new flat, if I find it, while I wait for the landlord to refund the deposit from this one. I feel gutted about that. I had been really looking forward to going back to Italy. I'm finding it harder and harder to get out of bed in the mornings, even at weekends, and I've pretty much stopped socialising. I don't have it in me to be upbeat and fun anymore. I just want to sit in front of the TV and drown out my worries with wine I can't afford, eating food that comes on plastic trays.

I feel like I've lost my motivation. I've lost any sense of

fight. I just want to lie down and let life roll all over me. Being awake for hours at 3 a.m. is now standard, with my mind going through every worst-case scenario possible, to make sure I feel even lousier than I did before I went to bed. Here I am, nearly thirty-three, single, about to become homeless and, if things keep going the way they seem to be, unemployed. It's not bad enough that I could end up on the streets – I could go back to live with Mum and Dad. *God help me!* It would feel like the last fifteen years since I left home had been for nothing

I wish there were a law that if a landlord wants to sell a tenant's home then they were forced to find them somewhere equally lovely to live, at the same price. Fat chance.

"Would you like to buy the flat?" the landlord asked, via the agent, after the first ten viewings failed to bring an offer. Yes, of course, but…! The asking price is so high there's no way a mere mortal could get a mortgage for it. You'd need to be half of a couple, both earning above the higher tax limit. I'm a million miles from that at every level.

I hate buyers being shown round. They go through my stuff. I even found my underwear drawer had been rummaged by some pervert last week. I felt violated. I'm sick of having to keep the place extra-tidy and clean – another request texted weekly by the landlord. Bloody cheek! He should be giving me a discount off my rent for this. But, as the agent said, it's the price I'll be paying to get my deposit back. And I can't afford to lose it.

I feel like I'm living under a black cloud. Everything I do goes wrong. When I think back to before Christmas, I can't understand the change in my life. How did it get this bad, so quickly? It scares me to realise how close I am to giving up hope. I hate feeling this way.

I made a decision while I was in Germany, which feels like progress. I'm clutching at straws, pretending to be positive. I'm going to accept Anna's offer of sleeping on her sofa from the end of the month. Just for a few weeks, I hope. It will give me time to find somewhere else. But it will mess up my job-hunting. What will I give as my address? How flaky will I look if I end up giving them three different addresses between my application and the interview? And I'll have no privacy. The sofa is in Anna's lounge, so I won't be able to go to bed until she does. I'll have constant company. The only place I'll ever get privacy is on the loo, and even then I'll know she's on the other side of the door.

And Anna doesn't have a bath.

34. An Unexpected Offer

I still can't get used to having Isabella back in the office. I'll be working at my desk and suddenly look up to find her staring at me. But unlike most women, who would look away with embarrassment, she holds my stare every time, and smiles. She is so self-assured.

Rumour has it that she has moved on from the record label owner she ditched me for and had hooked up with some Italian aristocrat who she met at a party on a yacht. Where else? Apparently he's loaded. Every weekend she's off somewhere else with him, always flying first class or being picked up by his driver. How could real men possibly compete?

But the wounds she left me with are healing slowly. Each day it gets easier to see her, to spend time with her, without asking myself why: why I was with her; why I wasn't enough for her.

Luca is almost calm with me again but my actions have made closing the Denucci case much harder and the client told him last week that he won't pay extra for all the work I'm having to do to collect evidence, because the videos should have been enough. Luca had the decency to tell him it had been a hard drive failure, rather than a one-night-stand, that destroyed the evidence.

Isabella and I were standing by the photocopier. She was

using it. I was waiting, doing my best to ignore her. She turned to me and, expecting small talk, I smiled at her.

"Will you go for a drink with me, after work?" she asked, moving closer to me, so close it brought back memories of old times. I found myself wanting to kiss her, closing my eyes for a fraction of a second longer than necessary, reliving that memory. That wasn't what I had expected – or what I wanted. I shook myself free from her spell and stepped backwards, needing the space. "I've got something I need to talk to you about." Genital herpes? Maybe I was being uncharitable. I found myself agreeing, on autopilot, too scared of putting a foot wrong in the office.

So now I was in the bar, having ordered our drinks, waiting for her to come back from the ladies. I was sticking to mineral water. I don't trust Isabella unless I'm fully aware of what I'm doing and I remember what happened the last time I drank alcohol in front of a woman. She wanted a double measure of a herb-infused grappa she spotted, which she told me reminds her of home.

We took our drinks out onto the terrace. The bar has a beautiful view of the city. It's a long way out of the centre, but it's worth the effort.

"You said you had something you wanted to talk to me about," I started, not wanting to spend more time with her than I had to. Disappointment showed in her eyes, but only for long enough for her to put the mask back on. I watched her debating what to say next, which move to pull. Knowing Isabella, anything she wanted to say to me had been carefully planned and she would have thought through all contingencies.

"I miss you," she said, with a straight face, "I want us to try again."

I spat my water across the table, half-snorting it. It wasn't the reaction she had expected.

"That's just not happening, Isabella," I said with a conviction that, for once, I felt, "I will *never* trust you again!"

The arrow hit its mark. Her expression dropped and I saw the briefest flash of what looked like sadness in her eyes. "I've changed, Christof, really I have."

"Really? Prove it!" I had no idea how I expected her to do so, but the ultimatum came out anyway.

Before I realised what was happening, she was leaning over towards me and had cupped my chin in her palm, pulling my face closer to hers. I closed my eyes. It was involuntary. We kissed. I could taste the herbs in the grappa. I remembered how good this used to feel. Long, slow, lingering kisses. Her hands running through my hair, over my body. I felt what could come next, how easy it would be to fall back into that old life, how much I longed to be with someone exciting and passionate. But not Isabella. Not again.

I pulled away sharply. "Don't you have a boyfriend? Some royal something or other? Why are you doing this, Isabella?"

"I miss you, Christof," she whispered, ignoring my first question, trying to kiss me again. I didn't let her. It wasn't what I wanted any more. I would never trust her again. And, after what happened in Naples, trusting anyone had got a massive chunk harder after that, especially trusting myself.

"I don't care, Isabella. You haven't changed." And I was right. She hadn't. She might mean well, but I couldn't risk letting her back in. Not now, not ever.

I left her at our table with the excruciatingly beautiful view of the city at sunset, with my unfinished drink and with her conscience, if she has one. I went back to my flat, head swimming, but grateful to be free from the power she used to have over me.

I went for a long walk on my way home, to clear my head, and as soon as I let myself into my apartment I flopped down on the sofa, wishing I had remembered to stock up on beer for the fridge at the local shop. I couldn't be bothered to go back out now. My head was spinning with *what if* discussions about Isabella. Would it really be so bad getting back together with her? Yes! I still have my self-esteem and it had cost me dearly to rebuild it, after she dumped me. Though part of me would love to have dinner with her to find out why she had done what she had done.

I decided to distract myself by thinking about how to handle things with Pietro when I go back to the farm this weekend. I've got evidence on where the loan funds were transferred to now and I think he'll be shocked at how much I know. But the trail ran cold, so I need him to cooperate. I can't risk him clamming up.

It was as I was reaching for a magazine on my old cherry coffee table that it hit me: the paperwork I had left on the table last night didn't look right. I forced myself to focus, to let my unconscious mind tell me what had changed. It was a pile of papers with evidence for the potential Denucci inside man Court case. We've got nothing on Denucci so far, but plenty to put his accomplice behind bars. I had been pulling out the key data to send to the police last night, as I watched a film. And I had put the papers on the coffee table to continue with tonight, because I knew I would have back-to-back meetings today and no time to go through them.

I forced myself to slow down the images in my head, trying to reconstruct the memories I hadn't been concentrating on last night. At work, I would have picked up the pile of papers and banged it on the desk, arranging it into a neat stack, before locking them away in my filing cupboard. Had I done that last night? Had I? Why couldn't I remember? What was my mind trying to tell me?

An ice-cold draft blew up my back as I remembered. I hadn't. I had sorted them into four piles, for each of the different aspects of evidence, and then placed each pile at 90 degrees on top of each other, so it made a messy-looking stack, to save me re-sorting them this evening, but without them being sprawled all over the coffee table. And now they were neatly arranged, as though I had done them at work. I was racking my brain: was I making it up? Was I misremembering? Or had someone been in my flat? I don't have a cleaner.

35. Rock Bottom

I must have been utterly desperate. There was no 'must' about it. I was.

When Jamie phoned on Saturday evening, asking if I wanted to go to a party with him, I felt like I didn't have a soul left in the world. Anna and the girls were out at a hen do for someone I didn't know, so I wasn't invited. Lucy was struggling with Emma's sleep patterns, so she cried off our afternoon tea. Jem was still in Australia – not back until next week. Even Mum and Dad were on a romantic weekend away at some stately home's Murder Mystery weekend, where they would get to pretend they were actors and figure out who killed the parlour maid, while gorging themselves on exquisite food and free-flowing wine in full evening dress. It made a change from the three-month cruise they have already taken this year. I've barely seen them since Dad retired.

So I said yes to Jamie. He was so charming. He caught me with my defences down, spinning me a sob story about how no one has lived up to the standards I set in his life and that he needed to see me. I should have spotted it for the bullshit it was and drowned my sorrows in front of yet another TV dinner.

So I put on my little black dress, the painfully high heels and the tummy-tuck support tights, and grabbed my coat and bag, before getting the Tube to Soho to meet him at one of the exits at

Oxford Circus Tube station. My heart skipped a beat. I hadn't seen him in ages, having managed to fob him off for the past few months. But he was just as gorgeous as I remembered: tall, handsome, dark brown hair, bright blue eyes, ultra-white teeth and perfectly manicured hands, making the statement to the world that he gets paid for his brain, not his manual labour. And that's important to him, as I well know. He likes to put himself across as an intellectual, though I always thought he was masking a massive inferiority complex. I brushed those thoughts aside. I needed a night out and he had offered. No strings attached.

Or at least, so I thought.

"You look great!" he lied. I knew I didn't. I had put in some effort, but the last half year has seen wobbly bits arriving in all the wrong places and I now needed to wear at least three times as much foundation as before, to avoid looking like a morgue resident.

"You too." I was telling the truth. I totted up his clothes: at least a month's salary, and fairly new, from the look of them. Where does he get the money?

"So where's the party?" I asked, more reluctantly than I had intended. I wasn't really in the mood, but I couldn't face staying at home on my own and I didn't have any other offers.

His face dropped. "I'm so sorry, Soph," he drawled, so laid back he'd make a glacier look like it was in a hurry. "It's off, I'm afraid. The host's parents got back from skiing in Klosters earlier than planned – the Dad had sprained his ankle – and they canned the idea. Didn't want the mess – vomit in the Ming vase and all that."

Relief mingled with confusion in my face.

"I can see you're disappointed," he apologised. I wasn't, but I didn't correct him. I'd much rather go out for dinner than to a party with people I didn't know. Less effort and probably more civilised. Anywhere but staying at home again. "I thought we could have a quiet night in instead?" he continued, "Just the two of us? Some takeaway and a nice bottle? Catch up?"

No! That's not what I wanted. I didn't want to watch a film at my flat and have it stink of takeaway food tomorrow morning, as I tried to scrub the spillages and crumbs off my beloved sofa. It was the whole reason I made the massive effort to go out – the only reason I had said yes to Jamie's invitation – so I wouldn't have to be at home.

"How about your place?" I asked, knowing already what his answer would be. I have never seen his current flat – he has moved, so I had heard, in the last few months. Even when we were dating, I was only *allowed* to go to his place once in a blue moon, usually when he had forgotten something and we were running too late for him to leave me at home.

His face darkened, as he made an excuse. What was he hiding?

"So it's my place then?" I replied, already knowing the answer. He smiled and ushered me back down the steps I had just walked up. Why couldn't he have texted me before I trekked halfway across the city to meet him?

My place was a tip. I had started sorting, getting ready to pack for the move. But I didn't want to tell Jamie that. I didn't want to let him in on my world. Not yet. So he was going to have to think I was slovenly. I didn't really care. He might be heart-meltingly handsome, but he just didn't do it for me anymore.

We barely chatted on the Tube; just small talk interspersed with awkward silences. We walked back to my flat talking about the shops we passed. He was trying to bring back memories for me, as though he wanted to rekindle our relationship. He pointed, shop by shop, and asked me, "Do you remember the time, when…?" The harder he tried, the less I wanted to remember.

We walked past his favourite takeaway and he stopped, staring in the window. "Please, Soph?" he asked, knowing I would give in. I always had. We went in and ordered. He was generous, wanting something of everything of all his old favourites. The man behind the counter, who hadn't seen me since Jamie and I split up, rang up a frightening total on the till. Jamie didn't even have the decency to rummage in his wallet and pretend he was looking for cash. "Sorry, Soph, the party was meant to be a food and drink-supplied thing. I haven't brought my wallet with me. Could you sub me?"

Really? What kind of idiot goes out in London without money? Like I needed to ask. So we were back there again. History was repeating itself. I paid, in silence. And Jamie suggested we should head to the off-licence, two doors down, while we waited for them to prepare the food. He bought two bottles of his favourite semi-vintage Chablis – a white wine I quite enjoy when someone else is footing the bill. But, of course, Jamie didn't expect to have to spend any money tonight, so it was my treat again.

He even got me carrying the takeaway home: two heavy, white plastic bags that cut into my fingers until I was sure there would be blood on them as I put them down to hunt for my keys when we reached my door. "Don't want to risk getting it on my suit, Soph." So how was he going to eat it, then?

I should have realised.

"Do you still have those old jogging bottoms I left here, Soph? And that old t-shirt? I really don't want to get my suit stained."

So it would have been fine to drench it in Champagne and cover it with canapés at the posh party, but his favourite takeaway at my flat wasn't good enough. I've never been a good liar, so I didn't bother trying, though I'd have loved to spite him and watch his suit get ruined. I hunted around the back of my wardrobe and found them, hoping they would be full of moth holes. He went to the bathroom to get changed, asking me for coat hangers for his suit and shirt. Instead of taking them from me, he handed me the clothes to hang up, as though I were his valet. I slipped them onto the hangers and put them on a hook by the front door. "You were always so good at it, Soph!" All of this had to be finished before we were allowed to eat, in case I got greasy fingers on his beloved clothes. It was tempting, so tempting. I was ravenous.

Demolishing the take-away didn't take long and then Jamie remembered he hadn't ordered any dessert. For a brief moment I thought he might ask me to go out and get some, but the daggers I shot him warned him that would be a demand too far. Instead, I got the cherry *clafoutis* I had been saving for a treat tomorrow out of the fridge.

I had been drowning out how dull he was by drinking my fair share of the pre-chilled Chablis until, between us, both bottles were empty. I could feel tomorrow's hangover arriving ahead of schedule and I was about to go for a pint of tap water when Jamie remembered the emergency bottle of gin I used to keep in the cupboard above my oven. I still did. Vile stuff. I never used to think so, but there was one night when I enjoyed rather too much of it and ever since then I couldn't handle the smell, let alone the taste.

Between us, we finished the bottle.

I didn't even notice the film he had put on the DVD player. He had certainly made himself at home. He hadn't asked me a single question about me or my life. He didn't know about Stuart or about the flat move. He still didn't care about anyone apart from himself. And he gave me a two-hour monologue that would have made a character actor at the Royal Shakespeare Company proud.

It was well past midnight and I wanted to go to sleep. My head was throbbing and I downed the pint of water, whether or not Jamie liked it. It was as though he wanted to get me drunk.

I was sitting with him on the sofa. Next to him, not touching. Very deliberately. The film ended and he switched off the TV, turned to me, put his arm around my shoulder and drew me towards him. Then we were kissing. I couldn't be bothered to protest. It had been so long. I went with the flow. I was drunk and I didn't care.

Hands started meandering, on both sides. Things were warming up. Clothes were being removed. Before I knew it, we were down to underwear, hiding under the blanket for warmth. I knew I was likely to regret this in the morning, but right now I didn't care. If we shagged, we shagged.

We were racing towards the point of no return and part of me was definitely in the mood, when Jamie whispered in my ear, "Soph, are you still on the pill?" In other words, it was my job to bring the condoms. I froze. I didn't want to do this.

"Soph?" he asked again, impatient for an answer. I suddenly remembered how much I hated it – the way he said my name. "So-oaf", like 'sofa'. He always turns it into two syllables. Whingy, whining, like a spoilt child calling 'Mu-um!'

Then I saw the remains of the cherry *clafoutis* on the table and my mind zoomed back to Paris – the last time I ate it – when that total stranger was kind enough to let me have the last slice. Jamie would never have done that for me.

Someone, somewhere, threw a bucket of iced water over my head. I couldn't do it.

"You have to leave, Jamie," I told him, my voice shaking. "I don't want to do this. Not with you."

"Oh come on, Soph. It'll be good! So good! Old times' sake!"

"No, it won't. I want you to leave. Now!" I stood up, pulling the blanket tightly around me to give an illusion of decency, of privacy. It wasn't like he hadn't seen it all before, but I didn't want him seeing it all now. Or ever again.

"But, Soph!" He stood up wearing gorgeous, figure-hugging designer boxer shorts that made it perfectly clear how happy he would have been to keep going. "I don't want to leave! I love you!"

"Then why did you ditch me and run off with that heiress? Not even a fucking text message! Do you have any idea how shit that felt, sitting and waiting for you? What happened to her?" I screamed, the pent-up emotions pouring into my words.

"I was scared. I ran. I didn't realise how much I loved you. I was stupid." He chose to ignore the heiress part of the question. "Please give me another chance!"

I did a blanket-shuffle to my bag and dug out my wallet, finding the two twenty-pound notes I had taken out of the cash machine earlier this evening, and threw them towards him. He didn't move. They fluttered to land at his feet like rectangular butterflies.

"For your taxi." I turned my back on him and started to shuffle towards the bathroom, where my dressing gown was waiting for me.

"But, Soph, I had something I wanted to ask you!"

I turned round and he caught the full force of the disgust in my face. I loathed him. Right now, I loathed myself, as well. "Don't tell me," I replied, "I'm a professional mind-reader. You want some money?"

He reddened. I was spot on.

"How much?"

He stood up tall, the bulge in his boxers now significantly subdued from the shock of unexpected rejection. "A couple of months' rent, that's all. Just to tide me over. I'd pay it back!"

"Like hell you will!" I screamed at him. He nearly bankrupted me. That was why I've got near-zero deposit saved up to buy a flat now. It's why I'm stuck renting. Then he had the cheek to ask me out, to spin lies about still caring, about wanting to get back together, just so he could borrow money I don't have, because of him! I almost wondered if there might be another woman waiting for him, back at his flat. I wouldn't put it past him. I felt cheap and used. But I wouldn't let him win.

"I'm going to bed," I said firmly, with all the dignity I could manage. "I want you to leave. Your clothes are hanging by the front door. Make sure you close it behind you." I turned and walked away, closing my bedroom door loudly. Then I cursed myself because I was desperate to pee and now I would have to wait for him to go, or I would lose all the ground I just took. It took him ten painful minutes and then he left.

I cried myself to sleep and woke up with a vile hangover, expected and deserved. *Is this how desperate I am? Yes, I guess it is.*

36. The End of the Line

"You're off the case, Christof," Luca told me, looking genuinely sorry for me. "There's nothing I can do about it."

That was my reward for catching the inside man. I felt absolutely broken about it. I had been loving this case; the first meaty project that had come across our books for over a year and I had blown it.

"It's not a punishment," Luca continued. "Please don't see it that way."

"Then what is it?" I demanded, feeling churlish and wondering why he was lying to me.

"We have to protect you!"

"What do you mean?"

"Come on, Christof, you're not that stupid, are you?"

I didn't answer.

"Do you really think that total strangers break into hotel room safes and randomly delete videos from cameras?" I knew where he was going on this. It was the obvious fact that I'd been denying to myself since what my brain now calls *Naples*. "They're onto you, Christof." Yes, I knew they were, but I hadn't wanted to admit it.

He was right. Somehow, someone knew I would be at the stake-out and they followed me, guessing that Miss Italy would be enough to tempt me to drop my guard. Every time I think about that night I feel like the world's biggest idiot. But how did they know? We maintained absolute secrecy. The only people who knew about the stake-out were inside our team and none of them would have let it slip. Even the owner didn't know when it would be. How could Denucci even have known he was being investigated? That we were on his trail? It just didn't make sense.

"They found you that night; they could find you again, Christof. I have put the word out in our network that we're off the case."

I hadn't told Luca about the other night, when I had been sure someone had been in my flat. I couldn't find any sign of a break-in; nothing else had been touched, as far as I could see and there was no way anyone could have got hold of my keys. Given that the papers were left the way I always leave them at work, I had to conclude it had been my mind playing tricks on me – being paranoid. I was still on edge, but I hadn't taken the threat seriously.

"It's over to the police now."

"Is that true?" I asked, knowing that working on this was a good earner for the firm.

"Yes, I'm afraid it is, but it's also for the best. We can't risk the safety of our team members. And the client doesn't feel the need to pay us any more at the moment. That might change. I don't know. But I've got some good news."

I sighed. Feeling hopeful was a bit alien for me at the moment. There was still no progress on Dad's loan and things had been really tense at work since 'Naples'.

"Go on," I said, sounding frustrated. Luca ignored my tone.

"You don't have to testify. The inside man has confessed! So the police have agreed to overlook how the information reached the company owner and what led up to the confession. There will be no mention of our involvement when it comes to trial."

That wasn't good news. It was brilliant news. Testifying would have taken the risks for us – for me - to the next level. Our involvement would have become public. And if someone wanted revenge, it would have been much easier for them to find us.

"This case is now closed for us, Christof. We've been paid our fee, despite not quite delivering everything we promised. You owe the inside man for that."

I had identified him from the personnel records. It was easy to do. I could still remember the name of the person whose desk he had used. When the inside man was approached by the police – something the company owner still had to fight for because the police were still refusing to investigate the matter – he had told them exactly what he had been doing, though he said he didn't know who for. We believed him. The police were suspending charges in return for him providing evidence they might be able against Denucci. There's no guarantee he won't end up floating in fresh cement – and he knows it – so he accepted the offer of the police witness protection programme. He was single and his parents died years ago, so it would be easier for him than for most, but it still wouldn't be fun, having to walk away from his whole life, spending the rest of it looking over his shoulder. That's the price he would pay for getting involved with the wrong kind of people. I have often wondered what motivated him to do it. But I guess I'll never know.

Luca was right. It was for the best that this has closed down. But there was still a danger. Someone knew I was involved. They knew how and when and where to find me. Denucci would be angry at losing his revenue stream. Things have tightened up at our client's company since the inside man confessed and there's no way Denucci will be able to pull that scam again.

He had been clever, keeping it to internal fraud rather than obvious theft. It was a mixture of overpayment of bogus supplier invoices – all firms suspected as being owned by Denucci – and changing shipment quantities on deliveries, after Denucci's bogus firms had been paid, often receiving five times the inventory they had paid for. Simple. Hard to trace, unless you knew what you were looking for.

"Christof, you're going to have to watch your back for a while. We still don't know how anyone knew how to find you in Naples. We can't find any trace of a trail. I can't believe I'm saying this," He watches my face drop, triggered by his serious tone, "but it's actually a good thing that you shagged that woman, or we might not have known that there had been a leak. We still have absolutely no idea where or who. That's why you've got to watch your back. It wasn't a coincidence that she knew to delete those videos."

I clenched my fists and tried to stop the anger I felt at my own stupidity, but I could see Luca had a point. It was better to know that to get caught unawares. But who on earth could have known, outside of our team? And we knew each other far too well for it to have been one of us.

"Just be sensible," Luca interrupted my thoughts, trying to soothe me. "The usual stuff: no dark alleys, making sure people know where you are, checking your car before you get in it, watching for signs at your flat." He didn't notice me flinch. "If things stay quiet, you can relax soon enough. It's just as likely that Denucci has taken this one on the chin and taking you off the case will fix everything."

I hoped that was right. It put me on edge, even thinking about having to consciously keep an eye out for danger.

"Luca," I asked, knowing now was the best time I was likely to find to get the *yes* I needed, "I have been thinking of taking a week off at the start of June to represent the farm at the annual cherry festival. It would get me well out of the way while things die down with Denucci. Do you think it's a good idea?" I knew I was pushing my luck, but after our conversation, Luca couldn't really say no. I was relieved that I wasn't going to get the grief he had given me when I needed a couple of days off to see the Bank Manager. He cleared it and even told me to enjoy myself.

It's not for a couple of weeks yet and I'm sure Luca is right. If Denucci's contacts wanted to get me, they'd have done something about it by now. It's been over a month since the stake-out, with no sign of anything other than the false alarm at my apartment. And yet again, I find myself regretting that night in Naples. It keeps coming back to haunt me.

37. A Life-Changing Dinner

I flunked another interview yesterday. It was a sideways move again, and I knew I could do the job. But I just couldn't find the enthusiasm any more. In the olden days, I'd have spent a week's worth of evenings researching the company and coming up with ideas they could pitch for clients, highlighting the strengths of their research team and suggesting opportunities they might not have spotted – in ways that wouldn't offend them. Now I show up in my bulging-at-the-seams suit, wishing the interview were over before I even start.

Combine that with the *Eau de Desperation* that must be streaming from every pore and it's no wonder I'm never making it to the second round. I don't really want the jobs. I used to love the one I have, but I need a new one. It's not optional. Each rejection letter drives me more deeply into panic.

I don't even feel angry any more, just numb. It's like living under a black cloud, as though someone has turned the sunshine off – in May. I hate the way my thoughts make me feel.

Yesterday's interview was a disaster. I knew it was over when I asked them if I could keep my mobile on the desk in front of me. "My boss thinks I'm with a client." Their faces said it all. If I could lie to my boss about being at an interview, which other lies would I be telling, once I was working for them? They wrapped things up shortly after that. I didn't care. It's like I wanted to fail, to somehow punish myself. It doesn't make sense. I don't want a sideways move. Lucy and I were working on getting me promoted, but I just don't have the confidence to go for promotions. How can I sing about my strengths when every day I'm so plainly reminded of my failings? I don't even have the energy to hate Stuart any more.

I've got another interview next Friday. It's one that Lucy has set up: a Planner position. I'm only going because Lucy has arranged it. If I can't get sideways moves, I've got no idea how I'll get a promotion. I told Stuart the sofa that was taken back is now being replaced, so I have to work from home again. He's not buying it any more. A smirk of satisfaction contorted his ugly face as he pointed out that, "There are only so many sofas a girl can get delivered." He knows that I know he's onto me. And we both know I don't care.

"Look, if you're job-hunting that's fine. More than fine. It's what we both want. But shall we stop this bullshit with the sofas? How about just being honest and taking holiday days for the interviews? And remember you'll be needing a good reference." I shuddered at the memory of the offer he had made me at the party. He didn't need to remind me it was still on the table. I have been keeping my head down. He doesn't know about my back-up plan with Lucy.

In sheer despair of ever finding a way to leave, I phoned one of our former clients this morning, hinting that I might be looking to leave and asking if they knew of anywhere I might apply – or if they ever hired freelancers for their qualitative work. We had worked well together and I knew they would want to help me. I wasn't expecting the answer their Head of Research gave me.

"Yes, Stuart said we might be hearing from you." *Shit! He got there first. Who else has he been talking to?* "I'm sorry, but we don't have anything available for the foreseeable future." Stuart was being thorough. How could I stand a chance? The market research industry in London is a small world. Everyone knows everyone. And seniority counts. There was no way anyone would believe me about what Stuart has been doing. Sometimes I find myself wondering if I imagined it all, then I see the putrid gleam in his eyes as he stares at my breasts as he leans over my shoulder to correct an email and I know it's all true. There is no way I'm ever going to get a job with him spreading rumours about me. It must be his punishment for me trying to put in a formal complaint about him. Harry is bound to have told him. He will have guessed why I wanted to see Sally.

And Jamie is still texting me daily. I keep ignoring him. How clear do I have to make it that I'm not interested? I cringe at the thought of what might have happened had I not come to my senses at the weekend.

The only ray of hope is that Jem is coming over for dinner tonight. She's bringing food with her – she has experienced my cooking. It will be the first decent meal I've had all week. Saturday night at home. I can't wait to see her. She's just back from Australia. When she phoned yesterday to catch up on my news, I couldn't talk to her. I just burst into tears. It's not like me. But it felt so good to know that someone still cares. She told me she's dropping everything to come and see me. I really need a hug. I don't think I can take much more of this.

"How long have you feel feeling like this?" Jem cut straight to the chase, after I took her through what had happened since I last saw her.

"Since Christmas."

"And you didn't tell me?"

Why didn't I tell her? Same reason I didn't tell Lucy, I

suppose. I didn't want to bother her. And talking about it would have made it more real. I have been feeling so desperately low that I even went to see my doctor yesterday, on the way home from work, to ask if he could give me something to help. I explained this to Jem. I didn't want her to think I've been wallowing and not helping myself.

"What did he recommend?" she asked softly, holding my hands and staring into my eyes with so much love it made me want to cry.

"He can't help me." The floodgates opened. The tears came. She held me as I sobbed. She didn't care about her designer blouse. It reminded me of what a shit Jamie is. He wouldn't have ever let me sob on his precious suit.

"What happened?"

"He said he can't give me medication for depression unless I have been feeling like this for at least three months and that countdown started yesterday, with my first visit and even if he did give me pills, they can take six weeks to work and we might need to try a few different ones to find one that help, so it could be months before I would feel any better."

Depression. The word I hadn't wanted to admit to myself. Mental illness. I was a statistic. I felt like a failure. I've studied psychology. I should have seen the signs. It wasn't fair. I didn't ask for any of this.

I sniffed noisily, taking a delicious glacé cherry from the box Jem had brought with her as my present from Australia. It had taken guts to go to my GP, to admit how low I was feeling. He tried to be sympathetic, but he didn't have time to listen to me. He didn't understand why it was so important that I get help with this. I'm about to be made homeless and I will never find a new job while I'm feeling this way. I told him I couldn't take much more. I guess he hears that twenty times a week. I don't know what I would have done this evening, had Jem not been here.

"What else?" she asked, stroking my hair gently.

"He suggested I might want counselling, but the waiting list is six months, unless I want to go privately. I worked out how much that would cost. He says I might need twenty sessions – or more – and that would take all the money I have saved for the deposit on my next flat. I just can't afford it. He told me to do more exercise and to get out more. How can I find the energy for that? He can't help me. Nobody can."

"That's simply not true, Sophie. I'm here now. I wish you had told me sooner. I could have helped. It's what I'm here for."

She tightened her hug and I let her support me. In that moment, I let go of the weight of carrying all of this for the past few months. I hadn't realised how heavy it all felt. I cried again. She stroked my hair. Jem understood. In my heart, I knew it was going to be okay now. I just didn't know how.

Finally my sobs subsided and Jem's calm, confident voice moved from comforting to action.

"Look, you're not the counselling type. It would make you relive all the shit you've been through and over-analyse it. You're good enough at that already. You need to channel your energy into action."

I knew, deep down, she was right, but I didn't have any energy at the moment to channel.

"Dahling, there are two types of depression. There's the one that's down to chemical and hormonal imbalances. That's one that doctors can help with, with their pills. And there's the one that's down to environmental factors: going through brown stuff and getting stuck in negative thinking. That's where you're at. We can put a plan together to help you through it. I'm here for you."

In that moment, I suddenly realised that she meant it – she really was there for me. The cage of blue ice I had locked myself in started to show signs of melting, drips sliding down its surfaces, warmed by the glow of Jem's love and unconditional support. Rays of hope started to reach me.

"You're going through a rough patch, that's all." I gave her a look that told her 'that's all' didn't even begin to describe things. "I know it feels like the end of the world. Really, I do."

"I'm about to be made homeless and my boss has sexually harassed me, so I'm going to be unemployed too. I don't call that a *rough patch!*" I spat at her. I needed to take my anger out on someone. She didn't flinch.

"Sophie, you're stuck in the doldrums, in the literal sense. The wind has gone from your sails, but you've forgotten that when there's no wind, you can still row. You've turned yourself into a victim over all of this. You've allowed Stuart and Harry, and Jamie and your landlord to steal your oars – to take your personal power. You've given them control over your happiness."

I gave her an evil look. I wasn't impressed. Where did the sympathy go? "I know you don't want to hear this, Sophie, but someone's got to tell you the truth." I wasn't quite sure how I managed not to explode on her. She was talking bollocks. I pulled away from her hug and planted myself firmly on the opposite end of the sofa.

We sat in silence for a while.

"How much have you been drinking lately?"

I didn't answer. It was none of her business. I wanted to hate her; to give her the hate I wished I could have aimed at Harry and Stuart and Jamie. But it didn't work. I couldn't hate her. Not quite.

"Your skin has that sallow, grey look of someone whose

liver is working too hard, and you're struggling to make eye contact with me. You're moping around, feeling sorry for yourself, when you know you should be out every night looking for somewhere to live. You're not putting in much effort, are you?"

I looked her defiantly in the eyes, to prove her wrong.

"Great! That's progress!" she clapped her hands with child-like glee and her smile lit up her face. She was going bonkers. I just didn't understand her.

"That was anger! How does it feel to get angry with me?"

I didn't reply, but it had felt good. I needed to get angry. I needed to throw the rage I have been suppressing at someone.

"Firstly, you've got to get rid of Jamie." She was in practical mode. I felt like I should be making notes. "Just send him a text telling him to fuck off and never contact you again, and then never read another message from him."

She was right. It might be that simple. She saw the possibility of action in my face and handed me my phone. "Now!" she insisted. I did it. It was scary when I hit 'send', like I was going to end up single for the rest of my life if I turned him away. But I knew, after last Saturday, that living with him wasn't a price I was prepared to pay. I let a chink of relief in.

Jem smiled at me.

"Now, on to Stuart." My heart sank. I didn't want to think about Stuart. I certainly wasn't about to text him, too.

"Do you want me to get the girls to check him out? To find the dirt on him?" She was talking about her Godmother Club – the one no one is supposed to know about. "We could get someone to sort him out, if you want. Scare him off?"

The thought of getting revenge on Stuart really appealed. But I wasn't sure I want that kind of thing on my conscience. Not yet, at any rate.

"By all means do some research, Jem. It might come in useful, but please don't ask anyone to do anything to him. It might backfire."

She nodded, accepting my terms.

"You need to understand this isn't really about you."

"Then who the hell is it about?"

"It's his own shit being projected. This isn't about you at all. His behaviour isn't your fault. The Native Americans have this saying about all criticism being borne of someone else's pain. You haven't done anything wrong other than not stand up to him as much as I would have done, but that's part of learning and growing. This is all happening because he is feeling crap and needs someone to kick. You showed up with a neon target sign above your head."

"That's not fair! Are you trying to make me feel sorry for him? After everything he's done to me?"

"Maybe it's not fair, but it's true. You've got to stop letting him decide how you'll feel, and how you live your life."

"But how?"

"I've got stuff I want to teach you about mindfulness and yoga and other stuff, but that's too much for tonight. I'll find some local classes for you and come with you for the first few sessions, so you don't feel like you're on your own. But for now, all I want is a promise."

I gave her the hesitant 'Yeeees' that meant 'maybe' or more likely 'no'.

"I want you to promise me that you're going to stop obsessing about his behaviour. You're going to reclaim your power over your life and how you're feeling. You've decided not to fight him and that's your choice. You're going to leave. You've got a back-up plan for your reference from Lucy. So how about pretending he doesn't exist until you can find another job?"

"And how the hell do I do that?" I could feel anger welling up inside me again.

"Imagine you're walking round inside a disco ball. You know, those mirror balls they have in ballroom dancing competitions?" Yes, I knew what she meant, but I was confused. "Any shit he flings your way is reflected right back at him. You're safe inside the ball. He can't touch you: he can't affect how you feel or the decisions you make. It'll help him realise there's no point in trying to hurt you. Reckon you could do that?"

I wasn't sure.

"Try it out, now." I felt really stupid. I didn't want to. "Look, think back to something he said recently and replay it in your mind, but this time with you standing inside the mirror ball. How different does it feel?"

I gave in and ran it through my imagination. I wasn't going get any peace from her until I had. It took a few minutes to drown out the frantic objections of my Inner Drama Queen.

"Well, what happened?" I couldn't lie to her. I was really surprised.

"It helped."

"In what way?"

"He didn't get to me as much. I didn't feel the usual knots in my stomach – that tension – the nausea. I felt more able to handle it."

"That's my girl! It's a really useful thing to remember. It might not fix everything, but it gives you a moment to pause – to choose how to respond. It helps to stop the automatic, emotional response when he does something unkind."

I mulled this over and realised how automatic that has been. Even seeing Stuart in the distance was enough to get me feeling miserable and overwhelmed by dread these days. "Do you really think this could work, Jem?" I wanted to hope.

"Yes, it will. It's a great place to start. There's plenty more we can do, but we need to take baby steps to turn this around. You've got pretty deep into the brown stuff while I've been away. Your mirror ball is an emergency fix."

I gave her a look that told her I wanted to believe it, I really did, but I wasn't there yet. She didn't seem to mind.

"There's another thing."

"What?" I was feeling tired and I wanted to go to bed. Part of me knew this was just an avoidance strategy.

"That mirror ball has mirrors on the inside, too."

"How do you mean?"

"Any shit you want to send out at him gets reflected right back at you."

"But why would I want to do that?"

"Because, my Love, you take yourself with you."

"What are you on about now?" I was losing patience. I was too tired for riddles and games.

"Do you want to spend the rest of your life bouncing from one crap boss to another, being stalked by abusive ex-boyfriends – because Jamie *was* abusive – and living in fear of your landlord selling your flat?"

"What kind of a question is that?" I couldn't believe she had even asked it.

"Then you need to change."

"But I didn't do any of this! It happened to me. I couldn't help it."

"You might not be able to prevent the brown stuff hitting the fan, but you *can* change the direction the brown stuff flies in."

I gave her a confused look. She continued patiently, as though trying to teach a young child their alphabet for the tenth day in a row.

"When someone treats you badly, it's like the two of you are dancing a dance. They do something bad, you react; your reaction feeds their need to hurt someone – even if that need is subconscious – and so the cycle continues. They dance, you dance; the two of you keep dancing. The only way to stop the dance is to change the steps you are choosing. You can't force them to change theirs. But here's the thing: even if that person moves out of our lives, we're so used to the steps in that dance we used to dance with them that we somehow attract others to fill their role. It's why so many people see history repeating itself – same story, different actors – over and over again."

She paused for effect. "Eleanor Roosevelt said that 'no one can make you feel inferior, without your consent'."

"That's not true!" I protested, with passion.

"Yes, it is. Think about it. How can someone else *make* you think or feel or do anything?"

"Easy! They behave in a way that forces you to do it."

"How? How do they remove your power to choose?"

I didn't have an easy answer on that one.

"No one can *make* you feel angry or sad or inferior or hurt – or happy for that matter. It's the stories we tell ourselves about things that trigger off the emotions. It's why the same thing can happen to different people and they'll have totally different responses."

"But how can I feel happy when Stuart touches me up or threatens me, to make me sleep with him?"

"I'm not saying you can, Sophie, or that you should." She was edging towards me on the sofa, sensing that the wall I had thrown up between us might be ready to soften and fall. "His behaviour is completely unacceptable. But you can choose whether to spend every waking moment telling yourself stories about how awful it is, diving into that drama, giving him power over every thought you think, or you can choose to channel that energy into positive action... to do something to fix this mess. He can't *make* you sad or angry or hopeless. Yes, he can provoke you, but how you respond is and always will be your choice."

I was struggling to get my head round what she was saying and my Inner Drama Queen wasn't letting go lightly.

"I know this is a lot for you to take in, Sophie. The thing is, though, if you find a new job and you're still dancing the steps from that old dance, you'll find someone new to be your dance partner and history will repeat itself. It might look a bit different, but the music will be the same. You take yourself with you. If you want to break free from the cycle of ending up with shits like Jamie or bosses like Stuart – and Harry, who is far from blameless in this – then you have to change yourself. You'll never change them. That's what I mean when I say you take yourself with you."

"How do you know all this stuff?"

"I've been there, done it and got the t-shirt, Sophie," I looked at her, surprised, "I'm living, walking proof that you can come out the other side."

We paused to make a cup of tea – that classic British 'fix-everything'.

"But, Jem, this is all well and good, but I'm about to be made homeless and I need a new job."

"I know. But that's storytime again. Can't you see it? 'I'm about be made homeless'; that's quite a strong victim-theme, don't you think?"

"But I am!"

"There you go, defending your side of the dance. Life is happening *to* you. You're giving circumstances outside of your control the power over how you feel. You are not about to be made homeless. Yes, it's rubbish that your landlord is selling your flat, but you have somewhere else to live – Anna's place.

And, in an emergency, you could commute from your parents' place. It's not that far out of London. It might not be what you want, but you're not about to be made homeless. That's your Drama Queen talking."

I slammed her tea down with a fury that spilled half its contents over the worktop. The hot, milky brown liquid dribbled over the edge and down the front of the cupboard.

"Aren't you going to do something about that, Sophie?" she asked me, not moving a muscle to help me, "or are you going to tell me I *made* you spill your tea?"

I seethed silently, as I grabbed a tea towel and wiped up the mess. She watched.

"Had I jogged your elbow, then you could claim I *made* you spill the tea. I didn't. I spoke to you. Your anger made you spill the tea. And your anger was your choice, not mine."

My jaw was clenched tightly. I didn't want to hear any more of this. I wanted to push her away.

I headed back to the sofa and put what was left of my tea on my coffee table. My head was swimming.

"So basically it's all my fault?" I asked petulantly.

"You know that's not what I'm saying, Sophie." There was no chance of getting a rise out of her. "I'm just suggesting you take a bit more responsibility for how you feel – how you react – with all the stuff that's going on around you. You've got so stuck in the worry and the drama of the stories in your head that you've used up all of your energy. There's nothing left for taking the actions that could actually fix things."

I sipped my tea. I didn't have any more to say. I needed to let this stuff to sink in. It was all so new: such a different way of looking at things. I wasn't sure I was convinced yet. Then I remembered, "But what about finding a new job? How can I do that when Stuart has ruined my reputation?"

"That wasn't fair of him, I agree. It's hard for you to fix on your own. But… I've got a plan."

My Inner Drama Queen tried to drown out the faint rays of hope those four words brought me.

"Think about it: why do most people move company if they're staying in the same area? Because they hate their old one or they want a promotion that isn't available where they're currently working. What are people going to be assuming about you asking for sideways moves?"

My brain had stopped working. Jem answered for me. "They will either be worried that you're just looking for another name on your CV and a bit more training, before you leave them for something more glamorous, or they'll assume you're in some kind of trouble with your current job and you have to leave. And here's the rub: recruiting managers know that new employees bring themselves with them. If you hate your current job, you'll end up hating them soon enough. If you're bored where you're currently working, you'll be bored working for them at some point too. If you're not getting on with your current colleagues, chances are you'll find that with your new company as well."

I could see her point. "But how do I fix it, Jem?" I was clueless. "I'm not good enough even to get sideways moves. How can I possibly go for promotions?"

"Didn't you say that Lucy was grooming you for a job-share promotion?"

"Yes, but…"

"No 'but'. You are ready to become a Planner for an agency. Sure, it'll be a stretch, but you can do it. You're qualified and you have experience that proves you can do it. I can help you with your confidence. And there are three extra advantages of approaching it this way."

"Really? I'm not seeing any." I could feel my bottom lip

trying to stick out in a childish pout.

"One: you'll get a pay rise that means you'll be more likely to find a flat you like with a bigger budget, and your referencing will be easier. You'll be able to prove you can afford the rent more easily."

I nodded.

"Two: they will stop worrying about why you're leaving. Tell them how much you love working with Lucy and the opportunities she has given you to stretch yourself, but that she's not leaving any time soon and there is no way you can be promoted to Planner while she's still there. So – very reluctantly – you're having to leave. Don't mention Stuart or Harry, or maternity leave cover. Tell them your boss is a good friend and you don't want to do anything to jeopardise her role or the company, so you're leaving to be able to stretch yourself to the next level. Your current firm doesn't have those opportunities. Tell them Lucy knows you want a promotion and fully supports you in leaving to achieve it."

Genius. This might just work. "And the third advantage?"

"This one's my favourite!" Jem looked excited. It was contagious. Hope was threatening to win. "Stuart can't see beyond his own nose." I was looking confused again. "He has been sabotaging your interviews, yes?" I nodded in confirmation. "But he's busy. So he will have been looking through the same magazines as you to see who is interviewing for jobs at your level. Yes? A quick phone call here, an email there?" I nodded again, still confused. "He probably thinks he's done such a good job on destroying your confidence that there's no way you'd be going for Senior Researcher jobs, let alone applying for Planner positions?"

I suddenly thought I could see where she was heading on this.

"So, that's your answer. He can't have sabotaged *all* of your chances for promotion because there are only so many people he can bad-mouth you to. And he'll be concentrating on the sideways moves he expects you to go for; he will have considered sabotaging promotions as a waste of his time. Apply for promotions and you'll get a fair crack at the interviews."

I was about to smile when suddenly I felt totally overwhelmed. "But how on earth am I going to manage all of this, as well as pack and move house and keep up with my current job?"

"Ah," Jem smiled, knowingly, "that's where your fairy godmother comes in. I've decided I'm not going to stay with Julio, after all," *Who on earth is Julio? I can't keep up with Jem's love life.* "I'm moving in with you for the next two weeks. I'll do everything I can to help, to make sure you're all sorted before you have to move. And to make sure that you don't 'take yourself with you' into your new job. I'm going to support you."

"But, Jem, I don't know what to say!"

"Say nothing. It's happening. But you can sleep on the sofa. I'll take your room. I love you, but I love my back too."

She kissed my forehead as she gave me a bear hug and, for the first time since December, I finally dared to hope that things might work out.

38. Pietro's Secret

I still haven't sold the harvest that is only a few short weeks from ripening. Pietro doesn't need to give me *the look* to let me know how disappointed he is in me. I feel it in myself, too. Dad always had a small group of buyers who took a portion of the harvest, year after year. Occasionally one might drop out, but it was easy enough to replace them. We have a great reputation for quality, flavour and reliability and Dad could always find someone in his network who knew someone, who knew someone. But this year something has gone really wrong. All three of last year's buyers have backed out, with no explanation. They won't return my calls.

I can't understand why, and they won't talk to me about it. It doesn't make sense. They were old friends of Dad's, having bought at least some of our harvest nearly every year for at least the past decade.

Fewer than four weeks until we start picking the first harvest and I still don't have anywhere to send 100 tons of fruit this summer. Not many people will want to take on that kind of surplus and do something useful with it, before it rots. If I can't find a buyer, the farm will go bust.

It's my fault, in part. I had assumed that the buyers would carry on with business as usual, despite Dad being gone. I didn't chase them when the orders hadn't arrived by January. It slipped off the table. Had I done so, I'd have had an extra four months to find a buyer and we wouldn't be having a panic now. Pietro made sure to remind me of this.

I had a long talk with Pietro about it last week and he doesn't know why our usual buyers backed out, either. They are running from something and won't talk to us. There aren't even any rumours to pick up on.

"But surely you could have pointed this out months ago, Pietro?" I tried to defend myself. After all, he would have known they should have placed orders by now. I could have guessed it, but this was my first year of doing this and I hadn't known what the process was.

"Not my job, Christof, remember?" The gleam in his eyes showed he was pleased to have caught me out, even though my mistake could cost him his job and Nonna her home. "You make the decisions. I carry them out."

I could tell he was still bitter that I am – as he sees it – having fun in Milan while they all work hard on the farm, underappreciated, earning money to pay for my profits. I know that's not how it is, but I can't pretend that the dynamic hasn't changed, now that the farm owner isn't mucking in with the hard work, there for them to see, each and every day.

So we have made a decision. As I discussed with Luca, I'm going to take a week off work at the start of June and go to the annual cherry festival in our neighbouring town, hoping to meet with buyers who will take at least some of the crop off our hands. The rest we will process into products we can sell at markets and to department store deli counters, via our distributors, over the rest of the year. It's much more labour-intensive, but it brings a good profit. And we have to be realistic – showing up at the cherry festival, looking for a buyer for the entire crop, at this late stage of the year, makes us look desperate. We're not going to get the best price.

Then yesterday I received the letter I had been dreading: the final demand from the bank, threatening to foreclose on the loan. I knew what it would say even before I opened it. I had managed to find the funds to restart the repayments, but I hadn't been able to address the arrears or the penalty fees. They have given us five working days to cover the backlog of payments or they will begin official proceedings to repossess the farm, forcing a sale by auction to clear our debt. I feel sick every time I think about it. I didn't sleep much last night, tossing and turning in the bed I have slept in since I was a teenager, in the room that has been mine since soon after I was born, in the house that has been in the family for generations, which we could lose before the summer's crop has ripened.

The farm's financial future is precarious, but I have decided I need to do the one thing I have left, to buy us more time – raid the *tredicesima* account. We put aside one-twelfth of the wage payment into it each month, to make sure we have enough cash for the Christmas bonus payments. There are funds in there that would help us to clear the €40,000 in late payments, if I empty pretty much all our other accounts as well, but that leaves us with no cash reserves. And it means I can't leave the cherry festival without a hefty down payment or I won't be paying the June wages or invoices. But it's the only way I can see of doing it. And not having sold this year's crop means I have no guarantee that I'll be able to top up the *tredicesima* account in time for December. Having defaulted already on such a large loan this year there is no way any bank would give us the funds to cover it. It's a really high-risk strategy, but it's the only one I have left. So I'm taking the day off work on Monday – Luca isn't impressed – to go to the bank and arrange it.

And it would give me time to keep my promise to myself

and have it out with Pietro. That was why I came to the farm today, though I told Nonna it was because I wanted to spend the weekend here, before sorting some stuff out at the bank on Monday.

I got confirmation last week of something I really didn't want to know – something I find hard to believe – that the payment of the €200,000 went into Pietro's bank account. He's been lying to me. I can't think why he would have done this. I feel so angry with him. I have been through every emotion in the few days since I found out. It was such a shock. He has betrayed me – Nonna – the farm. And he has lied to my face. I need to know the truth. I'm sure he knows more than he is telling me about the emptying of the emergency account too. I can't allow him to clam up again. This is too serious. So I have asked him for a formal meeting this afternoon and I'm not letting him leave until he has told me. I hate the thought of having to be tough with him. I have looked up to him as an uncle for as long as I can remember, but I need to know everything he knows, or we'll all lose the farm. It is taking every ounce of self-restraint I have not to rage accusations at him. I know him too well to think that would ever work.

I had agreed to meet Pietro at 3 p.m. The deadline came and went and there was no sign of him, just as I had expected. He knew what I wanted to talk about, so he was bound to get caught up with some convenient crisis to avoid our meeting. I headed out to find him and, sure enough, he was up to his elbows in oil and grease, repairing some machinery that couldn't possibly wait until later.

He heard me approach and rubbed his hands on an oily rag, looking up from his work and making it clear that a 'real' farmer would be helping him, instead of wearing clean jeans and a white shirt. But that wasn't how I wanted to run things. There was no need for me to pretend to be Dad any more and, since I had found out the mess he has left us in, my level of hero-worshipping has subsided.

"Our meeting?" I asked.

"Emergency," he pointed at the engine.

"This can't wait."

"Nor can this."

Which one of us would blink first? I decided to bring the meeting to the farm manager.

"Fine. You can do it while we talk."

He was stumped. He couldn't reasonably object.

"I'd like you to start by telling me what's going on, Pietro." A nice open question that would help me, I hoped, to get to the bottom of his sulks and his petulance. I could guess some of it, but I wanted to hear it in his own words. By letting him vent at me first, he would hopefully have his anger out of his system by the time I pushed him for the truth on the loan.

He was silent, scowling. Jaw clenched. "I mean it, Pietro. This is a formal meeting and I want to hear what you have to say." He sighed loudly, as though I were a child who was irritating him when he would rather be concentrating on what he needed to do. Then the floodgates opened.

"We've had enough of you in your ivory tower, living like a prince up in the city while we work our fingers to the bones so that you can walk away with the profits. And you're greedy, too. Don't you realise that changing our suppliers to the big names has put local businesses in danger? All so you can save a few euros? That's not how we do things round here."

So that was our starting point. I waited, giving him time to say more, if he needed to.

"It's not how this farm should be running. You should be

here, with us, helping. It's not fair. Your dad would never have done it this way." He was using precisely the attack I had thought he would. I waited again. But this time he had finished. He was hammering a component on the engine with a ferocity I was quite sure it wasn't designed to take. I got a sense he wished it were my head.

"Pietro, firstly, I don't live like a prince, and I haven't taken a penny out of the farm so far. My life is fully funded by my job in Milan, not by the farm-workers."

The hammering didn't slow. He knew this was the truth, but it wasn't the story he wanted to tell himself.

"Secondly, Dad is dead. And the way he was running things wasn't working. That's why we were making a loss most months. We were squandering money on overpriced contracts with so-called friends who were ripping us off, and the farm wasn't earning enough to pay the bills. Things have to change. If suppliers in town were giving him a bad deal, then *they* were the ones profiting from the farm-workers' hard efforts, not me. Each supplier was given the chance to submit a competitive quote and some did, but most didn't. We are running a business, not a charity. I stuck by the terms of the contracts when I gave notice, where they existed. Cutting our costs is the only way we will survive. I had to reduce our expenses to keep the farm, so you and everyone else could keep your job. That was my priority: keeping everyone in a job. I've managed to cut our monthly outgoings by a third, without making anyone redundant. Personally, I think that's a good thing."

The hammering was getting harder. Heaven knew what kinds of stories Pietro had been sharing with his friends at the local bars. There was no way he would want to give up the sympathy his complaints were bringing him. Whiffs of 1950s communism still linger amongst the 'oppressed workers', as they still saw themselves, forgetting that they were fairly paid, had decent working conditions and got their *tredicesima* bonus each December.

"Thirdly, I am not moving back to the farm. I never wanted to be a full-time farmer. That is why I asked you to hire someone to do the heavy-work stuff Dad used to do, so you're supported. It's not my fault that you haven't done that yet. You've had all winter."

The hammering stopped, but not because peace was in the air – quite the reverse. I saw wisps of white rage floating around Pietro. He stood as still as a stone carving, trying to control his temper. I decided that now was the time to strike.

"Pietro, I have a question I need to ask you." He didn't respond. His knuckles were white on the shaft of the hammer.

"Where are the letters from the bank where Dad took out the loan? Why weren't they in the pile? This is really important." Still nothing. "Remember that loan I told you about? The one you said you hadn't heard of?" I waited for some indication that he was listening. If anything he looked even more tense. "Do you know what happened this week?"

At last, he shook his head – a tiny movement, but it was there.

"They have been writing to Dad for nearly a year now, telling him he was defaulting on the monthly payments for the loan. The loan was for €200,000 and there's a further €100,000 missing from the emergency account. This isn't a game. As you know, I only found out about this a few weeks ago. I haven't been able to find the money to cover the missing instalments and this week they wrote to *me* – at *my* home in Milan – telling me they are foreclosing the loan, if we don't pay immediately. That means they would own the farm and would sell it off to the highest bidder at auction. Given that we haven't sold this year's harvest and our regular buyers have backed out, that price wouldn't be high. After costs, there won't be much left to pay off the workers. They will all lose their jobs and Nonna will be homeless."

I paused to let this sink in, before asking the question that I was trusting would start to unlock this mystery. "Did you know about the letters, Pietro?"

He gave a nod so small I wondered if I had imagined it. Then I watched the colour drain from his face.

"Please tell me, Pietro. Everything."

In a voice almost too quiet to hear mumbled, "I burned the letters."

No! This wasn't what I wanted to hear. I had been hoping to be able to fall back on the bank not having informed us of the debt following Dad's death, so we could buy more time.

"Why?" I tried to stay calm. Losing my temper with him would just make him clam up again. For what felt like a very long time, he said nothing. It was probably only a minute, but I wished I could squeeze the truth out of him, like water from a wet towel. I slowed my breathing, to try to stay calm. I needed to think clearly.

"I didn't want you to know. I thought it would be okay."

I wanted to scream at him. In what way would it suddenly be okay? Having a massive debt and not making the payments and hiding the warning letters, as though any bank would ever let this go away? I knew he must have been really stressed to have done this and I needed to know why. He must be involved at some level, to have wanted to hide the trail from me. I knew the funds went to his bank account, but I strongly suspected that was not where they had stopped.

"Tell me everything, Pietro. Please." I used as soft a voice as I could, knowing this must be hard for him, but also wanting to strangle the answers out of him. "Come over here, please. Sit with me. I need to know everything, no matter what it is."

Slowly, methodically, Pietro put down the hammer and moved over to the grassy bank I was standing on. I sat down and waited for him to follow. He didn't. He stood near me. I was looking up at him like a schoolchild to his teacher in morning assembly. I didn't care. If this was what it took to get to the truth, I would do it.

He stood still, shoulders hunched, staring at his feet, looking twenty years older than he did before Dad died. It hit me. What a self-obsessed idiot I have been! Dad was Pietro's best friend. They were like brothers. They worked together every single day, for most of their adult lives. He will have been missing him as much as I have been. He has had to cope with this change, too. I suddenly felt selfish. Guilty again – a new bucket of the stuff to swim in. I realised in that moment that so much of Pietro's anger and aggression towards me had been his way of coping with the grief of our mutual loss, and the stress of the extra responsibility.

I let this realisation soften me a little and it seemed to help. Pietro started to talk.

"About two years ago, your dad and I were talking about how risky it was to have the business dependent solely on the cherry harvest. One of our buyers for the crop had threatened to pull out and tried to negotiate a bad price. Your dad managed to find a compromise, but it still hit us hard." I nodded, remembering what the accounts had looked like that year, glad to now understand why.

"He was looking for other ways to bring in money, so we could be more independent of the harvest. Supermarkets were changing the way crops were sold. A farmer could lose everything overnight if a buyer in the city changed their mind. The contracts were harsh. We could see the industry changing and we couldn't keep up. We weren't big enough to automate. Our farm is still too labour-intensive and we were getting uncompetitive."

I felt relieved that Dad had seen this too. It was one of my big worries. In fact, it was one of the reasons I was looking into getting certified as organic – so we could command a permanent premium for our crop. We grow organically anyway, but certification is an enormous amount of paperwork. The annual fees are high, but it would open new doors to us, especially in export markets. Everyone round here *grows* organically, but few can prove it to consumers.

"I told your Dad about my cousin's business idea. Francesco wanted to set up a shop in town, selling hardware: tools and stuff." He looked at me, as though hoping for approval. I nodded, hoping he would take it as encouragement to continue, even though I had now guessed where the money went. Although how his cousin expected to make a profit with a town-centre hardware store when most people buy at the out-of-town warehouses, I didn't know. "He needed to buy premises. He didn't want to risk a landlord putting up the rents once he was successful. You know how it is," I nodded. "He wanted to own the shop and have a flat above it. And he needed to get stock in and do the place up and start advertising."

"But he didn't have any capital?"

"That's right."

"So Dad went in as a business partner?"

Pietro shook his head, almost making eye contact with me. I was confused. "Not quite. He was a silent partner. He didn't want anyone to know he was involved, in case our harvest buyers thought he was going to ditch the farm. Or in case locals thought he was drowning in cash and our suppliers raised their prices yet again."

At last, Pietro was admitting that our local suppliers had been screwing us. But that was a conversation for another time.

"So it all went through you?" I asked, already knowing the answer.

He stared at his boots again, scuffing the dry earth beneath him with the toe of his left foot, as though it might hold answers, or a means of escape.

"Yes."

"The loan money was paid into your account?"

The 'yes' was almost inaudible, but it was there. I knew already, but he didn't need to know that.

"It bought the premises." That sounded about right. If they wanted a place that needed doing up they could have got somewhere small for that in the town, especially if it was somewhere that hadn't sold for a while. There were so many old properties either boarded up or with whitewashed windows, owned by families who argued about how to split it up when someone died, or just left empty because everyone knew how hard it could be nowadays to run a business in a small farming town.

"And the money from the emergency funds account?"

The slightest nod confirmed this, too. "Payments to suppliers, for stock, and renovations."

"And where is the money now?" I was really not sure I wanted the answer to this question. The likelihood of a small hardware shop in a farming town making enough profit to service a €4,000 per month loan was very low. Pietro didn't answer. I tried another angle. "Was there a business plan?"

Pietro shook his head. Of course not. That wasn't the way it would have been done round here. That kind of thing is for us city whizz kids who prefer talking to action.

"A contract?" I had already guessed the answer on this one.

No, there wasn't. More head-shaking confirmed this.

"So we can't prove that Dad invested €300,000 in the project?"

My heart sank as though it were made of lead. Pietro's silence confirmed my suspicions. After a long pause, he explained, "Your dad didn't want people to know he was involved, as I said. Francesco never asked where the money came from. He knew it was legit. He dealt with me. He was my cousin. We shook hands on it."

"So, no contract, no formal agreement, no evidence?"

Pietro's continued silence confirmed this. He was expecting me to explode. It took restraint not to. But I needed the rest of the story if I was going to have any chance of fixing this, so I kept quiet and waited.

"Francesco agreed he would make the monthly repayments. We would get half of the profits the shop made."

Well, that would explain why there was no trace of the first two monthly repayments in any of Dad's bank accounts. "All based on handshakes?" Pietro nodded. He knew as well as I did how stupid that had been, now it had all gone wrong. "Did anyone ever talk about what would happen if the business didn't work? If the loan wasn't repaid?" He shook his head. Of course not. Pietro would have trusted his cousin completely. "And where is he now? How much profit is the shop making?"

Pietro's cheeks flushed: a rare display of emotion from this man-of-the-earth.

"He's gone. My aunt – his mother – doesn't know where. The shop never opened."

He looked like he might cry. This bulk of a man was shaking silently. I felt for him. I really did. But he had kept this from me for so long that it was now a disaster, and the chances of us getting any of this money back were much lower than they would have been just after Dad died, now the shop project had been abandoned.

The situation was desperate. Pietro's cousin's name would be on the deeds. There was no written record of Pietro or Dad giving him a loan. And now he had run away. Who knew what state the building might be in and, under law, it belonged to Frencesco. We could lose the farm so that a virtual stranger could indulge a business idea and then disappear when things didn't work out. How could Dad have been so stupid? But I knew the answer to that question. He was trying to protect us, to give the farm a future. And he trusted Pietro.

Pietro didn't move as I tried to get my head round what to do next, whether there might be any way to fix this. The birds sang in the background and the cherry tree leaves rustled around me in the breeze, warmed by the spring sun. But I didn't care. It felt like I was going to lose everything and have to auction off the farm, or have to sell my flat in Milan to cover the debt and move back to the farm, which was another way of losing everything.

Then, out of the blue, a thought struck me: this was the proof I needed! There might not be any contract, but Pietro's cousin had made the first two repayments on the loan. He must, at some level, have been taking responsibility for the loan if he covered the first two instalments. And that was done before Dad died, so he couldn't say it was in sympathy for our loss. I could find the evidence I needed.

I mentally went through the steps I would take if I had to do this for work. I knew I could do it. I needed to take legal advice and I might need Court Orders, but there was a glimmer of hope. I might be able to prove that Dad gave Pietro's cousin the money – that the shop belongs to us – and then it could be sold, to cover at least some of the debt. But it would be better if I tackled this from both directions at once: the official route and the family pride path. I needed to get Pietro's cousin to admit this. Proving it through the Courts could cost more than the loan. Somehow, I needed to get Pietro's cousin to sign a statement, in front of a lawyer, but the fact that he had already done a runner meant he wasn't likely to want to own up to the debt. And I had to find him, because we couldn't sell the shop without him, and I had no idea how many months that could take – or how much time it would eat up. I could hear Luca's complaints already. But at least I now had a trail to follow. I had somewhere to start. I had hope again.

Pietro's shuffling increased, as though he were desperate to end this discussion. But I needed one more piece of information from him. I grew up round here. I knew how things worked. And sometimes the indirect approach works best. I had an idea I needed to test out.

"Thank you for telling me all of this, Pietro." His face risked a glimmer of relief.

"So you're not going to fire me?"

Was that what he was expecting? Actually, it wouldn't be unreasonable. "I'm not going to fire you, but I need you to help me to fix this, please."

He nodded slowly, reluctantly, in confirmation.

"Tell me. Your cousin … was he living with his mother?"

Pietro looked confused, but confirmed that he was.

"When can we go and see her?"

39. The *How* Will Come

J em was true to her word. After popping back to her apartment to grab some things, she was back at my place by lunchtime on Sunday, well and truly 'installed'. My head was still swimming with everything we had discussed. It really helped to have her around.

"You take yourself with you." I made a decision last night. I'm not taking this version of me with me, wherever I end up working next. She's not happy. She's unfit and overweight. She doubts herself. She lets people like Stuart freak her out and destroy her confidence. She doesn't believe she's good enough. She's tempted to get back together with Jamie. None of that is who I really am – or who I want to be. I'm just not clear on the 'how' yet.

"Don't worry, Sophie," Jem reassured me, when I asked her about it. "The *how* will come."

Once I started seeing the games I had been playing, it was all too tempting to beat myself up, making everything worse. How did I let Stuart get to me that much? How did I manage to get so stuck in feeling like a victim? Why did I let Stuart and Harry demote me? Why didn't I stick up for myself?

Jem's advice was to treat myself with love, as though I'd just had open-heart surgery, which about how massive these changes were, according to her. But it was hard to treat myself

with love when my Inner Drama Queen had been treating me
with self-loathing for so many years.

That, apparently, is where the yoga and mindfulness come
in. Jem has had me practising mindful breathing several times a
day, for ten minutes at a time. It was really hard to concentrate. I
hadn't realised how much my mind flitters and flutters, like a
butterfly on a caffeine high. She has made me a recording to keep
on my phone, complete with some kind of bell chiming every
minute or so, to remind me to bring my focus back to my
breathing instead of feeding stress thoughts. It's really hard to sit
still and I had never noticed how much I think – or the kinds of
things I have been thinking. Jem has promised me she'll teach
me techniques to let my thoughts 'drift on through like passing
clouds' over the next couple of weeks. Apparently there are ways
to slow them down and even turn down the volume. I'm curious,
but I'm not convinced yet. Either way, the sessions are helping
already. Whenever I find myself diving into drama stories in my
head, a couple of minutes of the breathing really help me to get
grounded again.

Tonight was our first yoga class. It was with a lovely lady
called Simone, someone Jem has known for years. I didn't know
that Jem was into this kind of stuff. She has arranged for us to go
to Simone's house each evening this week for a private yoga
lesson. 'Yoga intensive therapy' Jem called it. I'm massively
grateful to her. The thought of donning Lycra to wiggle my
wobbly bits in a room full of elastic-band-bendy magazine cover
women contorting their legs into pretzels didn't appeal. That's
why Simone was such a shock.

She's short, size 14 and definitely endowed with wobbly
bits. I relaxed the very moment I met her. There was something
so reassuring about her. I didn't feel the need to impress her. I
didn't feel her judging me in any way.

She started us off with some gentle stretches, dancing to music. It felt like an aerobics class for the energetically challenged, but I loved the sensation of movement in my tired and stiff muscles. It has been too long since I moved my body. Then we did some warm-ups, ready for the postures – *asanas* she called them – we were going to do this evening. She said she wanted to keep it easy for me, but to get the most from it, I needed to focus on being present, right here in my body, rather than allow myself to be distracted by my mind. Easier said than done.

I've played with yoga a few times in the past, but this was different. Her movements were flowing. She told me not to lock my knees or my shoulders. The way we got into the posture and out of it was as important as the posture itself, she said. It took all of my concentration not to wobble and crash into her wooden Buddha as she got me moving my arms and legs in a flowing sequence for her version of the Tree posture. It was a far cry from the locked knee, foot in the groin and hands reaching for the sky that I remembered from past yoga classes. At first, I found it surprisingly difficult. There was so much to focus on. But after a few rounds, I found myself 'landing', getting into the flow of it. I could sense the strength in my supporting leg. I could feel the movement flowing up through my body. I could almost imagine being a wise, old tree, blown by the wind, yet flexible enough not to be snapped in two by a storm.

Then she taught us the Flowing Cat, to help me bring gentle movement back in my spine. She got me down on my hands and knees, trying to let my spine to move like a wave. At first my spine acted like a solid lump, but after a few rounds I was able to move some of the vertebrae independently. Then we did a similar movement, but in the Flowing Bridge, lying on our backs. She said it will help me to be more flexible in life. I'll wait and see on that one.

Our final posture was the Seated Spinal Twist, which she said would help us to digest and absorb the experiences that happen to us in life. I wasn't totally won over yet, but I had to admit it did feel good afterwards. Despite all the movements being slow and intentional, my body felt like it had worked hard and I was feeling much less stressed.

My favourite part of the evening came at the end with a wonderful deep relaxation. We were wrapped up in thick cotton blankets, supported by cushions and bolsters, and Simone talked us through how to tense each muscle in turn and then relax them in a specific order, to release tension and recharge our batteries. I could do that all day, every day.

She finished our session off with some mindful breathing. It was like the stuff I'd been doing with Jem, but instead of running from my thoughts, she got me turning to face them, to watch them, as a silent observer, without the need to dive into their drama. It was really hard, but it was easier after the relaxation. It helped me to see how all the stress and tension and worry of the past few months (make that years) has fed the thoughts that were making me feel bad. It is all a bit overwhelming at the moment, but Simone said that later this week she'll teach me how to press 'pause' on those thoughts.

I got home feeling tired, in a good way, for the first time in ages. I snuggled up on my sofa, with Jem in my bedroom, and realised I was looking forward to tomorrow night's class already.

40. Out Of Options

It was such a relief to finally know the truth; I was grateful to Pietro for telling me, at last, though I wished he had told me when I first asked him. At least this way I would have some positive news to report to the bank now.

I didn't see any more of Pietro at the weekend and it was good to get to spend time with Nonna, without the usual bustle around us. She knew something was wrong, but I didn't want to worry her, not before I had the answers. I didn't want her feeling stressed. I had to admit though, that I hated hiding all of this from her.

First I met with our Bank Manager. I must have checked my sums ten times to make sure I wasn't kidding myself. If we emptied the *tredicesima* account and took out most of our other surpluses, I could pull together enough money to cover the backlog on the loan, plus this coming month's payment. That would leave me with enough cash for the May wages bill and that was it. After that, we would empty. June's wages would be relying on me getting some of our overdue invoices paid *and* getting a good deal at the cherry festival.

However, we wouldn't have any money to pay the farm team or our suppliers in July, unless I could get an advance payment on this year's crop. In other words, I have to find a buyer, which we don't currently have.

The Bank Manager was relieved that we weren't going to lose the farm – yet – but he could see how big a risk I was taking today.

"Are you sure there's no other option, Christof?" he asked me, as he prepared the paperwork for the confirmation of the electronic funds transfer for me to take to my next meeting.

"I wish there were. I don't like emptying our accounts like this, but I am grateful that doing so will be enough – for now."

"And how certain are you that you'll find a buyer at the cherry festival?"

"I have to be certain. Otherwise I might as well give up."

"But you need a back-up plan, Christof, in case you can't sell the fresh crop and have to wait for department stores to pay you for your cherry products. They might not do that until next year."

I nodded, not wanting to comment. My fallback plan was to see what we could sell – equipment, maybe even land – to tide us over. But it wasn't one I wanted to think about and it wouldn't bring us enough to keep us going until the end of the year. Any crop we could sell at local markets might help towards the wages bill, but it wouldn't enough to run a farm. It's not really not an option.

He shook my hand and wished me well, saying that he hoped the next time he saw me the first payment for this season's crop would be making us solvent again. And he warned me that the bank wouldn't be able to give us an overdraft. That didn't surprise me. Our credit rating had been trashed by the unpaid debt.

My meeting with the other bank's Debt Manager was much less friendly. His beady eyes looked almost disappointed as I handed him the proof of payment and assured him that the next instalment would be covered by the end of the week, when it fell due. Had he hoped to see me grovel? Was he secretly looking forward to foreclosing the loan and taking our farm off us? I wondered from the look on his face whether he might have been.

I gave him the news that we had found where the money went. He looked surprised. He said he knew the family concerned – and even the shop involved. He told me where to find it and I decided to go past it on my way back to Milan. Knowing that I owned it – morally, even if not legally – I felt a strong interest in it.

We parted on civilised terms, but he warned me that if we defaulted again, even for just one month, we would risk instant foreclosure and that the security against the loan was still the farm, not the shop.

I'm loving how everyone I meet today is reminding me about the worst that could happen. I want to be celebrating, having found a way to pay the overdue debt, keep the farm and keep everyone in their jobs, but the banks just want me to be miserable and stressed. I guess they've seen it happen too often: someone starts feeling more positive and they slack off on finding solutions until it all goes disastrously wrong again. They don't know me. I won't let that happen.

Pietro was visiting his cousin's mother this afternoon. Francesco was missing – *allegedly* – but Pietro hoped to persuade his *mamma*, Marisa, to talk some sense into him. I was reluctant to agree to Pietro doing it on his own, but I could see how having a stranger – an outsider, despite being born and growing up here – at the meeting could make it harder for him to talk her round. So I walked past the shop on my way back to the car, before heading back to Milan.

It was every bit as run-down as I had imagined. I could well understand why it had been such a bargain, why no one else had wanted to buy it. It must have been someone's inheritance from the look of how long it has been neglected. I peered through the dusty windows and I could see some evidence of work having been done: the ground floor windows had been replaced.

As I looked at the new glass I became aware of a reflection of someone on the other side of the road, standing, watching me. I looked at them in the window for a few moments. They didn't move. My inner radar kicked off. There was something about his bulky frame and the baseball cap he was wearing that felt out of place. My heart started to speed up. "Watch your back!" Luca had said. I turned round to confront the stranger, to show I wasn't scared.

There was no one there. I looked up and down the street. It was empty. I could hear my heart thumping my ribs like a bongo drum. I took a deep breath. It must have been my imagination. But that was a crazily detailed trick for it to be playing on me. Was I being paranoid again?

To help calm myself down again I turned my attention back to the shop. It was a four-storey building in a row of similar properties, many of which were boarded up, but some of which were optimistically trading, trying to sell fruit and vegetables and tobacco to non-existent customers. I wondered where the €50,000 of stock had gone.

I couldn't understand how Francesco had thought he would make a profit here. The property would work much better as rental flats than a shop. Had it been a beer-inspired venture one weekend, with the sun shining and Dad all too willing to help the family of his closest friend?

I debated putting a note through the door, to ask Francesco to contact me, but I knew it won't work. It might work in Milan, in the business world, but not here, in the rural farming community. Best to let Pietro start the process off and hope he made progress.

In the meantime, I was going follow this up with the systems we use at work, to see what I could trace, what evidence I could collect. I had arranged a meeting with a lawyer in the city later this week, to find out what my legal rights were, both if Francesco was helpful and if he wasn't. Being practical about it helped me to stay calm. It was the only thing that did.

41. Two Gifts From Jamie

I walked out of the office today to find Jamie there waiting for me, with a sheepish grin on his face. He didn't even give me a chance to say hello or ask him what the hell he was doing there, before he thrust a gift bag into my hands.

"An apology," he muttered, looking like he might just mean it. "Well, aren't you going to open it?"

He's one of those people who has to see a person unwrap any present he gives them. It's as though he's getting more pleasure from the reassurance of his flair in choosing a gift you like, rather than joy at the recipient being happy. For him, giving is an ego thing.

I opened the bag. Its rope handles were tied together with a red ribbon. Inside was a sea of scrunched-up tissue paper, creamy white, and nestling in the bottom was a plastic tray, with a cellophane lid. It stopped me in my tracks. This was perhaps the first and only kind thing Jamie had ever done for me.

"Well?" he asked, craving reassurance, like a young boy whose parent was reading his end-of-term school report.

I lifted out the package, to make sure it was what I thought it was. 300 grammes of the royalty of early spring cherries – the Turkish ones – the first of the season, purple-black, insanely sweet and dripping in juice.

I smiled at him. "Thank you. That was kind of you."

His face relaxed with relief.

Cherries are my absolute favourite thing ever. I get so excited the first time they arrive back on the shelves each year. I've always had a 'thing' for them. It was one of those family 'received wisdom' assumptions, when I was a kid. Father Christmas brought presents. The summer holidays were rainy. Sophie loved cherries.

"Can I just check exactly what it is you're apologising for?" I asked. There was no point assuming. With Jamie, it was more likely he was apologising for not having persuaded me to lend him money, rather than for his unreasonable request or for literally eating the surplus from this month's salary by intentionally forgetting his wallet.

"I was crass. I screwed up. I want another chance, please."

The first two I could handle. But number three? I couldn't help myself with my sarcastic response. "What, exactly, do you want a second chance at, Jamie?" I asked, though I was sure I knew the answer: that getting money from me would be involved, though I was sure he wouldn't admit that... yet. He looked lost, then defiant.

"Us."

"Us?"

"Yes, us. I want *us* to have a second chance, Soph."

And with that single statement, it was as though he had wiped the mist from the mirror through which I had been seeing myself. Suddenly I could see the real me; the person behind the people-pleaser, the person who knew what she wanted, and what she didn't. The old habits that had kept me stuck, saying yes when I meant no and begging for approval, were all laid out in front of me. I felt like I was at a market stall, getting to choose which bits of me to take into the next stage of my journey, and which to leave behind, no longer wanted, not worth the price.

I found myself standing there, mentally flicking backwards through a photo album of the bad choices I have made, over the years. Jamie was in there a lot. And Harry. And Stuart. Then I went back further in time. There were plenty of photos of me trying to please my parents, my teachers, my examiners, Louise Jones and her team of bullies when I was ten, even my first boss on my paper round for the corner shop. Whenever there was a choice to be made, I would choose the option I thought they wanted me to, even if it wasn't the one I wanted – even if it didn't work.

The photos on the pages turned into mini videos, showing how things had gone. I focused on one and imagined pressing pause. It rewound to the beginning. I wanted to give the 'me' in the video a chance to do it differently, to play with what might have happened, had I chosen what I wanted instead of what I thought was expected of me. It was a scene with a teacher from school. I played the video in slow motion, making my own decision, and I was blown away by what happened. Absolutely nothing. The teacher didn't care.

Wow. I tried it again, this time with an old memory from Mum and Dad. When I made the choice I really wanted to make, I saw a row, some slamming of doors, but it soon blew over. I did what I wanted to do and it didn't really bother them. I felt a spark of excitement as I found myself flicking over page after page, rewriting those scenes with the decisions I had truly wanted. In nearly every case, it didn't matter to the other person which choice I made – at least not long term – but it mattered a lot to me. And in the few cases where they did react badly, I could see that wasn't really fair of them. It wasn't about me being callous or selfish. It was about me being true to myself and realising that it wasn't my job to make them happy.

My thinking mind knew I wasn't really changing the past,

but I could feel the difference this was making. I didn't want to let myself drown in the regrets these realisations were offering me, though. Instead, I could see myself changing and growing and becoming more of who I really am with each turn of the page, with each rewriting of history.

Then I reached today's page in the album, with Jamie standing in front of me, asking me to make a decision. An important one: to let him back in, or to tell him to leave me alone. I sensed the empty space in the pages waiting for my future choices and, in that heartbeat, I found the courage to reclaim my power, to take responsibility for those choices, instead of abdicating them to others through my old people-pleasing addiction.

I became aware of Jamie's mouth moving, realising I wasn't paying any attention to the sounds, which had a distinctly whiny tone. I knew what I had to do.

"Well, Soph?" There it went again – *So-oaf*. "What do you say?"

I looked at the cherries and felt genuine gratitude to him, for both of the gifts he had given me today.

"No, Jamie." He wasn't taking this in. He had been so sure of a yes. "I don't want us to be together again. But thank you for the cherries. Apology accepted."

I smiled and walked off, almost skipping home, aware that he was probably standing there, frozen to the spot, doing a guppy impression. His problem, not mine. I finally felt free.

42. New Beginnings

I never would have dreamed that a week of daily yoga would lead to me telling my boss to fuck off.

Stuart pushed me too far this morning, and it felt great. I know that sounds crazy, after the five months of hell he has given me, but I finally snapped. It was long overdue.

He was doing his usual Monday morning 'let's make sure Sophie feels like crap' routine, by asking me to tell him my plans for the week and then pointing out the holes in them, even though there weren't any. He needed to be right, even if it weakened the quality of the research we were doing. I could always tell it was coming because his beady eyes would narrow until they were almost closed and the corners of his mouth would twitch, as though they were attached to invisible strings that were being controlled by the rumbles of a distant earthquake. His pen would tap absent-mindedly on his desk, to make sure I knew I wasn't worthy of his full attention.

When that happened this morning, I jumped into my invisible mirror ball and let him have his say, venting his irritation on the inadequacies of my work plans and I found myself genuinely not caring. It was amazing. I've had a week to play with the technique and this was its first big test: the weekly assassinate-Sophie's-confidence meeting. Last Monday I had been too wobbly to try it, but this week I finally understood why

Jem had been so insistent.

The more I didn't react, the harder Stuart tried to get a rise out of me. At a few danger points, I found myself getting indignant, wanting to defend myself, but I let it go. I've realised how it rewards Stuart when I object, giving him the fix he is looking for. The more I let his insults and digs float on by, the more ridiculous he got. It was hard not to laugh at him. After ten minutes he finally reached the point of desperation and the insults started getting really personal. He started talking about my clothes and my appearance, starting with my fingernails.

I know they're not perfect. When I'm stressed, I bite them, but they're not that bad. So when he launched into a tirade about how no one will ever take me seriously as a research professional with 'fingernails like those', I had had enough. I stayed inside my mirror ball, but I decided to stand up for myself. I wasn't about to take advice on personal hygiene from a bloke who smells like he only showers once a week and whose teeth are so badly brushed that some of them are orange.

"You need to take more pride in your appearance, Sophie. If you ever want to get promoted, I strongly suggest you–"

"Oh just fuck off, would you?" He stopped, mouth open, ready to speak.

"I beg your pardon?" he retorted, in his best school mistress voice, "That is no way to talk to your superior!" That was the final straw. Jem had been talking to me about the difference between 'acceptance' and 'acceptable'.

"Some things you can't change, Sophie," she had explained to me the other night. "And to feel happy and at peace, you need to get to a place of acceptance about them; where you stop telling yourself stories about how awful everything is, how life happens *to* you, and how you're the victim of circumstances beyond your control."

"But what about if everything *is* crap?" I asked, not sure I wanted to 'accept' things just yet.

"That's where 'acceptable' comes in," she replied, "you can accept how things are, but it doesn't mean you can't take action to improve things. The great thing is that taking action from a place of acceptance tends to produce much better results than action from a place of resentment and 'woe is me'. You have more energy to put into it because you're not giving your power away to your discontent."

I wasn't sure I had understood what she meant at the time, but right now, I got it. I could accept that Stuart's behaviour was bad, but that didn't mean I had to be his doormat. I felt a surge of energy in my stomach area as the words he needed to hear came out, at full volume, for everyone in the office to hear.

"Look, you're not my superior." Stuart's face contorted with anger, but I was only just getting started. "You're Harry's best mate from uni. That's the only reason you're senior to me. And I won't take you putting me down any more." He was slowly turning red and his eyes were like arrow slits. "We both know I can do this job standing on my head." He was turning a nice shade of puce. He wanted to retaliate, but I didn't give him a chance. "I've had enough of you putting me down and making me look bad in front of Harry. You have broken so many laws with your behaviour."

I had to pause to breathe, which he used to butt in.

"What about your reference, Sophie? You'll never get a new job if I give you a bad one. Remember my offer?" He was trying to make me give up. I wasn't going to. I knew I was worth more than this.

"Fuck that, Stuart! And, no, I won't ever fuck you, no matter how hard you try to blackmail me into it. You repulse me." I was yelling by now. Harry's office door was open and everyone had stopped working to listen.

"I don't need a reference from you!" He looked like he wanted to explode. His whole body was quivering. Everyone was staring. I wasn't sure we had ever had entertainment like this in the office before.

"And we both know I know you've been fiddling your expenses, which is why you had to leave your last job because they caught you out. So fuck off and leave me alone!" Stuart stared at me in stunned silence as we both saw Harry standing in the doorway. He had heard every word.

I mentally picked up what remained of my dignity and walked back to my desk. "Morning, Harry! I wonder if you might have a minute for a chat later?" I couldn't stop grinning.

How did I manage to do this? Well, I knew something they didn't know. I got confirmation of my new job this morning! And Lucy had already sent over the most wonderful reference. She had heard about a Planner position on the grapevine. It hadn't been advertised yet. She had phoned the agency owner who was someone she knew well from her old job. She had told him all the reasons why she thought I would be great for the position and explained that there was no way for me to get promoted while working for Harry, without her leaving.

I had been to the interview on Friday, after an hour's pep talk from Lucy. I was reluctant to go for it, feeling really nervous, but I did the breathing stuff that the yoga teacher taught me and it worked. I really enjoyed the interview. The job sounded exciting and I liked the team I'd be working with.

As I left the interview Jeff, the agency owner, took me to one side. "I've got one more question for you, Sophie," he smiled. I tried not to feel nervous again. "I hear you're working for Stuart, over at Harry's place?" It was a question, even though he knew the answer. I nodded. "Between you and me, the guy's a total idiot. I can understand why you want to leave. Has he been giving you a hard time?"

"I couldn't possibly comment," I smiled, grateful to Jeff for giving me the chance to prove to myself that I *can* do this, after all, by giving me an interview. He sent me a text with the job offer an hour later.

I was so excited all weekend, but I didn't want to believe it until I had the offer in writing. I received the contract at 9 a.m. this morning – Jeff was keen – and I had signed it and faxed it back ten minutes later. The deal was done. By 10 a.m., after my outburst at Stuart, I was sitting in Harry's office handing in my notice. It felt so good to see the confusion on his face: that the woman he had convinced himself was useless had got a promotion to be a Planner. He asked a few tentative questions about Stuart too. I knew he had heard our row. I could see that seeds of doubt had been sown, and that was enough for me. I knew they would grow and that was enough revenge, for now.

Jeff, my new boss – oh it felt good to think about that – is flexible with when I start and my notice with Harry is just four weeks. I could almost imagine getting through that, but I was jumping-for-joy happy because I didn't have to. I've barely taken any time off this year so I've built up a massive seventeen days' leave that I'm owed. In theory, Harry has to pay me for these if I work my full notice, but I'm taking them as holiday instead. That means I leave on Thursday. I can't quite believe it!

Harry objected, but all I had to do was to point out how useless Stuart says I am and drop hints about bullying and harassment and he gave in. I could easily tie up the work I need to do for a handover by then. And I've decided to take a couple of weeks' holiday. I can't really afford it, but I need it. I'm going to give myself a week to pack and move out of the flat, then I'm going to go to Italy: to Florence for a week and then a bit of touring. I used to study Italian at evening classes and it will be fun to try it out, and to enjoy plenty of pizza and red wine.

I can't believe the difference ten days can make. It feels as though someone turned the light back on at the end of the tunnel. And I know, in my heart, it was me who found my switch.

June

First signs of harvest
Tentatively ripening
Red and purple gems

43. A Confession

P ietro visited Francesco's mother nearly two weeks ago now and we've heard nothing. I was back at the farm to prepare for the cherry festival in just over a week's time. When I pushed Pietro for more of an update he just shrugged his shoulders.

"These things take time," he replied.

But in the meantime I have had to make the June repayment on the loan, which has wiped out the farm's final reserves. If I can persuade our final two overdue customers to settle their bills then I can pay the July wages. But if not, I can't. That's how desperate things are. I wished I could make Pietro understand it, but I was asking him to stand up to an aunt who has been like a mother to him since his own mother died, twenty years ago; and to stand up to a cousin he treats like a brother, albeit a distant one. I also have to remember that Pietro was the orchestrator of this mess. To put passion into fixing it would mean admitting it existed and I could see his reluctance to do that. But we didn't have time to worry about his sensibilities.

I couldn't help thinking there must be another way. My legal research had confirmed my worst fears: unless I could get a confession from Francesco, I couldn't prove anything. The bank trails prove the money went via Pietro and I could trace them from his account to Francesco's, if Pietro would agree to that. I could also show the €200,000 had been used for the purchase of the property. But there was no way I could prove the money wasn't just a gift from Dad to Pietro after so many years of friendship. And the €100,000 for the repairs and stock was very likely to have been spent in cash, under the table.

I was sitting at our kitchen table in the farmhouse with my head in my hands and I didn't notice Nonna walking into the room. It was empty when I arrived, devoid of its usual delicious smells and bubbling pots and pans and hot ovens. Not like her. She made me jump as she walked up to me and said hello, giving my shoulders a hug and my cheek a kiss.

"We need to talk, *caro*," she said, not even asking me how I was. A quiver of panic rushed through me. Was there something wrong? Was she ill? She saw it on my face.

"Don't worry, Christof, I'm fine," she reassured me. "It's you we need to talk about."

"Me?" I was genuinely confused.

"Yes, you. What is it you haven't been telling me?"

I didn't reply. I didn't want to worry her. It was my problem. The longer I've kept everything from her, the harder it has felt to tell her.

"Nothing, I'm fine, really," I lied, hoping I was being more convincing than I felt.

She smiled, just with her eyes. It surprised me. She had her cheeky look on her face. "That's great, *carissimo*," she almost giggled, "but I'm not cooking dinner until you tell me what's wrong. And," she patted her ample backside, "I've got plenty of reserves, so if we don't eat this weekend, I'm sure I'll do better than you."

Food was the way that Nonna showed her love and support. It had been for as long as I could remember. If the farm was in crisis, she cooked. When a baby was born, she cooked. When someone was sad, she cooked. When we were celebrating, she cooked. So for her to withhold her cooking was a big deal – she meant business here. But, even so, I didn't want to talk. It had taken so much for me to confront Pietro and I've taken so much flak over the changes I've made, I couldn't risk Nonna judging me too.

She waited, patiently. I said nothing.

"How about we start with the harvest, *caro*."

I looked up at her, feeling like a rabbit being chased by a fox into its hole, wondering if the entrance would be small enough to stop it from following. But Nonna's eyes were filled with love, not anger. Suddenly I felt a need to let her in. She wasn't a fox. She was there to protect me. I let her hug me. I didn't want to cry. But I felt I needed to. I swallowed back the tears and took a deep breath.

"We don't have a buyer for the harvest, Nonna."

I studied her face for a reaction: for anger, for a rejection, but it didn't come. It was still full of love. She didn't hate me for screwing up my first summer running this place. The bit of my mind that beats me up at 3 a.m. was confused. It didn't know how to handle this.

"Okay. What else?"

"Isn't that bad enough?"

"No, *carino*, it isn't. Not bad enough for you to look the way you do. Have you used a mirror lately?"

I knew I looked washed-out, drained, with clear signs of long-term stress in my face. But I hadn't thought that others could see it too.

"We'll process them and sell them through our other channels." She was practical and calm about it.

"But you don't understand!"

"You're right, I don't. Try me."

"If we don't have a buyer, we'll lose the farm!"

"Christof, this has happened before and we have always found a way through."

"Not this time, Nonna." She raised an eyebrow at me to show me she didn't believe it could be as bad as I thought it was.

"I've had to make economies, Nonna, to help us to meet our outgoings."

"So I have heard. It's a small town." I was still looking for criticism, for that judgement, but it still wasn't there.

"Pietro said I was betraying Dad's memory by stopping doing business with his friends."

"Christof, your Dad should have done what you have done years ago. He never had much of a business head. Somehow he made it work, but there were people who took advantage. They might not like it that you've put a stop to it, but it was time."

She sat and waited, not moving, giving no indication that dinner might start any time soon. It was her way of telling me that she knew I was holding out on her. I didn't want to tell her any more, but this was a battle of wills now: my frayed nerves against her seasoned, grounded calm. And she was going to win. We both knew it.

"Nonna, Dad took out a loan for €200,000 shortly before he died, and he emptied the emergency account of €100,000 too."

She looked surprised. This was new news for her. She soon recovered her composure.

"Do you know why?"

"Yes. He was worried about the farm's future relying solely on cherries, especially with the way things were changing with supermarket contracts with his customers." She nodded sagely, showing this was something they had discussed. "So he decided to invest in a business, someone else's business, a shop in town."

Nonna looked curious now, "Whose shop?"

"It never opened. Francesco's. Pietro's cousin."

Her brow furrowed. "Marisa's son?"

"I believe so."

"Well, it's no wonder it never opened. What did your father want to go into business with *him* for?"

"Apparently he needed a loan to buy the shop and the flat above it, and to cover the renovations and the initial stock."

"Don't tell me. He's run away from his problems? It wouldn't be the first time."

I nodded.

"Where is he now?"

"Pietro went to see Marisa a couple of weeks ago and she promised to get a message to him, but we've heard nothing."

"How bad is it?"

I wasn't sure I want to tell her. She might freak out. So I stayed quiet.

"There's no dinner until you tell me."

I hesitated, but the look in her eyes made it clear she wanted the whole truth. "The deal was that he would make the repayments. He did for the first two months, but then he stopped."

I didn't want to tell her any more.

"Go on."

"Pietro was burning the demand letters from the bank." Nonna raised her eyes to the heavens. "By the time I found out about it the outstanding repayments and fines were over €40,000 and the bank demanded immediate payment. The loan was secured against the farm and the bank wanted to foreclose. This week."

I could see Nonna was trying hard to stay calm, to allow me to feel safe to tell her everything. "And now?" she asked. "Do I need to start packing?"

"I had to raid the *tredicesima* account and all our other

surpluses to cover the debt. I had enough to pay the June wages but not July, unless I can get a down payment on this summer's crop at the cherry festival."

She took this in in silence; calm, accepting, non-judgemental silence.

"Why didn't you tell me?"

My heart sank. Why didn't I tell her? Because I was the owner of the farm, it was my job to sort out this mess. I didn't want to worry her. I couldn't answer. I stared at the floor. She squeezed my hand. She wasn't angry, just sad.

"I can help you, *caro*."

"You can?"

"Of course! I've been watching this game with the harvest every year for over sixty years. Don't you think I've learned a thing or two?" I felt really stupid now. "Tell me what happened with our regular buyers."

I took her through the little I knew. She agreed it was highly unusual, but she had her sources, she said. "Give me a couple of days and I'll know more by then," she promised. "Now, back to that loan. What are we going to do about that?"

I told her about the legal advice I had taken, about how I could trace the route the funds took, but not prove what was agreed with Dad, and how we needed a sworn statement from Francesco to have a chance of saving the farm. She took it well, looking serious. But she didn't shout or get angry. I didn't know why I had thought she would.

"I know Marisa. I've known her since she moved here to marry that no-good husband of hers. It was a blessing to all when he passed on. But that son of hers inherited his father's wishful thinking when it comes to the success of his crazy plans. I've got an idea. Leave it with me."

I started to allow myself to feel relief, some hope. Maybe we could find a way through this.

"Now, is that all, *caro*?"

"Isn't that enough?" I ask. She heard my stomach rumble.

"For now, yes, it is. Shall we eat?"

44. Farewells

We did some serious partying last weekend. The team threw me a brilliant farewell bash. Neither Stuart nor Harry had been invited. Even Janet managed to come along and I saw a whole new side to her. It turned out she didn't like Stuart, either. Then Anna and the girls treated me to a spa day on Sunday, as a 'congratulations for surviving that prick' present (that's what the card said!). I'm feeling very loved.

Jem is still with me and she has been helping me to pack for the move – clearing out stuff I don't need any more and sorting out what I need to take to Anna's and what will go in storage until I find myself another flat. I couldn't have done this without her. I love her so much. There have been times when I nearly freaked out with stress, falling back into those old patterns again, but she got me right back on track. I'm pretty sure I'll keep the yoga going when I'm back from my holiday in Italy and I'm finding that the mindfulness stuff is really helping.

By the time we were done, the pile of boxes of stuff to go to charity or recycling was bigger than the pile I'll be keeping. It felt good, like letting go of the past. There was no way I would ever need my uni notebooks again or clothes I haven't worn in three years. Jem arranged for someone to collect them all. Then we spent two full days scrubbing the flat.

I had had to come clean with the landlord about the scratch

on the lounge floor, but I was surprised that he agreed to it being 'reasonable wear and tear'. The rest of the place was spotless – after some emergency repainting – so it barely looked like I had lived there. I couldn't help a few tears as I closed the door behind me for the last time. I was going to miss my flat so much. Of course, I'm grateful to Anna for letting me stay at her place, but it wouldn't be the same as having a flat of my own.

My Italy trip was booked. I was feeling so excited. I will fly into Florence and out of Bergamo. I've got a hotel room booked for Florence, but after that my time is free. It's the first time I have ever travelled abroad without every aspect of the trip tied up. It makes me a bit nervous, but I'm curious to see where it will take me.

Jem has gone back to Julio. She's still cagey when I ask about him. But she blushes. I think she's keen. It makes the gift she has given me of the past two weeks even more special.

Anna and I are getting used to each other. I still can't quite get used to not having a 'room' to go to if I want peace and quiet, but I'm sure we'll find a way to make it work.

We had dinner together this evening and Anna wanted to watch TV, so that meant I had to watch too, since we had to sit on my bed (the sofa) to see it. Anna loves travel programmes and she was excited: she had found one on the area of Italy that I was going to. They were covering a couple who were on a tour of Northern Italy. I was busy scribbling notes. I leave on Saturday, just a few days away.

The programme moved a couple of hours south of Milan, visiting a market town that didn't look particularly exciting, until the presenter mentioned the magic word – cherries. I was all ears. Apparently this town is an undiscovered gem on the cherry festival route. Cherry festivals? I never knew there were such things!

The town will host a four-day festival, celebrating all things cherry-related. And it wasn't too far off my route. I could probably make it there. And it would earn me massive brownie points for my new job. When I met with Jeff this week he had told me one of my first projects will be working for a client that wants to import an artisan brand of cherry brandy and kirsch into the UK. If I go to the festival, I can do some background work that might help with the research, giving me a head start.

"That's at the end of your holiday, isn't it, Sophie?" asked Anna, looking almost as excited as me. I was counting days on my fingers, trying to double-check if it would work out. She was one step ahead. "It is! You have to go! You can't miss your first ever cherry festival!"

She was right. It was perfect timing and too good a chance to miss. I could travel up from Florence and spend a few days somewhere in between, finishing off at the festival. Decision made.

"And look at *him*!" Anna was pointing at the TV, grinning. The presenter was interviewing a cherry farmer. I hadn't been paying attention to the screen, just listening to the sound, because I was too busy checking my calendar, trying to work out if I could fit the festival into my schedule. After all, a cherry farmer was likely to be late fifties and looking fairly haggard. I didn't need the visual to put me off going.

Then I looked up at the screen and saw him. Mid-thirties, tall, dark, chestnut-brown eyes and a smile that wobbled my knees. He looked familiar. He was gorgeous. His English was perfect with just the smallest hint of an Italian accent that made him sound so sexy! Then it hit me.

"It's Mr *Clafoutis*!" I yelled, jumping off the sofa in surprise. "I know him!"

Anna gave me a look that told me I was acting like a crazy-lady. "That's not bloody likely, is it? But yeah, he looks like half the male magazine models you've ever seen. You just want a good-looking man to make beautiful babies with! And what's with the dessert?"

I punched her in the ribs. I wasn't in the mood for men. Not for a long time. And the effect that Emma has had on Lucy has put me off babies for a long, long time to come too. I told her about the café in Paris and the really kind stranger who had given me the final slice of *clafoutis*. She was still sceptical, but I knew it was him. I'd know those eyes and that smile anywhere.

Anyway, the decision was made: I'm going to the festival. I can't wait. There's no way I could miss a chance to spend time at a festival for my favourite fruit *and* get bonus points for being super-keen with my new client when I got back. The TV slot on Italy finished and they move on to Alaskan cruises, so I mentally switched off. I had a lot to do before the weekend and it started with trying to find a hotel in the cherry festival town. Now I had made the decision, I needed to make sure I had got somewhere to stay, in case everywhere got booked up – especially after the feature on the travel show.

I was tired and luckily Anna decided to be polite and watch a film on her laptop in her room, so I could go to sleep. The past six months had left me utterly exhausted. I don't think I've ever needed a holiday as much as I need this one. I feel truly grateful for the way things have worked out.

45. Marisa's Offer

After telling Nonna the truth, I slept better than I had in a long time. Nothing had changed, except that I wasn't carrying the load on my own any more.

I went back to the farm this weekend, but I didn't get there until after Nonna had gone to bed. I could hardly contain my curiosity at what she might have sorted with Marisa, Francesco's mother, but she had refused to tell me over the phone. By the time I woke up Nonna had been up for ages. It was nearly ten. I must have been exhausted. As I walked into the kitchen and gave Nonna a morning hug she thrust an espresso into my hand.

"You look like you need this!"

It smelled divine, perfected by many decades of experimenting.

"I have news for you," she continued. "Sit, eat and listen." She pushed a plate of warm bread in front of me, with some cheeses and olives and jams. I was ravenous. I suddenly realised how little I had been eating lately, I had been so preoccupied.

"Firstly, do you remember Giovanni from the town?"

"Vaguely." I remembered him from my childhood, someone we used to bump into at the cherry festivals. I thought he and Dad would sometimes do business together.

"Well, he's agreed to take you on." I gave her my confused look. "He's going to find us a buyer for the crop. He says he's been hearing rumours – he wants to talk to you about them next week – but he doesn't think they'll stop us selling. He wouldn't tell me them over the phone. He'll want his usual commission. But if he doesn't have us a buyer for at least some of the crop by the end of the festival, then I don't know how to make pasta." I grinned. She makes the best pasta ever. "So there's nothing at all you can do until the festival. You can let that one go for now. But you know I could have set this up months ago, had you told me the trouble you were in?"

It was the closest I was going to get to a telling off. I knew she was right. It felt like taking a heavy rucksack off my back. I had been paralysed into inaction over selling the crop. I had had no idea where to start. I didn't have Dad's – or Nonna's - contacts and it would have been really hard for me to get a good deal as the 'outsider', despite being as local as I am. The thought of Giovanni helping is great. I trust Nonna on this.

"Now, Francesco, that slippery piece of–" she didn't finish the sentence, "I went to see Marisa. It wasn't easy, but between the two of us, we think we have a plan."

I looked up from my breakfast, holding my breath, hardly daring to hope.

"You're going to meet with Francesco. during the cherry festival."

Wow. That was progress, but it was also confusing. "How did you manage that? Pietro said there was no news."

"It turns out that he doesn't know how to apply leverage, *caro*. Sometimes you need to give people a bit of an incentive to help you when they have messed up."

I couldn't imagine what she has said or done to create that *leverage*. I hoped it was legal.

"How did you do it?"

"Simple! I pointed out to Marisa how many laws her son

has broken and how easy he is to find."

"Really? Even though Pietro couldn't?"

"He didn't try very hard. It only took two calls for me to confirm he is sitting pretty with his fancy woman and their two children up in her place in Piacenza."

I was genuinely in awe of Nonna and her network.

"Pietro didn't try very hard, then?" I asked.

"Not really. Marisa is a tough woman to stand up to."

"So how did you do it?"

"Let's just say I have my ways." Nonna grinned, looking proud of the power she holds in the area, earned through decades of learning how to get her own way without making enemies.

"I told Marisa to get Francesco to meet you and I offered her a deal."

For a moment I felt my insides tighten. We didn't have any money for a deal. Or time. Nonna saw the concern in my face.

"Don't worry, *caro*. Francesco will sign a statement, in front of our lawyer, agreeing to hand over the shop building and stock to you for €1, in return for us not pressing charges and releasing him from all future obligation on his debt. Marisa is over the moon. He had run away because he couldn't pay. He doesn't have a job or any other money. Now he can come back home, where he belongs. And she's hoping he might leave his fancy woman behind. Those women don't get on."

"And he has really agreed to this? She has spoken to him?"

Nonna shook her head and laughed at me. "She doesn't need to. She will just tell him that is how it will be. Trust me. It will be fine. I told her it all has to be done before the next loan repayment falls due. Sometimes you have to create a sense of urgency to get people to take action when they're reluctant. You'll need to phone our lawyer on Monday, to make sure he is up to speed on this, and then set up a meeting with him so he can draft the document before you meet Francesco."

She was looking rightly proud of herself. I gave her a huge hug.

"How can I ever thank you?"

She ruffled my hair like I was still the young boy she raised, after Mum left.

"Easy. Stop keeping secrets from me. Now, is there anything else you've not been telling me?"

The flood gates opened and I confessed how I had barely slept since taking over the farm, how I was awake all night worrying about how to keep everyone in their job and the stress of juggling it all with my work in Milan, about how Pietro resented me not being here, like Dad was, how everyone seemed to be ripping us off, how I didn't feel like I would ever be good enough to step into Dad's shoes.

"Is that all?" She was laughing, but I could feel she was taking it seriously.

"Do you want to be a farmer, Christof?"

I didn't want to answer her. I felt like I would be betraying generations of our family if I told her the truth. She looked me squarely in the eyes. She could see my answer without me needing to tell her.

"You don't have to, you know."

I held my breath. Could she possibly mean it?

"You can choose to walk away. We could sell off the orchards and just keep the house and a few acres. I wouldn't judge you. People would understand. Times change."

She was offering me freedom.

"What about the workers?"

"We would make sure we were fair by them. Some are ready to retire anyway. And we could make sure the buyer of the orchards kept the rest on, as part of the deal."

I imagined how it would feel to be free from the responsibility, from the worry, from the stress. It was so tempting.

"But, Christof, you know you don't have to do it all on your own. You don't have to carry the weight of the responsibility yourself. Your father used to lie awake at night with the same worries you have." This was a surprise. I had no idea. How did he manage to hide it from me for so many years?

"But how did he cope, Nonna? How did he do it?"

"He asked for help. He let us in. He told us how he was feeling – his worries, his fears – so we could help him to find answers."

I took my time to process this. I had held Dad on a pedestal, fed by Pietro's criticism of me, driven by his grief and love for Dad. I kept finding myself lacking, but now I could see I wasn't.

"I can see how alone you feel, Christof. It breaks my heart. It's not a surprise though. None of this was your fault, you know. Not your Dad dying. Not the mess he left the farm in. He didn't mean to. None of it. And you don't have to go through it on your own. But you do need to let us in."

I started to cry. She drew me to her and held me, stroking my hair.

"What is it you really want?"

"I love my work in Milan, but I don't want to lose the farm."

She didn't comment. She didn't try to fix me. She didn't offer solutions. She knew I needed time.

"So what's the problem?"

"I can't do it all, Nonna."

"So don't!"

"But how?"

She gave me the space I needed to let this internal drama die down before she replied.

"It's so much easier than you think, *caro*." She pulled away from me slightly, so she could look at me. "Just decide what you want and then work with us to get the support you need. I'll talk to Pietro to get him to stop hassling you. But you need to talk to us, too. You have to do this your way, not your Dad's or Pietro's, or even mine. And, from what I can see, what you're doing is working just fine. This farm's future is safe in your hands."

I squeezed her, unable to find words to express how much I loved her, right in this moment and every time she has helped me in the past. I was amazed by how good it felt to talk about what has been worrying me.

We spent the rest of the weekend together, with the key members of the farm team, drawing up our plans for the cherry festival. I finally felt supported. I wasn't alone. I could feel my shoulders starting to relax as I allowed the others to share the load I had carried since Dad died and, although it was still a bit scary, it felt great to let them in and to start to trust them.

But that calm disappeared as I drove back to Milan on Sunday evening. I had an eerie feeling that I was being followed. It was hard to tell in the dark, but it looked like the same set of headlights followed me all the way from the motorway, back into the city. The car kept its distance, never getting close enough for me to see it properly, even at junctions. I couldn't be certain, but something just didn't feel right. I lost sight of the car as I pulled into my side street.

I knew I was probably just imagining things, but I decided to talk to Luca about it this morning. After all, it was he who had warned me to watch my back.

He sat patiently, the tips of his fingers together as though holding an invisible ball in front of his chest, leaning back on his chair as I told him about everything from the feeling that someone had rearranged those papers in my apartment through to the man in the baseball cap opposite Francesco's shop, through to last night's car.

He sat in silence for a few minutes after I had spoken, thinking it over. "Here's the way I see it," he said, "if Denucci wanted you paving a new road in Naples, he'd have taken action by now. He wouldn't just be following you. You're not testifying in the Court case, so there's no need to wipe you out. Your evidence is already in. It wouldn't change anything."

I allowed him to reassure me; he was telling me what I wanted to hear. "But… I still think you need to watch your back – carefully. There's still a chance that he or one of his associates might want revenge. Someone knew where you would be the night of the stake-out and that still concerns me. So I want you to make me a promise?"

"Go on…?"

"Go and enjoy your cherry festival. Make the most of the time doing something different. Catch up with old friends. Sell your crop. But keep your eyes open; don't let your guard down. And call me – on my mobile – any time, night or day, if you notice anything suspicious. Okay?"

46. Buon viaggio!

"Get out of here!" Anna yelled, almost throwing my rucksack down the stairs outside her flat. The taxi had already been waiting for ten minutes. I grabbed the rucksack before it could fly past me. "Have a fantastic time and bring back a gorgeously eligible Italian for me!" She blew me a kiss as I closed the front door behind me. The taxi driver looked unimpressed as he tried to lift my luggage into the boot, as though considering demanding danger money to cover the cost of his future hernia surgery.

I was on my way to Italy!

Time flew, once I was there. It was as though the past six months hadn't happened. I was starting to reconnect with the Happy Sophie inside.

My Italian was rusty, but it seemed to be enough to get by. I had a fabulous week in Florence. The men were gorgeous. They made their English counterparts look scruffy, even the posh ones. They know how to wear clothes here – really wear them – to make them look great. It's just as well I'm off men or I'd have been in serious danger of a holiday romance.

I had so much fun in Florence. And today I was heading north for the cherry festival. I couldn't sit still on the train. Maybe the other people in my compartment thought I had fleas?

47. The Cherry Festival

I was so relieved that Luca was okay with me taking the time off. It was the right thing to do. So much was hanging on this festival being a success and I had a lot of negotiating to do – with Giovanni and Francesco.

I drove down to the farm to help load our van with the supplies we needed for the week and all the equipment. We had agreed that Nonna would stay at home this year. All the standing and selling would be too much for her. I was taking Pietro and three of the women who normally help with packing and shipping. They would take care of the market stall while I handled the networking and the small matter of finding a buyer for the crop.

I was going to be staying at Dad's old apartment in the town. It's a simple place, but so much more comfortable than an anonymous hotel room. I was looking forward to it.

It took us a few hours to get our stall set up and then it was time for the opening festivities. I wasn't really in the mood for partying, but I had a lot of work to do to convince the people Dad had worked with for years – his old friends – that they could trust me. All that talk about me living in luxury in Milan and abusing my farm team had damaged my reputation. This weekend was as much about me repairing that damage as it was about selling cherries. I was laying the foundations for selling next year's crop, too.

Everyone was friendly and it helped for them to see me here, pitching in. But each time one of them offered their condolences for Dad it hurt, reminding me of that empty place I do my best to ignore.

The first couple of days of the festival ran smoothly. It was hectic and tiring but it went well. I was given some good leads for selling our glacé cherries and bottled cherry sauce into a chain of speciality shops and a French department store. It might not work out until next year, but it felt like I was making progress.

I met with Giovanni, too, and he was just as I had remembered him – big and brash and fun to be around, but I also sensed he would drive a hard bargain to help make sure we sold the crop at a fair price. He wanted his commission. We agreed an action plan and a minimum price, below which we would walk away and process the cherries ourselves, instead of selling the fresh fruit. He was hopeful. I asked him about the rumours he had mentioned to Nonna, but he refused to tell me about them until he had confirmed them from a more trusted source. "I don't want to worry you unnecessarily, *chico*!" he had said, which didn't reassure me.

My meeting with Francesco was scheduled in the next couple of days. Marisa wasn't sure when he would show up. I guessed that was his last chunk of power. I tried not to worry about it – to trust Nonna's strategy. I knew in my heart it was likely to work and, once I had met with Marisa, I was sure she would do whatever was needed to make sure it did. I met with our lawyer this morning, so the papers have been drawn up. I make a point of carrying them with me everywhere, just in case I bumped into Francesco. I was daring to hope that it will all work out okay; that – between us all – we will save the farm. I know we're doing all the right things to make sure we will. I needed to let go and trust Giovanni and Marisa to deliver on their promises.

I had been out this morning, meeting up for lunch with some old friends who I had almost forgotten. I felt so ashamed at the thought. It was refreshing to see them. Everyone is so happy at the festival. They're on a high, celebrating and catching up with each other. It had a holiday atmosphere, despite the amount of business that was being done.

I got back to my apartment and went to unlock the deadlock, but it was already unlocked. Had I forgotten to lock it when I went out after breakfast? I was sure I hadn't. I opened the Yale lock, trying to ignore the fear that was crawling up my spine. Had someone been in the flat?

I almost tiptoed inside, my senses on high alert, listening, watching for any sign of movement. Nothing. I called out: *buongiorno*! No reply, not that I would have expected one. I tried stamping my way through the hallway and into the room that was both the kitchen and the living area. No sign of anyone having been there.

I was being paranoid again. I must have forgotten to double-lock the door when I went out. I have had my mind on other things this week and probably wasn't concentrating. I became aware of how the adrenalin had been rushing through my body, how I had been holding my breath. And then I saw it, on the floor, in front of the tall larder cupboard I rarely go to in the kitchen: a crumpled receipt. I don't screw up my receipts like that. The adrenalin started racing again as I bent over to pick it up. I unfolded it and frantically scanned the figures on it. It was from last week, from a petrol station. In *Napoli* - Naples.

Where was my sodding hotel? I felt like I'd walked for miles. The sweat was dripping down my back in little streams and I could feel my hair was wet-welded to my head under my sun hat. Bringing a rucksack instead of a suitcase had seemed like a good idea at the time. That was before I knew about these hills and the three million steps I'd have to climb in this heat.

All I wanted was a shower and to put my feet up. And some lunch. Did this hotel even exist? It looked like it did from the website, but I was totally lost. There was no one to ask for help, even if I could understand whatever they would say to me. My feet were killing me. They were melting in my hiking boots.

I was sure the hotel address was in my bag somewhere. It had to be in there. I couldn't stop to find it. If I stopped walking I wouldn't start again. I rummaged as I walked.

This thing is like a Tardis, it's so massive on the inside. Has it eaten that piece of paper? I can't find it.

It took me a while to calm down after that. Someone had been in the flat. I tried to rationalise it. Plenty of people in the town had a key. It wasn't uncommon for us to let family or close friends borrow it, when visiting from out of town. But I kept seeing the word *Napoli* flashing in front of my eyes.

I didn't want to believe what my mind was trying to tell me, so I blotted it out, resolving to ask our neighbour this afternoon whether she knew who might have been staying in the apartment last week. The receipt could easily have been there for a few days. I was so distracted at the moment I could easily have missed it. I remembered the promise Luca had asked me to make, about phoning him if anything happened, no matter how small. But if I called him about this, it would make my suspicions feel real. I decided to wait until I had spoken to my neighbour, then I would decide whether I needed to do anything.

I wanted to clear my head, so I went for a walk in the old part of town, with its steep hills and narrow streets. It's an area where tourists rarely bother going, because there are none of the stunning views they crave and the architecture isn't exciting enough. I still had so much to achieve in the next few days. While I was walking, I got a phone call from Marisa. Francesco was back in town!

I held my breath as I let her tell me what was going on. She said she had told them about our offer and he had agreed to sign the papers. He would meet me at my lawyer's office at 3 p.m. I could hardly believe it! The only caveat he had asked for was for me also to sign an affidavit confirming I would never press charges against him for defaulting on the loan. Of course I would! I phoned my lawyer to brief him.

I was wandering around the streets, enjoying soaking up their calm and quiet, away from the festival. I was distracted, counting down the hours and minutes until my meeting with Francesco, when I would be able to start fixing the mess that loan had created. I was excited and nervous.

Ahia! That hurt! Why wasn't she looking where she was going?

I had tried to get out of her way but she veered right into me. It was an empty street, for God's sake. Bloody tourists. This place is full of them this week. But she was well away from the festival track. What was she doing up here?

She looked lost. Not my problem. I wanted to walk away and leave her to it, I've got too much to do. But I couldn't. She had grabbed my arm. It took me by surprise. I stood there, looking at her. "Are you okay?" I asked, out of politeness.

Ouch! That hurt. He just walked right into me. Okay, maybe I walked into him. I wasn't looking where I was going. I was rummaging through my bag for my hotel address.

Hang on, chestnut eyes… That smile. My brain was whirring. It was *him*! Mr *Clafoutis*! He looked nervous, just like he did on camera.

Shit! I'm grabbing his sleeve. He must think I'm a crazy woman. But I have to stop him from walking away. I don't know why yet. I've got his attention now. Let go of his sleeve, girl!

"It's you!" The words were out of my mouth before I realised how bonkers they sounded.

To be continued.

Want To Know What Happens Next?

Christof and Sophie have finally met – properly – will they just walk away again? How will Christof react to Sophie's crazy behaviour? Will he run or could this be the start of something life-changing?

And what about the threat from Denucci? Surely now he won't be testifying, Christof was just being paranoid? And what will happen when Christof finds the buyer he so desperately needs for the cherry harvest?

Will Sophie make a success – at last – of her new job? And has she really seen the end of Stuart and his hunger for revenge?

All this and much, much more is waiting for you in the second book of the Denucci Deception series:

"The Tainted Diamond"

Get instant access to the first two chapters here:

www.clarejosa.com/thetainteddiamond

Join The Readers' Club:

www.clarejosa.com/youtakeyourselfwithyou/club

Members Get Access To:

Exclusive deleted scenes
Casting sheets for your favourite characters
A Spotify playlist for the big scenes
Recipes from Nonna's kitchen
Interviews with the author
Videos for the Yoga & Mindfulness techniques that
helped Sophie
The first two chapters of book two of the Denucci
Deception series: The Tainted Diamond

Join Free Now:

www.clarejosa.com/youtakeyourselfwithyou/club

Gratitude

I couldn't have written this novel without the unfaltering support of my husband, Peter, and our three young boys. Many's the time they found me distracted by a new plot idea or with a brain-turned-to-mush by editing. Their belief in me has been pivotal to it being published. My boys have already decided they are writing book ninety in the Denucci Deception series and it will be all about zombies, apparently. Watch out!

I want to thank Gale Winskill, my editor, who helped me to take my ideas to the next level. I also owe a debt of gratitude to Mel Parks and Julie Corbin, my creative writing teachers, and my fellow students in their classes. Thank you so much for your feedback, support and for inspiring me with your creativity.

Thank you so much to Andrew Becker, my cover designer, who has been a delight to work with, despite us being on opposite sides of the Atlantic. And to Georgina Aldridge at Clays St Ives – you astonish me with your infinite patience!

A huge shout out goes to my friends at my favourite hotel in the world – Hilton Sarigerme, near Dalaman in Turkey. Thank you for looking after me so beautifully, so I could concentrate on finishing this book – and starting the next one!

Thank you to my Tribe on social media for your support, encouragement and excitement for *You Take Yourself With You*. Your belief in me and this project helped me to believe in myself.

Thank you to Gita Faux and Hazel Shrimplin; two inspirational teachers who both had a major impact on my life, proving that a great teacher can change the world.

And thank you to you for reading this book. Without readers, there would have been no point in writing it. Thank you for allowing me to indulge my passion for stories. I hope this one has inspired you.

Message From The Author:

I really hope you enjoyed *You Take Yourself With You*. If you did, please could you leave a review wherever you bought it (or on Amazon) letting people know why you liked it? It helps more readers to find the book! And you can let my team know by emailing hello@clarejosa.com. I would love to hear from you.

About Clare Josa

Clare Josa speaks and teaches internationally on how changing the world isn't about what you *do*, it's about who you allow yourself to *become*.

She has been mentoring Passionate World-Changers since 2002. As an entrepreneur herself, the creator of over fifteen years of online and face-to-face training courses, and the author of six published books, she knows about the hidden blocks that keep us stuck, dreaming big, but playing small. She has been through most of them, herself.

But she also knows how to get past them. That's how she wrote You Take Yourself With You. For thirty years she had dreamed of writing a novel, but believed she couldn't write a story, following a throw-away comment from an English teacher. Then, one morning, she did some of her 'inside work' that she does with clients and cleared that out-of-date belief. Two days later and she had drafted seven novels, of which You Take Yourself With You is the first.

She originally trained as an engineer (she has a Master's Degree in Mechanical Engineering And German), but she is also an NLP Trainer (practical psychology) and a certified Meditation & Yoga teacher. She loves demystifying Ancient Wisdom into practical actions you can take to change your life in less time than it takes to boil a kettle. Her clients call it 'engineer-approved woo-woo'. And it all comes with a bucket load of common sense and a generous dollop of humour.

Also By Clare Josa

Dare To Dream Bigger: ISBN 978-1-908854-79-7

Dare To Dream Bigger distils 15+ years of mentoring entrepreneurs and passionate world-changers into exercises you can do at home, in your PJs, to *get out of your own way*.

If you're fed up with dreaming big, but playing small, then it's time to clear out those hidden blocks, so you can make the difference you are *really* here to make.

And Dare To Dream Bigger guides you step by step through how to 'be the change' you wish to see.

52 Mindful Moments: ISBN 978-1908854-44-5

Want to feel less stressed, happier, calmer and more at peace, but you don't have the time?

What if all it took to change your life was one mindful minute? Could you spare that long?

The inspirational mindfulness techniques in 52 Mindful Moments will help you to shift away from feeling stressed, worried and exhausted, to feeling calmer, happier, more at peace and more alive, in under sixty seconds.

A Year Full Of Gratitude: ISBN 978-1908854773

We've all heard about how gratitude can change your life. But where on earth do you start? And how do you create the habit if your thinking mind is making you feel miserable?

A Year Full Of Gratitude combines a gratitude journal with a year-long course, to help you retrain your monkey mind to think thoughts that make you feel happier, taming your inner critic and helping you to smile for no reason!

All of Clare Josa's books are available to order from local bookstores and from major online retailers.

www.ingramcontent.com/pod-product-compliance
Lightning Source LLC
Chambersburg PA
CBHW070643180626
46817CB00006B/2232